A Pirate Princess

By: Brittany Jo James

To Conlee,

Most husbands in the world wouldn't selflessly sacrifice for their wife the way you have. Without you, I couldn't have even attempted to follow my dreams. Words can't express how much I appreciate you.

I promised you that one day I would be able to pay you back for all the wonderful things you've done for me and our sons. Well, I wouldn't hold my breath if I were you. Maybe one of these days, right?

You're the best man in the world and I'm so blessed to have you.

I love you

PROLOGUE

May 2, 1649

It has been four months since I left France in search of new territories to claim for the country. My crew and I landed on several small islands. All have two things in common. First, Spain claimed them years ago from tribes of Arawak Indians. Second, their new Spanish inhabitants tried to kill us.

We were relieved this afternoon when we once again spotted land. This island, like the rest, is claimed in the name of Spain. The difference is that these people are friendly. We are encouraged to stay and discuss trade or cohabitation with them.

This beautiful island is called Cuba. And its capital is Havana. The land is not the only thing here that is breathtaking; the women are enchanting as well. One

1

young lady, in particular, caught my eye. She is the Spanish governor's daughter and her name is Amada.

–Marin St. Aubin

May 14, 1649

We are still in Havana, Cuba. The Spaniards are very cordial to us and we learned a lot about this land and the neighboring islands as well. I suggested a potential marriage between Governor Ricardo's daughter, Amada, and myself. I begged her to be my bride and her only reservation is that she refuses to leave Cuba and her family. She is very close to her father and has resolved that I should retire from the French Navy and move to Havana permanently. That is, if I want to marry her.

–Marin St. Aubin

May 21, 1649

Amada agreed to marry me and her family has consented. A big wedding is planned for tomorrow afternoon! On a more troubling note, three travelers entered Havana today. They had news for Governor Ricardo. They said that an unknown disease was spreading around neighboring islands. The messengers said it was extremely contagious, killing thousands by the day.

I hope that it is only a rumor. However, at dinner tonight, one of the men began vomiting and complaining of stomach cramps. The other two men looked fearful but the sick man said he was fine. I have faith that this disease is harmless. I am too excited about my bride to think of anything troublesome. –Marin St. Aubin

May 22, 1649

I am writing this with haste. Unfortunately, I have much more important things to concern myself with than writing now. However, in case I have been infected with the disease I need to explain what happened in Cuba today so that whoever reads this shall know of our demise.

I wrote yesterday about the travelers who came to Havana, and how one was sick at dinner. He was found dead this morning and his body was completely yellow, even his eyes! His two travel companions were gone! We spent the day preparing for the wedding in order to banish the thought of disease. I married Amada and our joy was overwhelming. However, by the time we were ready for our wedding feast to begin three of our guests collapsed with stomach cramps and nausea.

I hoped it was just a coincidence until the governor started holding his stomach as well. Amada ran to him and when he looked up at her I saw his eyes. The part that was once white had turned yellow, just like the dead traveler's.

He begged us to leave and I tried to coax Amada to the ship for a quick escape. I feared for her wellbeing along with the health of my crew. She still refused, clinging to her father and completely ignoring me. The governor said that we should leave for France so that I can return this ship and buy my own with the retirement money I shall receive. He assured Amada that by the time we return he would be well and everything would be back to normal.

Finally, I threw her over my shoulder and ran. Her brother and his wife came along. As soon as we sat sail I ordered my entire crew, including my new wife, to bathe in scorching water and use the strongest soap I could find! Several of my men are scrubbing the ship from top to bottom as I write this.

I hope that will kill any impurity. No one is complaining of sickness yet but the disease strikes rapidly. Amada swears she shall never speak to me again. If we are all on the verge of death then she will not have to!
–Marin St. Aubin

June 1, 1649

Amada's feelings for me are unpredictable. We have a normal marriage for one wonderful night then she glares at me for days, crying for her father. The good news is that we are all healthy. The disease struck at Havana so instantly that we would show symptoms by now if any of us were sick.

Instead of sailing straight toward France we circled the Caribbean Islands, hoping for a sign of relief from Amada's father. We sailed to Hispaniola today to ask them for information about Cuba but they refused to let us off the ship. They demanded to know where we came from and when I told them, they screamed "Yellow Fever!" With that, they shooed us away from their island.
–Marin St. Aubin

September 1, 1649

Although we still have not left the Caribbean to sail toward France, things have improved greatly with my wife. She has floated around the ship with a smile on her face for days! I am afraid to ask what has put her in such a wonderful mood. –Marin St. Aubin

September 5, 1649

We are finally sailing toward France! My wife consented yesterday to "go wherever I take her, happily as can be." It is such wonderful news! –Marin St. Aubin

September 6, 1649

I received even more good news from Amada today! She let me know the reason she is so happy now. She is expecting a baby! How wonderful life shall be, spending it in Cuba with her and a strong, healthy little boy! We will arrive in France by December or January if we have no delays. Amada says our son should arrive in March. –Marin St. Aubin

November 5, 1649

We are already experiencing delays on our journey. The weather is bad and we have been set back time and time again. Guillermo, Amada's brother, predicts bad weather for the next several months. Our son might be born right here on the ship. Amada's pregnancy is certainly not having any delays. It seems to be progressing as normal. –Marin St. Aubin

December 13, 1649

We have had more bad weather. At this rate we shall not get to France until February. Amada is growing larger by the day. Novia, Amada's sister-in-law, says that our son will probably be here sooner than expected. Since my wife is so small and this is her first child, Novia says it might be closer to the end of January. –Marin St. Aubin

January 1, 1650

Barely any progress has been made on our journey. We had an easy trip on the way from France to Cuba, but going home during the winter is hard. We have still not seen the arrival of our son but Amada feels that it will be soon. Novia, who shall deliver the baby, says that we have three or four weeks to wait. I am almost certain we shall not be home until the beginning of March.

–Marin St. Aubin

February 2, 1650

I am writing to calm my nerves! Amada is in labor. Novia says she is surprised our son has waited this long to arrive. I keep trying to check on my wife but Novia will not speak to me about it, just Guillermo, who relays information to me. He says Novia worries that my wife is to small and frail to have this baby on the boat. If we were in France with proper treatment it would be better. I am really worried. –Marin St. Aubin

February 3, 1650

This shall probably be the last time I write. My life is over anyway. My strong, handsome son is not even a boy. Amada gave me a skinny little girl with black hair. My beloved Amada was so happy, although weak. She named the baby Corisanda, which apparently means, "Flower of My Heart," in her native language. That was the last thing she said to me. A few seconds later, my wife died.

I was asked to pick Corisanda's middle name. I have thought about it through all of this, and have settled on Aleene. That means, "Alone," in my own language and that is exactly what this girl must be because that is what she has made me, as well. I cannot stand to look at her. If I cannot have Amada I do not want Corisanda Aleene either. I asked Novia to take care of her for now. I do not want to go back to France. I want to keep sailing the ocean until I die. —Marin St. Aubin

ONE

February 2, 1668

On other days, the calming water would have rocked the ship's passengers into a soothing, tranquil state. Today was a different story entirely. No matter how serene the ocean was, the mood of the pirate captain could not be tamed. This day every year brought the greedy, spiteful, unhappy man into a worse state of miserable agony. The pirate crew kept their distance and his daughter hid in her cabin beneath deck.

"CORI! CORI!" The gray-haired captain wailed. "Where is that blasted girl? She has less sense than a starfish."

"Yes, sir?" the brunette beauty answered hastily as she ran up the stairs and onto the ship's main deck.

"Where have you been, you ignorant child?" The pirating captain of *The Beloved Loss* demanded.

As usual, Cori did not know what to apologize for first. "I am sorry, Father. I was in my quarters. You told me not to burden you with my presence today, so I thought you wanted me to stay…"

"Shut your mouth! Do not talk to me today. Calling you to assist me run this blasted ship was a mistake. Get your *derriere* back below deck and do not let me catch you out again! Do not think about eating dinner tonight either! I would have one less mouth to feed if you starved to death!" Captain Marin dismissed her with a shove toward the stairs. Turning to search for his only helpmate in times of trouble, he screeched for his second wife. "SHARLENE!"

Thankful that she was forgotten once again, Corisanda Aleene St. Aubin rushed down the creaky stairs to her below deck cabin. Her aunt was bustling around nervously, waiting on the young girl to return unharmed. "Oh, Corisanda! I was hoping this birthday would be better than the rest."

"It is never better, Aunt Novia. It only gets worse every year," Cori said with a ragged sigh, fighting back her customary birthday tears.

"*Si*, this is a hard day on everyone. One beautiful woman was taken away but another replaced her. I must get back to work. Cleaning the ship without you is a tough job!" Novia said with a consoling hug.

Cori tried to smile, "The girls will help."

The ship's maid rolled her eyes with derision, "The poor children are still so homesick for their families they can hardly lift a rag. If only we could return them to Argentina without Captain Marin knowing it! Seeing innocent children ripped away from their parents to become pirate hostages should be enough to break even Marin's cold, black heart!"

Novia bustled out to continue her daily chores, leaving Cori sad and alone. She heard the story of her birth many times. Her uncle and aunt relayed the heartbreaking tale over and over again, trying to answer Cori's questions without crying.

Refusing to return to his homeland after Amada's death, Cori's father turned to a life of pirating and ale. He never returned the French Naval ship. It was converted into a speedy vessel, perfect for making a quick getaway with whatever treasure could be stolen or killed for. Gold, spices, jewels, children, or furs were worthy objects for illegal traders. At the present moment, *The Beloved Loss* was on course from Argentina to Hispaniola. More islands would be sacked and then the pirate crew would sail directly to Africa in order to trade all their gathered loot for gold and silver.

Cori knew with certainty that most islands in the Caribbean would be invaded before setting sail across the Atlantic, but one island was safe from Captain Marin's rage. The island of Cuba would be completely ignored. He circled it each year but had not stepped foot on it since the last time he left, over eighteen years before.

After Cori's mother died and Marin began pirating most of the original crew had been killed, traded, or abducted by other unlawful sailors. Only one of Marin's ex-Navy crewmen remained by his side. Yvet, the ship's Gunner, was the only enduring crew member with the same Navy experience that the ship captain had.

Other members had been picked up along the way. Guillermo and Novia, as happily married as possible under their captive conditions, had been on board since the Yellow Fever attacked Cuba. Cori's aunt and uncle were her only companions.

The rest of the pirates were as evil and immoral as the devil's own crew. *Perhaps the worst,* Cori thought, *is Falco de Vries.* Falco, a Dutch pirate from the Netherlands, seemed to be a man with no past at all! No one knew any details about his family or life before *The Beloved Loss* except that he had a mother who he rarely spoke of. All the crew truly knew was that he searched the sea on an old, rugged, slow, stolen boat until he found the one ship he was looking for, Marin and Sharlene St. Aubin's.

Now, at only twenty eight years old, Falco was Marin's Quartermaster. Sometimes called a First Mate, the Quartermaster was the ship's second-in-command, only under the captain himself. Excited about taking over *The Beloved Loss* as soon as possible, Falco had the most wicked goal Cori could imagine. Not only was he being rewarded with Marin's ship, he was also being gifted with Cori's future. Cori rolled her eyes, not wanting to think about the man she was being forced to marry within the year.

Falco did not see the marriage as an outrage, like his fiancé did. As a nickname, he called her *Mevrouw*. After years of questioning him about the meaning behind the word, he finally told her it was the Dutch term for *Woman*. Cori hated his term of endearment as much as she hated him. *Who calls their future wife, "Woman?" Dutch is a revolting language anyway, none of their words sound romantic!* She chastised him more than once, "Call me Cori or Corisanda, not *Mevrouw* or woman!" He forced his laughter, trying to ignore Cori's attitude until he could properly punish her.

Two crew members joined the ship with Falco. His lackeys, Zeeman and Klaas, were always by his side. She would stick her tongue out or glare at them when only the two of them were looking. Zeeman was the ship's Carpenter, taking care of any damage done to the vessel while sailing or attacking. With barely more sense, Klaas was the pirate crew's Surgeon. "Useless trash," Cori mumbled as she thought about Falco's two baboons.

The crew held one lone wolf who was almost as bad as Falco. A Frenchman named Laron, a notorious womanizer, was the pirate ship's Boatswain. Third in command, under Marin and Falco, Laron barked orders left and right, making sure every pirate took care of his or her proper duties. Cori caught Laron staring at her quite often and snarling his nose at Falco.

He wanted Cori for himself and hated the Quartermaster with a passion. *What luck,* Cori thought. *The idea of another man loving me enough to keep Falco away would be wonderful… if the man was any better than Falco himself!* Laron was not as coldhearted and malicious as Falco, but he had a totally different set of problems that Cori could not stand.

The last member of the pirate crew was Cori's stepmother. Sharlene, Marin's deceitful wife, joined *The Beloved Loss* when Cori was only five years old. She was French, like Marin, and turned to a life on the sea to escape a prison sentence she was wanted for in south France.

Sharlene was a thief, traitor, and deceitful con-artist, among other horrible things. She had hair even longer than Cori's and it was as bright red as a flaming fire. She was small framed and slightly shorter than Cori but had a grip tighter than any man on the ship. Sharlene hated Spaniards, Dutch, English, and basically everyone besides Marin. Although she kept her distance from most of Marin's crewmembers, she was very close to Falco.

Marin, on the other hand, only despised Cubans. Anyone from Cuba could not be tolerated by the captain; his heart could not handle anymore reminders. Sharlene and Marin made Cori's life as miserable as possible. Cori's stepmother lied to Marin, continuously trying to get her step-daughter in trouble. It was no secret that Sharlene hated Cori with a passion, almost as much as she hated Cori's late mother, Amada.

Before Sharlene came along, Marin detested Cori but only showed it by completely ignoring her. Once he remarried, Sharlene convinced him to punish Cori at every possible opportunity. Cori tried to escape and Sharlene encouraged Marin to let her go but he never would.

He had caught her trying to flee at least twice a year since Sharlene came into the family. She was whipped, criticized, humiliated, and deprived of food for days. Cori had not tried to escape for many months but she hoped for the chance to get away soon. She planned to successfully flee before being forced to marry Falco de Vries. Death would be heavenly compared to a life as the cruel and brutal pirate's bride.

The beautiful young woman sat on her small bed, cuddling her blankets closely around her. She contemplated her situation with Falco. He joined the pirate crew when Cori was only eight years old. Marin loved Falco like the son he never had and always wanted.

Six years after Falco joined the crew when Cori was fourteen and Falco was twenty four, Marin announced that Falco would be his successor as captain of *The Beloved Loss* whenever Marin decided to retire. The crowd cheered, they were happy Falco was being thusly rewarded. Cori had been in attendance, watching the festivities from the back of the room to not draw any attention upon herself.

When Falco stood to thank Marin and accept his reward, he surprised the whole attendance, especially Cori. "Captain," he said, "Honoring me as the future commander of this fine ship means the world to me. It is the second biggest dream I have ever had. There is only one thing in this world I would want to possess more than *The Beloved*

Loss. As a matter of fact, you are the only one who could give me that gift, as well."

Cori recalled every word as if it was only yesterday. Marin laughed heartily in high spirits and jokingly asked, "What on Earth could you want from me besides my ship, son? It is all I have."

"The one thing I want is Corisanda." Everyone on the ship went silent. No one blinked. Each pirate froze, not sure what to do. Then, all at once, the ship crew turned to stare at the captain's daughter. Marin seemed to be in shock for a few long moments before Falco turned to him again, "I am asking permission to marry your daughter, when she comes of age, of course."

Still silent for a moment, Marin's suddenly sad eyes turned to Cori and he considered the pretty little girl he barely knew. He cleared his throat and smiled, feigning cheerfulness again. "Why would you want Cori, son? Have you lost your mind? Surely you could find a more comely girl than her anywhere you wanted to look! Nonetheless, if you still want to marry Cori when she turns eighteen years old then she is yours. Let the drinking begin!"

When her father said the last few words, Cori came to her senses enough to run. She cried in her below deck quarters the entire night. If Cori had not known what he was truly like, she would be thrilled to marry Falco de Vries. The pirate ship Quartermaster was tall with darkly tan skin from being in the sun so much. His clean-cut hair was golden blonde, the color of sand.

Oh yes, Cori thought to herself, *Falco is a handsome man. He is vicious, heartless, conniving, and unjust but he is handsome.* Falco had a charming way with words, he could sound romantic and loving but it was all just a game. He was evil, through and through.

Cori looked into her small hand-mirror, trying to wipe the tears out of her eyes. Novia told her daily how closely she resembled Amada. "Which parts look like her?" Cori would ask in curiosity.

"All of them", Novia would always answer. "The only difference is that your skin is lighter than hers. It's like a perfect mixture between your father and mother's, not too dark but not too light."

Cori was definitely a beautiful girl, and Falco de Vries was aware of that. She had black hair that flowed down her back and ended barely above her derriere. Corisanda was very petite; her Uncle Guillermo teased her about being skinnier than a rail. However, Cori was taller than Novia by quite a bit, with long, slender legs. The young beauty was tan from spending her whole life in the sun and in shape due to exceptionally hard work for a girl her age and size.

Cori agreed with her father. *Falco must be crazy to want to marry me.* Being raised by pirate men was not a good idea if you want to create a ladylike, mannerly wife. Cori was extremely feminine in her looks, catching gasps and stares from every man she passed when she was allowed to venture onto an island. What made Cori so different from most girls was her enjoyment of adventure, love of games, and her bothersome tendency to get into trouble.

Her long legs were put to the test many times when she was caught pulling tricks on Zeeman or Klaas, her favorite morons to provoke. She never tried to anger Marin, Sharlene, or Falco out of complete fear for her life. Guillermo and Novia were safe, being Cori's only companions. And the only reason she did not antagonize Laron was because she did not want him to think she wanted his attention. Yvet, the only man besides Marin left from the original Navy crew, was never mean to Cori like the rest of the pirates were. He certainly was not nice to her though, out of respect for Marin. Cori felt that Yvet pitied her, somewhere deep down in his tiny pirate heart.

Cori did not care what anyone thought of her. She hated pirates. Every single one of them! For the most part, she even hated herself for having no choice but to be a part of it. *All pirates are bad, even Novia, Guillermo and me! They are nothing but murderers, thieves, kidnappers, and lawbreakers. I have been a pirate since the day I was born and it looks like I shall be forced into this life until the day I die, as well.*

Being forced to help the pirate crew was something Corisanda had trouble doing. Cori had many jobs on *The Beloved Loss*. She helped Novia with all the cleaning, and at times she was forced to help Yvet run the heavy cannons during battles with enemy ships. However, Cori's most important, and least favorite, job was to lure in boats for

Marin to attack. Sharlene thought up the horrible job as a punishment once and it worked so well that it stuck.

From the time Cori was thirteen they forced her to dress in one of Sharlene's scantily-visible night gowns and compelled her to stand on the deck, waving the other ships to come closer with a flag of surrender. Peaceable vessels and enemy pirate ships alike would rush to the rescue, hoping to help the young girl or attack an enemy. Then, when they became close enough, Yvet would start firing and Marin would hold the enemy crew hostage and raid their boat. Once everything of value had been taken from the enemy ship, someone would decide how to dispose of the hostages. If Falco was in charge, torment and death would be the chosen method.

Cori fought and begged for years not to be forced into such a horrible duty but to no avail. She was beautiful, and they used it against her. She had refused in the past but was always eventually beaten into submission. If a beating did not work they would lock her in her quarters without food for days. Finally, Cori gave up trying to ignore her "responsibilities". That was one of the many reasons she dreamed of escaping.

She paced around her room, looking at the small amount of toiletries she was allowed to have. Cori wanted to escape more than anything. She did not care where she would go or who she might meet, as long as it was far from the ocean and she did not come across any pirates.

Cori learned much about France from hearing her father tell the other pirates stories about growing up in the beautiful country. Cuba, Novia and Guillermo's home, would be just fine too. She thought that the only problem with Cuba is that they had to deal with pirates! *Anywhere would be fine,* Cori thought with determination. *Anywhere but here!*

The Count of Calais, Burke Landis Belcourt, stood on a wooden dock staring into the bright, blue ocean under him. His best ship, *The Heart of Calais,* was being examined for any damage done on a recent trip to Africa and back. The most sought after man in France was not a normal, wealthy, privileged Count. While the other French nobles were sipping tea and planning balls, Captain Burke Belcourt was sailing his ship from country to country, trading goods and serving his close friend, King Louis XIV.

Burke stared into the deep water, thinking about his life and the way it was soon to change. His plan to remain a life-long bachelor, sailing the ocean, working hard, and enjoying total freedom had recently been destroyed.

The Count stared at his reflection on the water's surface. The blue eyed man had thick, shaggy-cut, dark brown hair, lying a little longer than fashion allowed. It was styled in Burke's usual, quick and easy way, arranged flawlessly as if he spent hours working on it. He was tall with broad shoulders, tan skin, and an almost faultless face. The only flaw was one, small, crooked scar on his left cheek from a fist fight years before. The scarcely visible scratch just added to his carelessly gorgeous appeal.

Women swooned over Burke even in foreign lands where no one knew he was a wealthy, titled, French Lord. His money, title, and power with the King only made him that much more sought after in France where everyone knew him. Burke once considered his handsome face and flawless body a blessing but Odelia Vadeboncoeur turned it into a curse.

Odelia was a notorious flirt, conniving, deceitful, and extremely manipulative. She had her wealthy father, the Earl of Le Havre, wrapped around her pinky finger and whatever Odelia wanted Lord Orson Vadeboncour gave her. Unfortunately for Burke, he was one of the top items on Odelia's very large wish-list.

The father and daughter lived together in a spacious home in Le Havre. Odelia's alcoholic mother left them both for a happier life as a poor maid in England. Lord Orson Vadeboncour was average in height but awkwardly scrawny in form. He had light brown hair, not much darker than Odelia's golden-blonde curls. The Earl wore thick glasses, making his awkward appearance seem even more noticeable.

Burke had known Odelia since she was born, nineteen years before. At the age of eleven, Burke had cared very little for the bald baby who would still be demanding his attention almost two decades later. Odelia had her eyes set on Burke by the time she could walk, still chasing him when she turned sixteen. Even though she insisted profusely, Burke refused to court her once she was old enough to date. Nothing changed when she turned seventeen or eighteen.

Taking matters into her own hands, the brazen coquette showed up unexpectedly at Burke's grand chateau in Calais. She arrived in the middle of the night, demanding to speak with her *beau*, Burke. He yelled at her for risking her life by sneaking out of her home in Le Havre, only chaperoned by a smitten stable-boy servant.

The Count continued yelling at her when he brought up what irked him the most, *wasting his valuable time!* Burke gave her a room for the night on the one condition that she would be sent home at dawn. He wondered why she put up no fight, but he knew now. Burke fell right into Odelia's ploy. She had no doubt that he would deny her scandalous offers and send her home. Fortunately for Odelia, lying came easy.

As soon as she returned home to her father in Le Havre, tears pouring down her face, she laid out her devious ruse. "Oh Papa," she bawled, "I just wanted to spend time with him because he was my *friend*. But he *forced* me into his bedroom. He *stripped* me of my virtue and my reputation shall be ruined! Burke says he shall not marry me, Papa! Do something!"

Odelia had not owned her virtue for several years, but it was certainly not Burke who took it. Regardless, her father was powerful enough to demand King Louis XIV to pay attention to the *crime* done against his *innocent* daughter. King Louis and Burke were close friends with much in common. Both were thirty years old, both expected a lot out of the people around them, and both were energetic about their careers.

The King knew about Burke's plan to stay single and free for the rest of his life, and he certainly knew that Odelia was no innocent maiden. However, that was not something he could tell Odelia's Papa, so forcing Burke to marry Odelia Vadeboncour was the only option.

The captain took a long, drawn out breath, staring at his beautiful vessel sitting across the dock. He was born into his title, a Count by birth. The only thing Burke had never possessed was *patience*. His servants joked that Lord Burke could sit in a chair, never lifting a finger, and own riches greater than most of the country.

He just could not force himself into sitting still. Burke loved to work and stay busy. From the time he was a small child he dreamed of owning a shipping industry, being the captain of a glamorous boat, traveling to foreign countries. Trading goods made all of that possible and also made him an even *wealthier* young man.

Once he married Odelia there would be no more shipping. No more trading. No more *Captain* Burke Belcourt, only *Count* Burke Belcourt. He would be forced to sit at home, tending to his boring duties as a Count, piddling with his money, and listening to Odelia nag. Thankfully, it was not time yet! He had postponed their wedding over and over again until Odelia's father could stand no more.

They were supposed to be married in less than a month when Burke traveled to Versailles, right outside of Paris, to ask King Louis, again, if there was anything that could be done to get him out of it. "Actually," the King had said, "I need you to do something for me. It shall not get you out of the marriage, but it can postpone it for a few months! You are the only one I trust to handle this business for me but it is dangerous."

"That's fine, I'll take anything!" Burke had agreed.

That is when the King told his friend about the increase of pirating around the Caribbean Sea, half a world away. "I want it stopped," he told Burke.

"I do not understand." Burke said in bewilderment, "What does that have to do with France? As long as the pirates are not robbing us, why do we care who they steal from? Those islands mean nothing to us."

Ready to explain, knowing his friend would ask that question, he began with a nod. "You are correct! I care nothing about the islands. I never worried about it before because I thought the same way you do. *Spain owns the islands, so let them deal with it!* And England makes no excuses that they allow pirates to work for their country, robbing from Spain and bringing the goods back home. They are calling their legal pirates *buccaneers*! I would never do such a thing so I just stayed away from the subject. However, apparently there is one thing *worse* than a *legal pirate*. That, of course, would be *illegal pirates*! And by what I hear, the main illegal pirates who are robbing the Spaniards are *Frenchmen*."

The King shook his head in confusion, hoping he was making sense! "I have neighboring countries scorning me for allowing my people to do such horrible things to others. They are comparing me to England! There is one ship, in particular, owned by the reportedly worst pirate on the ocean. The boat is called *The Beloved Loss*. The gossipers say that the captain of the ship is French. I want it stopped," The King repeated.

"Consider it done," Burke said with a smile, all but skipping out of the King's Versailles Palace.

Burke was so excited he immediately rushed the short distance from Versailles to Le Havre to inform Lord Orson of the *terrible* news postponing the wedding. The Earl was livid, insisting that Burke was only trying to escape from his daughter. Odelia was even angrier. The scorned woman was not one to be reckoned with and she shot Burke's happiness straight down the drain. "I shall just go too!"

"YOU WILL WHAT?" Burke had screamed in unison with the Earl.

"I shall just go with you," she repeated. Burke tried to talk her out of it.

"It will be dangerous. It shall not be proper for an unwed woman to travel with her fiancé, without chaperones! I may be gone for months! What if the trip makes you sea sick?" He tried it all, but nothing would persuade the determined girl.

She was already aboard *The Heart of Calais*, getting her luxurious trunks of clothes organized in her spacious below deck cabin. Burke was dreading the trip in pitiable agony. *Why did I not leave when the King told me I could go? Why did I even have to inform Odelia's father? I should have just asked someone to tell them once I was safely out to sea!* He chastised himself.

"Everything's ready, Captain!" the ship's First Mate, Acel Belcourt, yelled.

Burke faced his cousin with a frown. "*Wonderful*, I will be right there," he muttered under his breath.

Captain Belcourt took a ragged breath, walking toward his beloved ship. He glanced at the sky as he quietly whispered, "God, if you have any mercy left for me, make that rotten girl stay out of my way on this trip. If I thought you would ever forgive me for it, I would push her off this boat at the first sign of sharks..."

TWO

The captain of *The Heart of Calais* was blessed with a *halfway* answered prayer. Odelia stayed out of his way during the journey. She was by no means pleasant, due to being afflicted with the worst case of seasickness anyone could possibly have, but at least she was out of Burke's way! From the moment the ship left the dock, Odelia's head spun and her stomach whirled.

She quickly found that as long as she was lying in bed, being waited on hand and foot by ship servants, she was fine. As soon as she tried to rise from her idle-state she would become nauseous and dizzy. It might have been her maid's worst nightmare, but it was a dream come true for Burke. He sometimes heard her screeching for him to visit, but knowing that she could not rise from her bed or see him from her below-deck quarters he just pretended not to hear her wails.

"How are you enjoying your last voyage, sir?" the ship's Boatswain asked.

"Now that my hateful fiancé is quiet, it has been fantastic, Karoly!" Burke laughed.

Karoly was a handsome man, strong and masculine. Nothing about him was graceful or classy but no one would have insulted the large man by telling him that for any amount of money in the world. He had a deep voice and a long, black beard that was beginning to turn gray. Everyone knew he was in love with the ship's maid, Leala, but no one mentioned that to him either. They had dated during their teenage years and had fought uncontrollably. Leala glared at him every second she could and cussed his name if he was mentioned around her. Karoly, not able to let go of his deep affection for the untamed maid, played pranks on her often.

No one understood how they ever dated but their attentive leader caught them staring at each other when no one else seemed to be looking. Burke teased Leala, accusing her of being secretly in love with Karoly as he so obviously was with her. She would ball up her fist and deck him then storm away in anger, leaving the captain laughing wildly.

Leala had a sixteen year old daughter, Miette, who had the same course, black hair that Karoly did. Leala never denied that Miette was Karoly's daughter and Karoly had eagerly taken on his role as a father. He begged Leala for years to marry him, making them a united family. She denied him over and over, claiming to hate him *for prancing around with an uncountable number of other women when he was supposed to be marrying her!* Miette helped her mother clean the ship and assisted her father as needed.

Lucky for Burke, Karoly handled all the ship's carpentry work when free of his Boatswain duties. It was a strange hobby of Karoly's but it worked out well for *The Heart of Calais* to use one person for two jobs. Karoly spent much time with Miette, teaching her the trade. Acel Belcourt, Burke's cousin and best friend, was always full of helpful ideas, making him the perfect First Mate.

The Heart of Calais had an expert Gunner, named Garner, who had been thrown out of the French Navy years before due to his overzealous killing efforts. Quain, the vessel's Surgeon was smart and continuously happy, despite any circumstance. The last member of Burke's crew was the cook. Davet could not boil a pot of water without messing it up; much less fix a suitable meal for the crew to eat. However, his love of sailing and admiration for Burke kept him around to practice.

Leala, Miette, and Davet took turns tending to Odelia's constant requirements and demands. Karoly and Acel could not stand the curly haired witch, Quain seemed afraid of her, and Garner avoided her as much as possible. Leala tried to protect Miette from the difficult-to-please girl but sometimes even the head-strong maid could not stand her ground.

Standing on the main deck at the helm, steering the magnificent vessel, Burke looked out across the deep blue ocean. Dismissing Karoly to his duties, the thoughtful captain picked up his binoculars to look across the beautiful water in hopes of seeing land. Although the experienced man knew he was getting close to his destination nothing was seen yet. After being on board *The Heart of Calais* for one long month, Burke's crew was ready to be off the ship. Even more ready to be on land again was Odelia.

Instead of traveling to the Caribbean just to locate *The Beloved Loss* and bring the pirate prisoners back to

44

France, the career-oriented French captain decided to make it a business trip as well. "We have never traded with the Caribbean Islands before," Acel said to his older cousin when Burke stocked the ship. "Are you sure the King will not mind you working for yourself before you work for him?"

Smiling ruefully, Burke replied, "Dear Cousin, King Lou knows how much I hate Odelia! He knows how much worse I hate the idea of marrying her. He surely expects me to prolong this trip as much as possible. Believe me, if I could extend this trip permanently I would! Nothing shall stop Lord Orson from demanding a wedding the second I return to France so let me enjoy my last couple months of freedom!"

Now, four weeks later, Burke had every trade worthy item he could find loaded aboard his ship and ready to unload once they reached an island. Like pirates, Burke was in the shipping and trading industry. But unlike pirates, everything Burke did was completely legal and ethically upstanding. He did not steal, kill, or attack. He bought items from one land and sold it to another, charging a carrying fee in order to make a proper income for himself and his crew. Also unlike buccaneers, Burke worked for no country or King. He owned his own ship, he paid his own crew, and he made his own rules. That was the way Burke Landis Belcourt liked to live, *free and in charge*!

It was an easy trip thus far. One buccaneer vessel passed and two smaller pirate ships as well. All stared at *The Heart of Calais* as if contemplating an attack, but Burke's strong reputation proceeded him and the enemy ships wisely decided to let him pass. Burke traded with many foreign lands and often ran into illegal traders but most wanted to live another day so they quickly disregarded the idea of attacking *The Heart of Calais* or any of Captain Belcourt's other ships.

Every now and then a pirate crew was brave and stupid enough to attack, but Burke had never been defeated. He took the pirates hostage and brought them straight to France for judgment. That is one of the main reasons, *besides Odelia*, that King Louis XIV chose Burke for this mission.

The subject of Odelia made Burke's temper soar. It seemed absolutely ridiculous to him that he was being forced into marriage with a lying, manipulative pest like the Vadeboncour brat! No one liked Odelia besides her father. She had no friends because she used and abused everyone in her life. Burke had an affluent family, much more powerful than Orson Vadeboncour, but when the Belcourts tried to argue the King's decision the *facts* were laid out on the table.

Odelia *was* a lady of class, someone truly had *taken* her innocence, Burke did *allow* her to spend the night at his home- without chaperone, and her story *never* waivered.

What could the Belcourts do? What could Burke do? Nothing. The only thing that could save Burke was if someone stepped forward and admitted that they had taken Odelia's virtue, not Burke.

That was unlikely to happen because no one else wanted stuck in a marriage with her either. The only other possibility was if Odelia felt bad enough to do the right thing and correct the rumors about Burke. That was definitely not going to happen.

Odelia had spread her lies about Burke's inappropriate behavior all over France. And, unfortunately for Burke, he possessed a reputation as a notorious lady's man long before Odelia came into the picture. That made her rumors even more believable. There was no way to prove that Burke had not slept with Odelia, especially since Odelia was no innocent young lady as her Papa believed.

Burke never forced a woman into doing anything and he most certainly had not stripped anyone of their virtue. Roaming a few brothels and bars had never seemed inappropriate until Odelia used it against him. Now he wished he had never met a woman in his entire life. The idea of marriage was not the worst in the world. No, he did not plan on marrying anyone, especially anytime soon, but it was not because he did not like women.

Beautiful women caught his eye often, as he did theirs, but none could hold his attention for long. It was just because he loved his career as a sailor so much that he did not think any woman was worth giving it up for. On the other hand, even if Burke was searching desperately for a wife he would not ever choose Odelia!

Trying to better his mood and forget the unfortunate situation he found himself in, Burke examined his surroundings. The ocean was dark blue and deeper than he could imagine. He smelled the salty water as it splashed through the air around his enormous and ornately designed ship. The sky above him was bright blue and full of fluffy, white clouds forecasting the beautiful spring weather. The May afternoon was just what he needed to relax his mind and enjoy the water.

As he stared into the sky above him, the first bird he had seen in months flew overhead. Throwing himself into action he grabbed his binoculars to search for any sign of land. Way into the distance he could see the very top of trees through the magnifying lens. "I see land, boys! We shall be there by nightfall," the captain called in excitement.

Cheers were heard all over the boat, echoing the captain's announcement. In the sleeping quarters below deck, Odelia raised herself from the small cot to hear what the fuss was about. To curious to not be a part of the action, the puny woman tried to steady her stomach enough to climb the wooden stairs. The bright sun made Odelia cover her face with her hands. After not seeing anything but her dark bunk for the last month it was hard for her to focus in the intense light. "What on Earth is going on around here?" She demanded with a pouty lip.

"The captain has spotted land! We should be relaxing on the beach by nightfall," Acel teased.

"Ha! I shall most certainly not be on the beach with *you* this night. You can *count* on that. Speaking of handsome, wealthy *Counts,* where is mine?" She huffed indignantly looking around for Burke.

Purposely riling the intolerable witch, Acel jabbed further. "Odie, Odie, Odie, you must understand that Burke only considers himself a *Count* when he is on land in France. When he is on a boat or in the middle of the ocean, like he is now, he is no Count at all. Only a *lowly captain...*"

Rolling her light blue eyes and poking out her bottom lip, Odelia threw her hands over her ears as if to block out the First Mate's ceaseless prattling. "Shut your mouth, Acel Belcourt! You are only jealous because you are a simple *commoner* while your cousin is an extremely prosperous *noble*!"

"Is that all you care about, Odie? Money, money, money and a few good looks?" He questioned, knowing she would deny the truth.

She just shrugged her shoulders indifferently, "Of course not! I care about Burke's personality, health, happiness, and all of that worthless matter too."

Acel threw his head back in laughter, "And I suppose you even expect me to believe you love him for all the right reasons, sickness or in health, until death do you part?"

"Why not?" she asked, still searching the ship for her fiancé.

"Name one thing you love about him, *besides* his money and handsome face."

"His, um," Odelia paused for a moment, honestly trying to think of something she cared about besides the Count's title, wealth, power, or appearance. "Oh! I know! I love his sense of style."

"Ahem!" Burke cleared his throat from behind the arguing youths.

"Oh, Burke, my darling, there you are! Acel says you have spotted land?" Odelia tried as she threw her arms around the captain.

"My sense of style is the only thing you love about me besides my money, Odelia?" Burke asked sarcastically with one hand over his heart, pretending to be crushed.

"Oh shut up, you fool! Who cares what you think? You are marrying me anyway, *my love*."

"Unless you grow a heart and admit that I am not the man who took your virtue…" Burke replied with a shrug.

Odelia's face turned red and her mouth dropped open. "Oh! How dare you? I shall *never* admit that!" she screeched. Catching her mistake, she corrected, "I mean, *of course* you are the man who stole my virtue! I am a lady of class! I never spent the night away from home without my father except for the one night I stayed with you, remember?"

Acel could not help himself, "And since we know Burke *truly* did *not* sleep with you that *night*, Odie darling, it must mean that you made yourself available enough to sneak away from your father with some unknown man *during the day*…"

Her eyes narrowed maliciously, "Burke! How dare you let him speak to your fiancé in such a manner?"

Burke could not answer her through his laughter. He chuckled so loud that the rest of the crew wondered what on Earth was so humorous. "Sorry, Odelia. Acel, how dare you speak to my straight-laced, prudish, proper, angelic fiancé that way?

"OH!" she shrieked as she stormed away from the cackling cousins.

"There we go, Captain. She shall never leave her quarters again, to be sure!" Acel saw with a wink, patting his idol on the back.

Trying to calm his laughter, Burke replied to the younger man. "Thank you, Ace. Back to work! Let us make sure everything is in tip-top shape and ready to be unloaded. We need to work as quickly as possible so that we can begin our search for *The Beloved Loss*."

Acel nodded in agreement and rushed away to carry out Burke's command. At the age of twenty four, Acel Belcourt admired Burke like an older brother. The two men were much alike in every way. The handsome cousins even looked like brothers. One of the only differences was Acel's absolute excitement to find a loving woman to marry.

Acel and Burke's fathers were born into the title of Dukes. Burke's father was The Duke of Bordeaux, and Acel's was the Duke of Tulle. The Duke of Bordeaux, Reule Belcourt married a Lady of nobility, the oldest daughter of the Marquis of Auxerre. Unlike Burke's mother, Lady Damica Belcourt, Acel's father married a common woman who was *not* from a titled family.

Ruskin Belcourt loved his wife, Elita, despite the dreadful treatment they received from many of the other noble families. Caring little about unnecessary judgments, Reule and Ruskin Belcourt remained best friends and inseparable brothers. With a simple decree from the King, all needless opinions were blocked. Ruskin was noble, making his wife and children noble as well. The Duke and Duchess of Tulle and their son were just as noble as the older Belcourt brother and his own family. No matter what any of the other nobles in France argued!

That worked well, until an unfortunate event brought the gossipers back into action. Ruskin Belcourt became ill at an early age, dying much younger than anyone expected. The other noble families shunned Elita and her child, Acel, insisting that they were nothing but commoners again.

No matter what Reule and Damica did to prevent such harsh treatment of their sister-in-law and nephew, nothing seemed to help. Acel was still noble, by law. He was the Earl of Lille and no one but the King could take it away from him. However, Acel's carefree attitude stopped him from ever reminding anyone, like Odelia, that he was indeed noble.

Acel Belcourt had a grand chateau, although it was much smaller than Burke's, and a whole staff of servants. If he ever married, his wife and children could live privileged lives as a noble family. However, he highly doubted that they would be accepted by society since he, noble as could be, was still being denied. Something like that would have infuriated Burke. The older cousin would have demanded respect for himself, just as he continuously insisted respect for his Uncle Ruskin's only son.

When Ruskin died, Elita and Acel came to live with Reule, Damica, and Burke. At ages ten and four, Burke and Acel became the best of friends. Nothing could separate the two boys and they had vowed that nothing ever would. Acel hoped for Burke's sake that Odelia would find some other prey. No one deserved such harsh punishment as being forced into marriage with Odelia Vadeboncour, especially not a fantastic gentleman like his cousin, Burke.

Hours later, they were close enough to land that they could see the sandy beach. "What island is it?" Quain asked.

"If I am not mistaken, I believe it is Hispaniola!" Burke answered with a wide smile.

"Have you been to Hispaniola before?" Karoly questioned in excitement.

Burke shook his head, "No. Never! But if we are right on course, that is where we should be! And I cannot see it clearly enough yet, but there is a large ship sitting right off the beach! Would it not be great if it was *The Beloved Loss*? Then we could just cruise around for awhile, not worrying about work!"

Karoly looked at Burke with a doubtful expression. "Why would a pirate ship be sitting right in the open like that though, Captain? Would they not be hiding somewhere instead?"

"Well, apparently that is what makes their captain such an intimidating one! He is not scared of a thing, and though he probably hides everywhere else he goes, he would not need to be sneaky at Hispaniola. They say he has many who work for him on that island, no one would try to take him down there. He has claimed control, so to speak, without the authority of owning it."

"I see. So that is why you wanted to go to Hispaniola first? You wanted to get information on *The Beloved Loss*!" Quain answered himself as understanding washed over the crew.

Burke replied casually, staring through his binoculars at the distant ship. "Of course, but who knows if this is actually Hispaniola! You know I get mixed up

sometimes…"

The crew talked with their easy going captain until

Burke was ready to claim their attention. "Okay, we do not

know what we are going to find here. We are accustomed

to trading with Africa, Asia and other European countries

where they welcome us, but this is different. We have never

been here before and they do not expect our visit. They

may be hostile or angry that we came."

The handsome captain took a breath and continued,

knowing what to expect from his crewmembers. "I plan to

go directly to *The Beloved Loss*, if that is it we see. If they

seem peaceful enough to talk to me, I want you to take the

ship and discuss trade with the islanders while I am gone,

Acel. And Karoly, I need you to stay aboard *The Heart of*

Calais to help me when I get ready. Be prepared for a hasty

departure though, in case we are not warmly greeted."

"Burke! You know we will not be welcomed if you march across *The Beloved Loss* and tell them you are arresting them!" Acel exclaimed in bewilderment.

Burke smiled at his worried crew, "No, no! I am not that ignorant! I plan to board *The Beloved Loss* to discuss *trade* with them. I will ask their captain to come aboard *The Heart of Calais* to look over our goods. When I get him on our ship, alone, I shall take him prisoner. I will then call the rest of his men aboard, a few at a time. Karoly and I together can tie and gag each until their ship is empty!"

He paused to make sure everyone was in understanding with him. "In the meantime, Acel, you and the rest of the crew must be discussing a real trade with the locals. We will hide the pirate crew below deck while we empty our ship and reload. By the time we finish it will be nightfall and we can take *The Beloved Loss* with *The Heart of Calais* and leave without anyone even knowing what happened. Understand?"

"Ay-ay, Captain!" the men shouted in unison, trusting their leader with no doubts.

Less than an hour later, Burke was rounding up his crew once again. "My good luck might be back, boys!" he bragged with a mischievous grin on his handsome face.

"Is it *The Beloved Loss,* Sir?" Quain asked hopefully.

"Sure enough! Says so right there along the side, *The Beloved Loss!* She is a pretty ship, is she not?" The captain nervously posed.

Acel, becoming tense and edgy, started rambling. Burke, knowing his cousin well, expected his descriptive answer. "Yes Sir, but she is an older ship. *The Beloved Loss* is not nearly as elegant or expensive as *The Heart of Calais.* Our ship is built with perfect taste. It is quick, easy to hide and maneuver, and top of the line in beauty and glamour. It's even spacious enough to have comfortable living quarters below deck. Plus, with the help of Karoly it's safe and solid."

Almost within firing range, the captain noticed the pirate ship crew raising a flag to warn Burke to keep their distance, or that they were waging war, it was too soon to tell! "Alright men, get to your stations. Garner, keep a strong command over your naval battalion. If *The Beloved Loss* starts firing or if I give you any signal of alarm, return their attack, understand? Quain, prepare bandages, medicine, and anything else you think we may need in case of injuries." As each man received their orders they nodded in acceptance and ran to their positions.

Burke continued after watching Garner and Quain rush to their duties. "Davet, boil water in case Quain needs anything sterilized. Mix up soup or whatever you can find that might soothe the weak, just in case. Leala and Miette, you two need to run back and forth between Quain, Karoly and Davet, assisting as needed. Take care of Lady Odelia. Ignore her if you want to, lock her in her cabin if necessary, but above all else, please, please, please keep her below deck and out of my way! Karoly, you are on carpenter duty! If *The Heart of Calais* is damaged I need you to fix it immediately. Steal Leala or Miette if you have to. Just make sure we stay afloat!"

All the men were dashing to their designated spot, leaving only one waiting for a command. "And Ace, my boy, you know your job is to keep everyone else in line and help me with whatever catastrophe I get us into. Alright?"

Acel nodded, whooping in excitement as he ran to check each man for the ready signal. With one thumb up and a big smile toward Burke, the First Mate approved that everything was ready for battle, trade, or fun, whichever came first.

The Beloved Loss was moving too. Still a distance from land, the pirate ship and *The Heart of Calais* were closing in on each other. Burke stood at the Helm of his ship, preparing for war with the other boat. He had his plan ready but the speed of which the enemy ship was moving clearly demonstrated that it was in no mood for peace and pleasure.

Then, to his extreme alarm, he noticed a pair of shapely arms waving him closer to *The Beloved Loss*. Burke could not believe his eyes. "Is that a woman?" He questioned out loud as he raised his binoculars.

Sure enough, it was a woman. It was an absolutely beautiful, breathtakingly stunning woman. She was a tan skinned goddess with dark hair flowing all the way down her back. The young woman was wearing a gown that left little to the imagination and motioned him forward, waving a white flag of surrender for peace.

"Hold fire, Garner. Stay on standby!" Burke yelled to his Ex-Navy Gunner.

Burke pulled the ship closer and closer until the two ships were side by side. "Permission to board, lovely lady?" he questioned to the enchantress of *The Beloved Loss*.

"Are you the captain of that ship?" she questioned.

Burke, mesmerized by her voice and entranced by her beauty had to think before answering her question. "Oh, yes, I am. My name is Burke Belcourt, and I am seeking the captain of *The Beloved Loss*. May I come aboard so I can speak with him in private, Mademoiselle?"

"Let me ask my Father," she whispered in fear, wondering what was going on. This script had been replayed hundreds of times through the past several years of Cori's life. Never had *The Beloved Loss* waited this long to attack! *Why are we not firing?* Cori wondered. *What has happened? Why is Yvet not blowing this ship to pieces by now? Oh Lord, surely my father has not taken my advice and grown a heart...*

Barely dismissing herself from the handsome captain of the other ship, Cori ran from the main deck where she had been standing to the enclosed helm where she knew her father would be intensely watching. "What is it, girl? What did he say?"

"Father, he says he has traveled here to speak with you. Why did we not attack him, Sir?" Cori asked anxiously.

"That is a French ship. It is also a very new vessel, expensive and elaborate. We could use that ship. If they are pirates then they must be quite successful. Or maybe France has started sending buccaneers, like England. Regardless, I need to know. So I told the men to hold fire. Did he say where he came from, or why he has requested me?" Marin asked his daughter, being unusually calm and patient with her.

"No sir, should I tell him he can board peaceably?" Cori asked.

Marin was quiet for a moment, contemplating his decision. "Yes. But he must come alone. If he is alone he shall be no threat to us. I will return him peaceably to Hispaniola to meet his crew when I have learned his reasons for locating me. Okay?"

"Yes, Father." Cori whispered as she turned on her heels and ran back to the enemy ship. She heard her father's words and his lack of hostility. However, she had been disappointed time and time again. Rarely did her father or Falco show mercy on anyone and she assumed this man would see the same fate.

For a moment, Cori just stood on the deck staring at the other captain, several yards away on his own ship.

Burke could not take his eyes off of the lovely girl. He could tell she was younger than him but she was a full-grown woman. She had a beautiful body and only the bare necessity was hidden from view in her seemingly uncomfortable outfit. As breathtaking as her body seemed to be, her face and hair fascinated Burke just as much. Trying to focus on business, Burke broke the spell they were casting on each other. "Well, may I come aboard?" He asked.

"Oh, right. Father says you may board alone. Your crew can sail to Hispaniola and wait for you, that is the island right over there. Can you see it?" She questioned in return.

Burke nodded his head in agreement, motioning for Acel to come forward. "Yes, Mademoiselle. I see it. My men shall not leave me unless they know I am in no harm. This is a peaceful visit, correct?"

Cori replied as honestly as she knew how. "I believe so, sir. This is as peaceful as I have ever seen pirates be in my life." She located the ship's long wooden ladder used for crossing during a ship raid. Cori struggled to pick up the large ladder, balancing it in an upright position. Easing the lumber onto the ship's ledge, she wiggled the piece across until Burke could reach it enough to pull it the rest of the way toward him.

"Ace, you heard her. I have been welcomed peaceably. Take the ship to Hispaniola. They promised to bring me there after we speak. We shall look over the goods there. Understand?" he asked, hoping his cousin understood the purposely misleading plan.

"Yes, Captain. We will wait at Hispaniola," Acel agreed as he moved toward the Helm to take over the steering of the ship. Burke knew his plan was not going the way it was supposed to but his luck seemed so great that

71

day that he decided to go with the flow, hoping that things would work out in his favor.

Hearing his words, she realized the man was in the trading business. Cori had only known one type of trader, illegal ones. She knew the difference between the buccaneers her father spoke of and true pirates, but to Cori they were all equally as bad. The thought of this handsome man being a pirate ruined him in her eyes.

She took a deep breath, watching the striking man climb across the lengthy ladder. Cori had not been around many men in her life, only the ones aboard *The Beloved Loss* or the few she encountered on her brief adventures on islands. Pirate or not, she knew that this man was exceptional. Cori hated luring innocent men or even other scandalous pirates onto *The Beloved Loss*. She hated to play a part in anyone's kidnapping or death and it hurt to see such a handsome and charming man be lost.

Cori took a footstep back as the attractive captain of *The Heart of Calais* reached the older vessel. He climbed into the boat and she noticed for the first time how he towered over her, even with her unusually long legs. As he pulled the wooden ladder back onto *The Beloved Loss*, he motioned for Acel to head for Hispaniola.

Now, standing in front of her, Cori realized what broad shoulders and muscled arms the man had. She raised her dark brown eyes to meet the crystal blue ones staring back at her. "Once again, my name is Burke Belcourt. It's a true pleasure to meet you, Mademoiselle. King Louis XIV, of France, sent me in search of your father."

Blushing in response, Cori felt the hair on her arms stand up. She knew that feeling well, it meant that Falco de Vries was standing in position, watching her closely. In a barely audible whisper, she said "I'm Corisanda Aleene St. Aubin, and my father, Marin St. Aubin, is the captain of this ship. I've been instructed to send you to him."

Cori turned to face the enclosed helm, where her father stood. Stepping out of his protective box and into view, the aging captain faced the younger man near his daughter. With a brief nod to Cori, Burke looked toward Marin. It was no doubt that the older man was French. Though he fit the part of a pirate well, there was no mistaking the same look of power and intelligence that most men of French nobility, including Burke, shared. Burke turned to Cori. "Thank you," he whispered.

"May God keep you safe, Sir. You're in the hands of *The Beloved Loss* now and most do not make it out alive," she replied as she fought back tears. Her words were cold and planned, Cori's only defense against showing her soft heart. "Goodbye, Burke Belcourt," she finished as she darted from his presence, straight to her below deck quarter to mourn for the handsome man she barely knew.

With her last sentence, Burke realized he made a dangerous mistake. Trusting pirates was nothing he should have considered. It dawned on him that it was not *normal* for a beautiful vixen to be standing in lingerie on a ship deck in the middle of the evening. She was nothing but a decoy. He turned to yell at Acel to turn *The Heart of Calais* around for help but they were already out of earshot. Taking a deep breath and holding his head high, he marched toward Captain Marin St. Aubin with the plan of having no plan at all.

THREE

"Who are you, who sent you, and why do you request me?" Marin asked the young man directly.

"My name is Burke Belcourt. I am an independent trader from France. I heard you were one of the most notorious pirates around and thought you may be interested in a business deal," Burke half-lied.

Marin did not buy it. This man walked, talked and looked like an upstanding man. He was of noble blood, no doubt. The man was well educated and highly intelligent. Marin knew the first part was true, he heard rumors of Burke Belcourt and his fancy ship being attacked by other pirates and buccaneers and that he took them all down effortlessly. His name provoked fear in many of Marin's accomplices and enemies. *He is certainly not the type of man to make deals with pirates, so what does he really want with me?* Marin wondered. Trying to get to the truth, he asked "Oh? What kind of business deal?"

Burke collected his thoughts and tried to sound truthful, "My ship is headed to Hispaniola with a full stock of Arabian rugs and chests of rare jewels. After I leave here we are sailing to the coast of America to collect corn and grain. I plan to speak to the Cubans about sugar. You are well known in this area and I thought if the two of us worked together we could both profit. If you do not want to be a part of my business venture, you should at least look at my merchandise. How would you feel about trading?"

"I want to know the real reason you are here."

"I just told you I am interested in a business deal."

"I know who you are, Captain Belcourt. Your reputation precedes you. You are not tight for money and have no need to make deals with pirates. That leads me to believe you have an alternative motive."

"Of course not, I am just looking to expand. Check my ship! You shall see that it *truly* is loaded down with goods."

"I have no doubt that it is. But that is not why you are looking for me."

"Why else would I need to speak with you?"

Marin smiled and leaned against the rail of *The Beloved Loss*. "Captain Belcourt, you are definitely intelligent. That is not in question. Most men would believe your story, but I have a feeling about you. It is a strange one. I can assure you that I will not be returning you to Hispaniola with your ship and crew. You might as well tell me the truth because you are going to be held captive on this ship one way or another."

Burke turned to run. His plan was simply to dive off of the ship and take his chances swimming to Hispaniola! Marin grabbed Burke by the sleeve of his white, half-way buttoned shirt. "Hey, son. Look around you! You are on my ship now and my crew has you surrounded. There is no escaping."

Burke knew there were men all around him. They had been hiding behind barrels, sails, and cannons the whole time. He saw them the second he boarded *The Beloved Loss* and knew now they were not there just for protection of the ship as he had hoped.

"Fine. I have been sent by the King of France, Louis XIV. He wanted me to demand your immediate surrender. Your reputation also precedes you, St. Aubin. It has been rumored that you are French and the King feels that you are hurting our currently passive status. I can assure you that they shall be looking for me with haste. You will not get away with holding me here," Burke conceded.

"Really? France wants me to stop, ay? Well, I doubt they can catch me. Your King can't, just as his father before him couldn't either. You are supposedly the only man who can outsmart me and I have you here now. I shall take my chances with the French." Glancing behind his shoulder he yelled, "Falco! Captain Belcourt wants to arrest us. What do you think we should do with him?"

A tall man with blonde hair sauntered out of a shaded area across the boat. He walked with an attitude of arrogance and sneered derisively at Burke. "Well, Captain, I think we should make an example of him. Feed him to the sharks, or maybe just snap his neck in front of his friends…"

"Those are good ideas, my boy. But we will hold off for now. Let's lock him up. Maybe we can make a better example out of him if we keep him alive. Think about it this way, if we sail around showing our hostage off to all the other pirates who fear *him* we shall be forever known as the crew who *defeated* Belcourt, right?" Marin pondered aloud.

"*Ja*, I suppose, but…" Falco began to object.

"Yes. Yes, I think we will do that. We shall be more feared than ever. Laron! Zeeman! Yvet! Lock him up in Cori's quarters. It is the only one with a bolt on the outside of the door."

"Where will Cori sleep?" Falco demanded. "Let her sleep with me, we are soon to wed anyway."

"Then how would I be able to lock her up when we stop places? She will escape in seconds. Our new prisoner needs to be locked in a room where he cannot lock us out. Cori's room is the only prisoner-safe place on the ship," Marin reminded.

Falco reasoned angrily, "You cannot trust this man locked overnight sharing a room with my fiancé!"

"Do not worry. I would not touch your woman. I have a fiancé of my own and I cannot stand to be near her.

The last thing I need now is another woman to deal with,"
Burke mumbled confidently. He had no doubt that he
would escape easily. He just needed to come up with a
plan. Burke knew he was not defeated. All he needed was
to buy his time wisely.

"It is settled then. He will not touch Cori. Now
throw him in, lock him up, and let us celebrate our victory,"
Marin laughed.

The three men who had been summoned grabbed
him forcefully by the shoulders. They heaved him up and
hauled him hastily down the creaking stairs of *The Beloved
Loss*. A door was thrown open and a screech was heard as
the men literally threw Burke into the room. He probably
would have sailed all the way through the room and landed
on the far side of it but something soft that screeched
loudly broke his fall. As he and his screaming *pillow*
crashed to the floor he heard the door being slammed
behind him and locked from the outside.

Sprawled across the floor, Burke laid still for a moment as he tried to realize what happened. It did not take long to figure it out as two boney fists pounded away at his back between him and the hard wooden floor. He jumped up hastily as he realized his pillow was a woman. It was the maiden in lingerie, now wearing a long flannel night gown but still just as beautiful and breathtaking as before. "What on Earth are you doing in my room, you moron? You could have killed me! You landed right on top of me! What do I look like to you, a bed?" The girl screamed irately with a stomp of her foot.

Burke stared at the dark haired angel for a few moments before remembering his anger toward the pirate decoy. "Well, if your father and fiancé had not arrested me I would not be here! Thanks for getting me held hostage, you little coquette!"

"Coquette? Me? Honestly? You are an imbecile, sir!" Cori blurted in defense.

"Oh, really? Correct me if I am wrong. You dress up in a see-through night gown, dance around on a boat deck, and purposely lure innocent men to your ship so Daddy can attack. Is that right or wrong?"

"You are nothing but a pirate too! How does that make you any more innocent than I am?"

"I am no pirate! I am allowed to trade by the King of France…"

Cori cut him off before he could continue rattling, "Fine, then you are a buccaneer. It is the same thing! Thieves are thieves, whether Kings let them do it or not! I might be a *coquette pirate* but you are a *thieving buccaneer*. We are *both* worthless, not just me!"

The girl threw herself onto her bed, pulled the covers over her head and turned toward the wall. "Do not even think about sleeping near me! There is a chair over there," Cori finished with a tear glimmering in her haughty eyes.

Burke was to confused and irritated to reply. He did not explain that he was not a buccaneer. *Let her think what she wants, why should I care?* Burke decided as he plopped into the uncomfortable seat. The girl seemed to hate pirates and he had heard Marin say she would escape in seconds if she had a chance. *Why does she work for them then? If she hates pirates so much she shouldn't help them.*

He was curious about the fascinating girl but he had more important things to worry about. If he did not make it to Hispaniola by sunrise his men would come looking for him. That was *comforting* but he could tell that *The Beloved Loss* was now flying rapidly in the other direction. Marin did not want *The Heart of Calais* to catch them. That was *discomforting.*

He had to think of a good escape. *The ship has to stop sometime and they do not plan to kill me yet. I am sure they shall let me out of this room once we get a fair distance away from land and my crew. Then I can hear when we plan to stop again. I need to find a way to loosen the lock on the door. When they leave the ship to raid an island or make a trade I can break the lock. Next, I can sneak off the boat and find a way to get to Hispaniola. If I know Acel, he will keep watch on that island. I can hide out until he arrives looking for me.*

Cuddling deeper into the uncomfortable, cold, cranberry colored chair, Burke took a last glance at the beauty in the bed across the room. He knew she was awake although she deliberately feigned sleep. The girl faced the other direction motionless but he knew she was conscious by the uneven rise and fall of her body as she breathed.

Burke could tell that she was quietly crying. The pirate princess seemed so strong, cold, heartless, and distant that he could not imagine what would make her hurt enough to cry. The gentleman in him wanted to comfort her, tell her she would surely be fine. However, the pirate-captive component would not give him the ability to pity the beautiful enemy

Rolling his eyes in disappointment that the day had turned out as unsuccessful as it had, Burke tried propping his feet up on a flimsy table close by. *What was I thinking?* Burke wondered. He was a man of complete control. He never lost a battle and never looked stupid. Burke was confident because he had proven himself to be capable. He was a leader, strong, fierce, and always the best at everything.

Why then, did I let myself act so foolishly today? I always focus! I always prepare! I do not let myself become distracted! But he knew that becoming distracted was exactly what happened. He saw the prettiest woman he had ever seen. She had an image more alluring than any other on Earth. The girl drew him in as if she was an enchanting sea nymph and he was her prey. He never saw it coming. Once he spotted the dark haired beauty he fell into a trance and forgot his entire mission. *Idiot!*

The boat was moving swiftly and he could hear the soothing sounds of the ocean under him. He almost felt that the ocean belonged to him. As if the water was created only for Burke to sail on. It was his career, his passion, and his life. It would soon be ending along with all the other things he loved to do. *It shall all be over the moment I marry Odelia...* Burke jerked himself to an upright position, throwing his legs to the ground.

That is it! He considered. *I haven't even thought of Odelia since I have been taken hostage! Maybe she will think I died! Maybe she shall marry someone else before I am found! The longer I stay aboard The Beloved Loss the better the chances of escaping Odelia!* He leaned back into his chair and smiled contentedly, *I shall try to enjoy this little cruise. My men can handle my ship and I will get home eventually... what's the hurry?*

Burke smiled to himself, closed his eyes, and let his mind wander where it would. He imagined the ocean, *his* ocean, swaying under him as he sailed through the deep, blue sea for a lifetime. His thoughts were peaceful and placid as he pictured himself walking across the deck of *The Heart of Calais.*

Then, there she was, the dark haired beauty he met only a couple hours before. She was wearing the same tight night gown and smiling seductively. Burke threw his eyes open with a jolt. He stared at the vixen who had finally cried herself to sleep. *No more thinking about her, Burke! Keep your head in the game.* He scolded himself. He closed his eyes again and drifted into a painfully uneasy slumber.

Burke awoke to a loud knocking noise pounding in his ears. Throwing himself out of the chair and stumbling unsteadily to his feet he twirled toward the door to look for the invisible, giant man undoubtedly charging into the room. To his surprise, all he found was the brunette beauty stomping one foot, both hands on her hips, staring at the door.

"Let me out this instant! Leave him here all you want to but you are not keeping me locked in this room one more second! Do you understand? Laron! Yvet! Klaas! Ugh, for mercy sake, Falco! Someone better let me out of here! Guillermo, Novia, where are you? Let me out this instant!" She screamed irately.

"What is the matter with you, woman?" Burke demanded.

Cori glared at the handsome captive. "Do not call me "woman", nor shall you call me "*mevrouw*", I hear that plenty from Falco! Because of you I am locked in this stupid room! They have just forgotten me here!"

He did not understand what *mevrouw* meant or what the crazy girl was talking about. Burke shrugged, "I was under the impression that they kept you locked away until they needed you. What happened? Did you get yourself in trouble and this is your punishment? How long does it take for them to forgive your mistake and return you to normal life?"

She began in a pouty whisper, hands still on her hips. "Punishment? Bah! Every minute here is punishment. My whole life is punishment! I am just as much of a prisoner as you, Sir, but I have earned the right to roam the ship when we are in the middle of the ocean and I cannot escape!" The last sentence grew louder and louder until she was screaming once again.

Turning back to the door and stomping her right foot, she wailed again. "Falco! Falco! Do you hear me? You better let me out this instant! Laron! Yvet, you stupid oafs! Klaas, I am sorry for putting that dead fish in your bed last week! Please, just let me out!" The door flew open, knocking Cori right into Burke's arms.

A short woman with auburn red hair stood in the doorway. Although small in stature and petite in frame, the woman held herself with an air of power and control. She eyed Cori with a hateful glare and a scowl across her lips. The woman's hair was braided, hanging all the way down her back and swaying quite close to her knees. "What do you think you are doing, Corisanda?" The woman asked condescendingly.

Immediately realizing that she was still in Burke's arms, Cori jumped away glaring at him accusingly. "Hey," Burke shrugged again, "you caught my fall yesterday. I just thought I would return the favor."

"Thanks anyway," she mumbled as she stared at the floor. Burke instantly noticed Cori's inability to look the older woman in the eyes as she whispered dejectedly. "I am sorry, Sharlene. I only want out of this room."

Sharlene ignored Cori's plea, pointing her eyes toward the newest man aboard her husband's ship. "You must be Mr. Belcourt, Marin told me about your interesting arrival."

"Yes. Are you going to let Cori out of here or not?" He asked. Why he felt the need to protect the teasing wench who put him in this predicament in the first place was beyond his imagination, but he could not fight the urge to leave her to her own defenses.

Sharlene stood motionless for a moment, still staring at the young man. With a wicked grin, the red haired woman turned to face her step-daughter. "Of course, Corisanda. You are no prisoner here, right? As a matter of fact, I suppose your new friend can do little harm now either. We are a good distance from land and his own ship." She pushed the door further open and turned to depart.

Cori picked her head back up and glanced at Burke. "Thanks, I guess," she whispered, hoping he would not ask her about Sharlene.

"No problem, let's get out of here." Burke shrugged.

"You should probably try to enjoy your day. As soon as the moon begins to rise we shall be locked in again," Cori advised sarcastically. With that, she strolled quickly out of the room, up the stairs, and onto the main deck before Burke could even reach the doorway.

As soon as Burke ascended the stairs to the deck, Falco stood waiting and ready. "Just so you are aware, Captain Marin and I were awake late last night discussing the best plans for you. I begged him to feed you to the sharks. However, he still thinks it is best to keep you alive for a *little* longer. So, while you are with us you will be working. Today you shall make yourself useful helping Yvet, our Gunner. Learn what you can. If you prove yourself a burden to us I shall get my way and you will be history. *Ja?*"

Burke nodded his head with an amused grin, "Sure, whatever you say, *boss.*"

His sarcasm did not go unnoticed by Falco. Before dismissing the prisoner, the Quartermaster of *The Beloved Loss* added one more piece of advice. "If you touch my fiancé, I shall kill you. Do not look at Corisanda, do not even speak to her." With that, Falco sauntered away to his other duties, leaving Burke to control his mischievous grin.

Burke approached Yvet as one would a skittish deer. By what he had gathered watching the Gunner as he took in his surroundings the evening before, Burke knew that Yvet was not very satisfied with his life. Burke first saw Yvet as Cori was walking away from him right before he met Captain Marin St. Aubin. Nothing fooled Burke; there was nothing that he could not understand or get the best of. *Nothing, besides Cori.*

"Need something?" Yvet asked bluntly when Burke approached him.

Burke shrugged, "Well, that little weasel you men call your leader *ordered* me to come *learn* from you today."

"Ha! Falco is *not* my leader. The Captain, Marin, he is worthy of being called someone's leader. Falco de Vries is not worthy of mopping the deck on this ship." Yvet was doing precisely what Burke had intended. Burke wanted answers, he wanted to know all the weak points about *The Beloved Loss* and it's faithful or unfaithful crew.

Liking the Gunner solely for the common trait of disliking the Quartermaster, Burke decided to give it to Yvet straight. "Listen, I am supposed to learn all about being a Gunner from you today. That shows Falco's ignorance by itself. I am the captain of *The Heart of Calais*, the most feared vessel on the ocean. Now, do you not assume I would know all about the ship's gunman position?"

Yvet pondered Burke's words for a moment. "Yes, you would. I have heard about you, Burke Belcourt."

"Really?" Burke questioned without surprise, "And what did you hear about me?"

"I heard other pirates and buccaneers speak of your keen ability to defeat anyone who stands in the way of doing whatever the heck you please to do," he paused for a moment as if he was finished speaking. Then, with hesitation in his voice he continued, "I also heard a few ladies on the coast of Peru gossiping about your good looks. I was listening to them prattle and I heard one say that you were reportedly such a good sailor because the ocean is all you think about. They said you hated all women and did not ever plan to marry."

Yvet chuckled for a moment before meeting eyes with Burke for the first time through the entire conversation. "Why do you have this reputation for disliking women?" Yvet asked in amusement.

"Well, I see where they would say that. You see, I did plan to remain a bachelor. Of course I notice women and enjoy dinner with a beautiful lady occasionally, but no, I did not plan to marry. However, I am apparently engaged, and no matter what I do, I cannot escape it. So I suppose I am off the market for them anyhow," Burke replied, not wanting to think about Odelia, much less discuss her. "Anyway, what should I do to *learn* from you, *Sir*?"

"Let's not fool ourselves, you probably know more about being a Gunner than I do. Help me clean a few of these cannons and pretend to watch for any ship getting close to ours. If Falco asks, I am teaching you all I can. Deal?" Yvet bargained.

Burke answered without paying much attention, "Sounds good to me." He constantly watched for Cori but she never came around. *She must be somewhere relaxing in a warm bath or sewing a gown for her wedding to Falco,* he surmised.

Cori seemed to be a ghost that morning. *Where is she?* He wondered over and over again. The ship was grand but it was not large enough to hide someone completely. Burke even saw Captain Marin and Sharlene occasionally. At lunch, it dawned on Burke where the enchanting sea nymph had been all day. She helped one other woman, a Hispanic maid, serve meals to the rest of the crew.

The pirate gang was provided according to rank, from the captain and his wife first, down to Guillermo, another Hispanic servant. Cori grimaced when she noticed one last platter of food on the cart. Searching desperately for Novia and frowning when she realized the woman was still occupied with others, Cori took a deep, exasperated breath, picked up the last plate and made her way toward Burke. Burke was sitting alone and he thanked her kindly when she brought his plate. "I wondered where you were today," he voiced.

"Oh yeah? I was working." She mumbled. There was a preoccupied tone in her voice making it seem that she really did not care to speak to him.

"Well your job is done, I guess. What will you do for the rest of the day? Bask in the sun? Take a nap? What does a privileged pirate's daughter do on normal days?" Burke questioned.

Cori sighed and rolled her eyes at the seemingly ignorant man. "As a matter of fact, I shall *still* be working," she said as she abruptly turned to leave.

Burke tried to catch her but she was gone before he could beg her back. Feeling eyes staring in his direction he glanced toward the large table where the captain, Quartermaster, and captain's wife sat. Marin was staring at Burke questioningly, Falco was glaring viciously, and Sharlene seemed almost jealous of it all. Burke smiled and waved toward them as if they were old friends. His gesture intensified the pirate leaders' reactions. Burke laughed and turned back to his plate of roast, carrots, and potatoes.

Cleaning cannons proved to be a shipping career less interesting than Burke's own. The lack of thought usage needed to work with Yvet gave Burke Belcourt plenty of time to think about his life. He thought of *The Heart of Calais* and his crew, wondering where they were at the moment and when they would be able to track *The Beloved Loss* down to retrieve their captain.

Or, if he would be required to escape the pirate crew and how long he would hide before Acel found him. That brought forth ideas of Odelia and the wedding he would soon be forced to participate in. Silently gagging, Burke wondered if he would still be on board *The Beloved Loss* when Cori and Falco were married.

Burke felt like an idiot for allowing himself to be so entranced by the beautiful young woman who was so *happily* betrothed to the most "intelligent idiot" known to man. *Why would Cori want to marry Falco?*

Burke questioned himself, *Sure, he is attractive enough for most women but Cori could marry a Prince or a King with her beauty. Plus, Falco is intolerable. Why any woman would want to marry him is beyond me! Cori is a pirate so I am sure she wants to marry another pirate. She probably loves this life more than she lets on and that is*

also detestable. It is a shame that someone as beautiful as

she would be wasted by such an awful lifestyle and career.

Burke allowed himself to mull over his thoughts all afternoon. He could not understand why he scanned the boat with his eyes every few minutes to see if he could catch a glimpse of the beautiful pirate princess. When evening came and the sun started lowering itself in the sky the voice of the captain was clearly heard across the ship, "Time for dinner, men! Clean up and relax for the night!"

Burke turned to Yvet with a grin, "I guess we are done."

"Until tomorrow at least, I have requested that you work with me another few days. I am sorry you are here, you do not deserve to deal with Falco," Yvet replied apologetically as they straightened all the cannons into a row.

"Well, it is my own fault. I should have never allowed myself to become mystified by your ship's decoy," Burke retorted.

Yvet seemed confused for a moment, "The ship's decoy? You mean Cori?"

"Yes. I think it's pretty cold for a woman like Cori to lure in ships so her father can attack," Burke explained as if Yvet did not already know all about Cori.

Yvet shook his head in a disagreeing gesture, "No, *Cori* does not trap ships or sailors. *Sharlene* does."

"Sharlene? No, it was Cori who stood on the deck last night in her lingerie to persuade me aboard her daddy's ship," Burke calmly argued.

"Yes. Poor, sweet, Cori…" Yvet mumbled quietly, shaking his head from left to right.

It was obvious that Yvet pitied the girl, but his reason for doing so was a mystery. *She is not forced to work on this ship and she is not forced to be a pirate. If she wanted out she could surely do it. This is what Cori wants to do, so why would anyone bestow sympathy on the pretty little criminal? I know she calls herself a prisoner here and she has tried to escape a few times, but no doubt those were only in times where she was being reprimanded or had a little lover's spat with Falco. She probably only does it for attention.*

Burke considered these thoughts in his mind as he shook Yvet's hand for a job well done. As he walked toward his shared quarters below deck, he realized that whether Cori deserved compassion or not, even he could not help but feel some for her. She was stunning and puzzling, something about her made Burke curious to delve deeper into her life.

FOUR

Burke was unsure what to do or where to go. Some of the pirates descended the stairs to their below-deck quarters and others went straight to the dining area. Deciding to find Cori, Burke went directly to their shared room. Once again, the room was empty and Cori was nowhere in sight.

Where does this girl hide? He wondered. *If I did not know better, which I do, I would think they keep her working with the servants or something! Of course that cannot be, her daddy is the captain and her fiancé is the Quartermaster. Surely she has a carefree life aboard this ship.*

Burke washed his face in a small water basin and left the room, closing the door behind him. He took a mental picture of the door, the locks, and the hinges so he could plan his strategy for escaping the room when he needed to. Walking briskly to the ship's kitchen and dining area, Burke took in his surroundings. Since lunch had been delivered above deck he had not even been sure that the ship's dining area was in use. Shockingly, the large room was a grand one indeed. Beautiful tables made from mahogany sat in the spacious, fancy room.

Although the area was a lovely thing to admire, Burke was more interested in seeing a form even lovelier, *Cori.* When he finally spotted her she was still wearing old clothes, obviously meant to work in. She passed out food, drinks, and bowls. For the first time since stepping onto the ship, Burke realized that it was full of people. He had met most of the crewmembers throughout the day but the ship also had a huge group of children living on it. "What do they have these children here for?" Burke asked aloud.

A voice Burke had not heard before answered him, "Falco kidnapped them from Argentina. We are taking them to Africa for trade unless their families offer us a worthy reward for bringing them home. Since their parents are all poor and cannot afford to do that, we are preparing them for Africa's slave market."

Burke took the young man in. He looked to be in his early thirties. The man was decently attractive and seemed passably intelligent. "Who are you?" Burke asked.

"I am the Boatswain of *The Beloved Loss*. My name is Laron," he answered.

Burke was troubled over the abducted children and did not see a reason to speak more to the other man so chose not to reply. Laron, on the other hand, was not finished talking to the newcomer of the ship. "Mr. Belcourt, I would like to speak to you about your sleeping arrangements," he stated.

Burke faced Laron with one eyebrow raised, "Oh? I did not know that anyone had a choice, besides Captain St. Aubin, in my sleeping arrangements."

"True, no one does. All I want to say is that you should respect Cori and her virtue. She has a hard life; do not make it harder by disgracing her. Cori has been sheltered on this ship. Yes, she has been subjected to a lot of bad things, but a man's advances are not one of them. If you pressure Cori into doing anything inappropriate, Falco will be mad *for himself.* I will be mad *for Cori.* Understand?" He prompted.

After being warned *not to touch or harm Cori* multiple times since boarding *The Beloved Loss*, Burke was beginning to be quite offended. *What kind of creep do these people think I am? I have never pressured any woman into doing anything with me.* For a moment he felt almost as if Odelia's rumors had spread even to *The Beloved Loss*!

Pirates are trying to teach me manners and respect for women, what is the world coming to? Burke had enough, he felt like putting the pirate crew in their place and letting them know that he knew more about virtuous and ladylike women than they did!

The look on Burke's face warned Laron that an argument was coming, "Laron, I am a French Count. Do you not think that a gentleman, taught proper manners from childhood, would know not to force anything upon a woman? Why do people keep telling me not to *touch* Cori, not to *harm* Cori, to *respect* Cori, and *pitying poor, innocent* Cori? *She* is a pirate criminal. *You* are a pirate criminal. *I* am *not* a pirate or a criminal. *I* am a *Count* and a ship *captain*. I am *educated* and *respectable*! Not to mention that *I* am *engaged*, happily or unhappily makes no difference. Why does everyone think that I might fall in love with Cori and whisk her away, get her pregnant, or some other heinous indecency?"

Laron calmly smiled at Burke. He understood why the dark haired man would be so angry. "Falco might be afraid that you would whisk her away or get her pregnant, Marin might be afraid of the same thing. Yvet and I might pity Cori. But none of us are afraid you will fall in love with her, because, the truth is that everyone does and you undoubtedly shall fall for her before you leave too. Believe me, you will. That is to be expected. I know you are a man of your word, respectable, and upstanding. If you fell in love with Cori you would marry her, and make her happy for the first time in her life. I cannot be worried about that. What I am worried about is not that you might fall in love with Cori, but that Cori might fall in love with you."

Laron paused for a moment to let his words sink in for Burke. When the French captain was obviously perplexed, Laron continued, "She has never been around a respectable man, Mr. Belcourt. Corisanda has been raised on a pirate ship with no one but four or five men to consider for marriage, half of which are twice her age. Do you not think she might be amazed by you, smitten with you, so to speak? I do. Cori has never fit in here. She is a sweet girl with a heart of gold. What if she fell in love with you, Mr. Belcourt? Falco would kill you and she would have that on her conscience for the rest of her life."

He paused for a moment and shrugged before continuing, "Or, you would escape without her and she would be forced to continue with her plans of marrying Falco, wondering why you did not save her. I am not concerned about you being a bad person for Cori to be around, I am worried about the opposite. You might be good, kind, and honorable enough that Cori might fall in love with you. Do you see what I mean, Mr. Belcourt?"

Burke felt horrible for being offended by the other young man's words. "I apologize, Laron. I understand what you are saying but if I were you I would not worry much. She despises me, of that I am quite sure. One thing I do not understand is everyone's pity of the girl. She chooses to be here and I am quite sure that she is treated like a Queen aboard her father's ship. She shall always be taken care of, right? I suppose I am just confused by all I am taking in, please forgive me of my earlier irritation with you."

The Count turned away, hoping the other man would leave. He did not want to be rude or hateful and he appreciated Laron's honesty, he was just to puzzled by everyone's devotion and sorrow for the girl.

"Mr. Belcourt, I will be leaving to take my dinner. But before I go, I would like to say one more thing to you," Laron interjected before leaving Burke.

Burke nodded his head, "What do you want to say?"

"Do not *assume* so much. Do not *assume* that Cori hates you by her protection methods. Do not *assume* that she is happy here or chose this life freely unless you were here all her life. Do not *assume* that Falco and Marin provide her with a privileged life like royalty where you come from would. Do not *assume* things, Mr. Belcourt. If you want to know, find out the truth. If you do not want to know, try not to look so curious," Laron said with a knowing smile.

Burke stared at Laron for a moment. He was not sure what the Boatswain meant by his statement. One question kept coming to Burke's mind and he decided to take Laron's advice and find out. "Laron," Burke began, smiling back, "If you worry so much about the girl and love her so dearly, why do you not marry her?"

"Do you remember how I told you that I do *not* think you are a bad person who might hurt Cori?" Laron asked in return.

"Yes," Burke agreed, not understanding where the man was going with his retort.

"Well, sir, I *am* a bad person. I know that I would hurt Cori. I am not worthy to be her husband. Falco is not either, and if I was any better than him I would fight for her. However, I do not want to free Cori from a life of pain and put her straight into another one. She deserves better than a pirate like *me*, Mr. Belcourt. Cori deserves a *French Count*," and with that statement Laron nodded his head in farewell and sauntered to a table, leaving Burke in complete disarray.

Burke sat alone during dinner, eating his meal. He made a deal with himself to assume less, as Laron had suggested. He searched the room with his eyes to look for Cori. She sat at a table with the two Hispanic servants. Cori would only eat a couple bites then rush to the three long tables of children nearby. She would separate boys from fighting, girls from giggling to loudly, and stop food from being thrown. Cori seemed tender and caring, disciplining the children with loving kindness. He could tell that the little ones all loved Cori also, and that was no assumption.

By the time dinner was over the moon had set in the warm night sky. Just as Cori had warned that morning, Falco, Klaas, and Zeeman approached Burke to lock him up for the night. Falco picked at Burke for a fight but did not get a rise out of him. No one threw Burke into the room that night; he walked himself to Cori's quarters and closed the door behind himself waiting to hear the clanking lock.

Cori sat on a small stool beside the water basin. She ran a silver handled brush through her long black hair. This was the first time Burke actually saw Cori's hair down, out of a bun or a braid. "Good evening, Mademoiselle," Burke greeted warmly.

"If you say so, Captain," she replied caustically. Cori was not sure what the man was up to with his manners and charm but he was not going to fool her! She had been warned immensely by Novia that men play mind games and Cori was determined not to be tricked by them.

"So, you help cook and serve meals during the day?" He asked, trying to start conversation.

"Yes, I do."

"What else do you do, Mademoiselle?"

"I clean."

"Oh," Burke replied. He knew her guard was up and she did not plan to let him get to know her. Regardless, he kept trying. "Do you clean dishes or the ship?"

"I clean both. I help clean whatever Aunt Novia needs me to clean. I help Uncle Guillermo cook whatever needs cooking. I help Yvet and the boys shoot when my father attacks a tough enemy. I help Zeeman when repairs need to be made to the ship. I help Klaas bandage wounds or tame fevers when the crew is sick or injured. I take orders from Sharlene and my father when they need me, as well. I even take orders from Laron when I know it is important. Do you have any other questions about my daily schedule, Sir?" Cori asked impatiently.

"No, it sounds as if you stay busier than I thought," Burke conceded.

"I do not sit around sunbathing or napping, as you suggested earlier. I work on this ship and earn my keep. I have no choice but to live this life of pirating so I live it as I'm told to," she explained testily. Cori was in no mood to deal with the handsome stranger. He was so attractive, smart, and charming. It was hard for her to hate him but she refused to admit any care for her fellow pirates, not even a good looking one.

"I understand that now, Mademoiselle. You work hard. Tell me what you mean by having no choice but to live as a pirate. If you do not like being here why do you stay?" He asked.

"I have no choice. My father says that this is where I shall live my life so it is where I am. A person cannot leave a pirate ship just because they want to. Surely you know that," Cori hesitantly replied.

Although Burke already knew the answer to his question, he posed it anyway, "Do you want to live your whole life on this ship?"

"Of course not! Why anyone would want to be a pirate is beyond me! Why do people choose that career anyway, Captain Belcourt?" Cori defiantly inquired.

Burke had already forgotten that Cori still thought he was a pirate as well, so not realizing that her question was directed at his own career, he answered, "Oh, different reasons I suppose. Some crooks want power and the only way they can get it is by attracting worse scoundrels to control with a quite unrespectable career. Others turn to pirating for prosperity. Maybe they are poor and hope for a better life? If you already have a bad life it could be hard to imagine pirating being any worse. Why did your father choose this career?"

Cori knew that she should always listen to her Aunt Novia. This man was not to be trusted, however, it was hard not to! He seemed like such a charming, intriguing, comforting gentleman. She decided to tell him some of the story, leaving out one important detail, the reason Cori's father hated her.

"He was a respected Navy captain in France. The story I have heard is that he left France in search of new land to claim. He stopped at Cuba and met my mother. Of course, Cuba was already claimed by my mother's homeland, Spain. Yellow Fever hit the island on their wedding day and they barely escaped before being infected with the disease. They were sailing to France for my father to retire, sale his belongings, and move to Cuba with my mother and her family."

Cori paused for a moment to catch her breath. The rest of the story was painful, "Nonetheless, before they reached France my mother died. By what I have heard, my father went crazy. He drank a lot, paced the ship at all hours of the night, did not sleep, and made a few really, really bad decisions. The crew thought that if they could get him to France then he would recover and be alright.

Then, one of his bad decisions ruined their hope. Out of anger he attacked a peaceful vessel and ordered the sailors killed. He stole what they had aboard the ship and claimed it all as his own. Uncle Guillermo said that he cried all through the night and no one could sleep for hearing his loud wails. By morning he was hard as a rock, cold, heartless, emotionless, just like he is now. He announced to the crew that he was not returning to France. From that point on, he was a pirate."

"I am sorry, Corisanda. Did she die of Yellow Fever?"

"No."

"Oh. Well, I am sorry for your loss," Burke could tell she did not want to discuss the details of her mother's death. He was not sure what happened to Cori's mother but he knew it must be a painful subject so he did not ask any other questions about it.

Cori feigned a small smile, "Thank you, it is alright."

"I know it is not easy to leave a pirate ship if you have been commanded to stay, but if I hated something as badly as you hate being on this ship I would find some way to leave!" Burke said encouragingly.

"I have tried to leave before," Cori sighed.

"Yes, last night your father and fiancé were talking about where to put me. Your father mentioned that your room was the only one with a door locking from the outside. He said you would escape if given any opportunity. So what went wrong with your previous escape plans?" Burke asked, refusing to end conversation with his roommate.

"Well, many things have gone wrong. I have tried to escape at least twenty times in my life. My father had been trading with islands and countries for a very long time. He knows his way around each of them and where all the hiding places are. I do not. Usually, if I escape on land I get lost because I have no idea where I am or where to go. My father finds me effortlessly. Another problem is that I look quite different than most do anywhere I have ever been and I am easily pointed out in a crowd," Cori explained.

Burke could not help but stare at the beauty before him. She was in a long, white cotton nightgown. It fit her body perfectly and showed her curves. Cori's long black hair flowed down her back and her clean, tan skin seemed to glow in the candle light. "Yes, you are quite beautiful. I'm sure everyone notices you."

"No, I do not mean that I am necessarily beautiful. I am half Spaniard and half French. I am darker than the French and lighter than the Spaniards. I am taller than most women but I am shorter than most men. I am well educated because I had nothing other to do on this ship than to study and read, yet I have no knowledge of the world. I just do not fit in anywhere and I stand out in a crowd." She sat down on her bed and faced the handsome man sitting across from her.

Burke shrugged his shoulders, "Have you ever thought that maybe fitting in is not a good thing? Standing out and being one of a kind is much more attractive, if you ask me!"

"Perhaps, but not if you are trying to hide from someone."

"I suppose that is true. Maybe escaping onto land is not a good way for you to escape then," Burke suggested.

Cori looked at Burke like he had lost his mind, "What do you mean?"

"Have you ever considered fleeing by a boat?" He asked. She turned her head sideways, silently urging him to continue his idea. "Does your father ever stop on land where other boats are docked?"

"Rarely, but sometimes when we are visiting South America we do not attack passing ships. We sail by peacefully so we can take the land by a surprise attack. Then, sometimes when we stop there are other boats coming or going. In Africa we go straight to the port as if we were legal as can be! The pirating cities there are feared and dangerous, illegal traders are a commonality and no one tries to arrest us as they would if we stopped in Europe." She quickly informed him.

"Okay, so what if you snuck off *The Beloved Loss* and onto another boat that was soon to be leaving. If your father noticed you were missing he would probably check the surrounding land. You could hide in the cargo area of the boat until you were days into the sea or until it stopped at another island where you felt safe and wanted to reside," he prompted.

"That is excellent! Oh, I have been trying to think of a plan for so long now, one that would not fail! This is perfect! You will not tell them where I am, will you?" She whispered.

He shook his head from left to right, "No, I plan to leave this blasted boat at my first opportunity also. If you do not tell on me, I shall not tell on you. Deal?"

"Deal!" Cori agreed with a smile.

"So when are you going to try the plan out?" He asked as he snuggled into the uncomfortable cranberry chair.

"I shall do it as soon as we get somewhere with other boats coming in or out! I probably will not have my chance until we get to Africa," she answered with enthusiasm.

"Africa? Is that where we are going now?" Burke questioned, remembering Laron also mentioning Africa that evening.

"Yes, we have stopped at all the places along our route in South America and the neighboring islands. Our last stop was Hispaniola and we left there right before meeting you! Now we are on our way to Africa with a loaded ship, ready to trade or sale and reload to head back this way."

"Interesting," Burke nodded. "I know my way around there pretty well. Maybe I could escape by that route too."

"If Falco does not have you killed first," Cori reminded.

The captive captain laughed loudly, "He already hates me so it's truly possible that he might try."

Cori smiled in response. The sound of the man's laughter made her heart race. She knew that this man was not trustable. He was just like any other man, only out to use whoever he needs to in order to get whatever he wants. The difference between this man and most was that he was so breathtakingly attractive. Cori thought he must be the most handsome man alive, but she knew that she had not seen many men.

She was nearly as tall as most of the men she had met in her life but this handsome pirate towered over her. Cori never denied being attracted to his strong arms and handsome face. She could outsmart most men, especially Klaas and Zeeman, but Burke seemed different in that way too.

Looking up, she realized he was staring directly at her again. "Do you love Falco?" He asked bluntly.

She answered as honestly as she could, "No. I loathe him."

By the time she finished her sentence Burke was already inquiring for more information, "Then why are you marrying him? Do you not know how beautiful you are? If you left this ship you could be a bride of royalty. You could marry a Prince, a Duke, or a Count. Men would fight over you left and right. You know, you are different than most women. Instead of being timid and meek, you are strong and brave. Would you not like to marry someone you love?"

"Of course I would! But it is not that easy, you see. My father promised me to Falco when I was only fourteen. There are a million reasons I want off of this ship, and Falco is one of them. I hope to escape before being forced to marry him but I have already been eighteen for three months. I am supposed to be planning my wedding as we speak. By the end of the year I will be his wife. Unless, of course, I can get off of this ship," she retorted.

Burke was not sure what he should say next. His heart throbbed as he stared at the beautiful maiden. He hoped she would not be forced to marry Falco de Vries, for her sake. For some reason that he could not understand, he even hoped she would not marry Falco for Burke's own sake.

Stop getting involved, he told himself. *I need to be concerned about getting myself away from this ship. Falco already thinks I want his woman; I shall get myself killed trying to help Cori. Besides, I am engaged to Odelia. I like that about as little as Cori likes being engaged to Falco. I have my own problems to worry about.* Still, he could not help but stare at the lovely girl and worry about her future. Deciding to clear his mind with some much needed rest, he looked toward Cori again, "Goodnight."

"Goodnight, Captain Belcourt. Thank you for the idea," Cori responded happily.

Burke smiled, "You are welcome. Hey, can I ask you one more question?"

"Sure, I guess. What is it?"

"What should I call you? Cori, or Corisanda?"

She paused for a moment, not sure what to say, "I like the name Corisanda because my mother picked it out. It means *flower of my heart* in her native tongue. Now the only person who calls me Corisanda is Sharlene. Just call me Cori, I guess."

"Okay Cori, see you in the morning."

"See you then, Captain Belcourt."

"You can call me Burke."

"Okay, Burke." She closed her eyes but was awake for many hours thinking of her grand escape. Sometimes the handsome man sleeping across the room entered her mind as well.

FIVE

Burke awoke to the sound of someone bustling around the room. "Cori, what are you doing?" he asked as he pushed his eyes open. "Is it already morning?"

"Almost, you will be expected for work soon but I am required to get an early start. Sorry I woke you," she quietly apologized.

"No, it's fine," he replied.

A light knock rapped on the door and the Hispanic maid rushed in. She glared at Burke, still sitting in his uncomfortable chair. "I was just checking on you," she whispered to Cori. The woman turned to leave and closed the door behind her.

"Does she dislike me as well?" Burke asked, wondering how he could have offended the cranky maid.

133

Cori grinned broadly at Novia's concern, "No, she does not dislike you. She is my Aunt and does not like the idea of any man sleeping in my room. It is not appropriate at all, but we are pirates so why should she expect otherwise? Anyway, she is fine, as long as you do not try to jeopardize me somehow… which you will not do, or I shall kill you myself. Okay?"

"As I have told everyone else on this ship, I will not harm you," Burke laughed. It seemed that everyone loved the spirited vixen and he was beginning to understand why.

"Any sign of them, Acel?" Quain asked worriedly.

Acel shook his head left to right, "None! They are at least a full day ahead of us, maybe more."

"We are sailing at full speed," Karoly yelled to the two men at the helm of *The Heart of Calais*.

"Our ship is faster, we are bound to catch up eventually," Acel encouraged.

Burke's crew sailed to Hispaniola as their captain instructed. Once they reached land the sky was very dark and they could not see *The Beloved Loss* from the island. They waited, and waited, and waited but *The Beloved Loss* did not bring their captain to shore. When morning finally came and they could see in the distance that the pirate ship was gone they began loading their ship quickly to search out their captain.

Unfortunately, the captain and crew of *The Beloved Loss* had a lot of power over the people of Hispaniola. Out of loyalty for Marin, the natives waged war with the crew of *The Heart of Calais* and captured Leala and Miette for bribery. Nothing could stop Karoly. Their flimsy huts proved to be no match when Karoly ran right through one.

He demanded his *wife* and daughter be released immediately. Since no one was able to stop him, he obtained his family back with ease. He regretted his word choice as soon as Leala and Miette were released; because Leala beat her poor savior all the way back to the ship. The crew finally boarded *The Heart of Calais* and raced after Burke, but they were way behind.

Luckily for the crew, an elder from Hispaniola was walking along the shore when they left. "Where is *The Beloved Loss* going?" Quain yelled as Garner aimed a gun directly at the native to ensure an honest answer.

"Africa! I would not chase them if I were you. You are not getting your captain back." The man yelled in a broken language barely understandable to the crew. Quain had to tackle Garner to keep the trigger-happy Gunner from shooting the old man anyway.

Now, after one full night of traveling they were becoming discouraged. "I know the man said *Africa*, surely that is where they are going and we are on the right route!" Quain reasoned.

Acel agreed through clenched teeth, "Yes, we must be. If they stop their boat at night we can catch up in a day or two. I hope they are afraid, very afraid. When we do find them, which we will, they shall regret messing with my cousin!"

The day was like any other for Cori. She helped the little girls scrub the floors, assisted Novia with changing the bed sheets and aided Guillermo with meal preparation for the pirate crew. Sharlene arose at her usual time, late in the morning. The woman seemed to wake in a bad mood. "CORISANDA!" She screamed as she entered the below deck quarters.

"I am here," Cori answered as she finished changing the sheets on Zeeman's bed.

"Let me tell you something, you stupid little coquette! You are going to marry Falco, and you better be worth something when you do. I do not like you sleeping in a room overnight with that man. Your father says you must and so that is where you shall stay but I want you to know that I do not trust you for one moment. I hope you know what must happen to you if you are defiled when Falco marries you! He shall have you fed to the sharks immediately. And do not fool yourself into believing that anyone around here loves you enough to save your life. I do not and neither does your father. You are nothing but worthless trash anyway. Do you understand all of this?"

"Yes, I understand. I will not do anything wrong," Cori answered as she tried to keep her voice steady.

"Good, now what are you standing here for? Get to work!" Sharlene barked as she stormed out of the room.

Once her step-mother was gone, Cori lowered herself to Zeeman's bed and wiped her eyes. Novia heard most of the words from next door in Yvet's room. "Corisanda, are you alright?" She asked.

Cori took a breath and stood up, "Yes, Aunt Novia. I am fine. I just hope to get to Africa soon."

Novia scrunched her eyebrows questioningly, "Africa? You hate Africa. Why are you looking forward to arriving?"

"Oh, never mind. It is nothing, let's get back to work," Cori dismissed. Although she loved Novia dearly she did not want anyone to know what her plan was. She hoped that Novia and Guillermo would be able to escape as well so that they could return to Cuba where they yearned to be. However, she knew that at this point she could not

139

make any mistakes or take any risks on her plan going wrong. Cori promised to bring up the subject to her Aunt as soon as they were closer to their destination.

She let her mind go back to Sharlene's harsh words. *It was hard enough to stay out of trouble before Burke came along, now it is impossible. What am I going to do when Falco kills him and I am to blame?* Cori had already been given a message that Falco needed to speak to her before lunch was served.

She was not sure what he would say but she knew it would be a lecture about Captain Belcourt and more threats as well. *Burke does not realize what trouble he is getting me into with Sharlene and Falco! I shall probably wind up dead because of this, or worse! They might space my wedding date up so that I will share a room with Falco instead of Burke! He probably does not even care that I am getting in trouble because of him. He is just a pirate, nonetheless!* Vowing to herself to no longer allow Burke to get her in trouble, Cori sat back to work with a vengeance trying to plan what she would say to Falco.

As planned, Burke worked with Yvet again. *The Beloved Loss* had enough cannons and equipment to be confident when waging war against enemies. Burke wondered where his own ship was at that moment and what would happen when they found him. Or, if they did not find him, what he would do to escape. It was impossible to stop thinking about Cori and how beautiful she was. He found himself searching the ship with his eyes for the pirate princess.

Although he was beginning to pity her and enjoy her company, he still felt resentment that she had low enough standards to work for the pirates. She was the reason he was in this predicament in the first place. Had she not been seen, he would have kept control of himself and took down *The Beloved Loss* right on the spot.

Wondering how many men had been killed because of Cori's trap made him flinch. He glanced up again, seeing Cori for the first time since that morning. She walked across the ship toward Falco. Her chin was held high and she walked proudly, confidently, and with an air of grace. They met eyes for a brief moment and she shot him a horrible glare.

What did I do to her? He wondered as he frowned back. *I should be angry at her for getting me into this mess. She is a deceitful pirate, why have I been so enamored with her? Not anymore! I shall not worry about her; she surely did not worry about me when I boarded this ship, no doubt about that!*

Burke turned back to the cannons, scrubbing angrily and working with aggression. He forced himself to not think about her for the rest of the morning but by evening it was impossible. Burke knew he would soon be locked in a room with her again and he hated himself for looking forward to it. *It is her fault I am here! She is no better than Odelia, they both used conniving snares to catch me. What has gotten into me lately? I have let two different women outsmart me, but it will not happen again! I shall get out of this mess and no woman will burden me again.*

Dinner came and went and the two were locked in Cori's room once again. They were silent and only glared at each other for conversation. Cori bustled around her room organizing chests and folding her raggedy gowns. Burke washed his face in her water basin and plopped down in his chair to glower at Cori. "What's your problem?" He asked.

"My problem? Oh, so now you care about my problems, ay?" She responded angrily.

Burke cocked his head to one side, "Well I don't know why I should care about your problems, since you don't care about mine! It's your fault I'm even here."

"Oh trust me, you're paying me back with plenty trouble of my own!" She countered.

"Trust you? Certainly not! I am not a fool."

"Oh, you want to talk about fools? I could call you worse names than that, *Captain*." Cori railed, implying his pirate career.

Burke shrugged his shoulders nonchalantly, "It would not bother me, and at least I do not trick anyone into taking their last breath aboard this ship just so your daddy can make a few gold coins!"

Cori spun on her heels and faced him with her hands on her hips, "No! You do all your dirty work yourself. I try to stay out of trouble on this boat, Captain Belcourt. You are making that difficult!"

"Well, I do apologize that you brought me here!" He sarcastically retorted.

"It's not like I wanted to!"

"No, but you did it anyway! You just bow down to your little fiancé and your daddy! When they tell you to jump, you jump. Is that not right?"

Cori stomped one foot, "If my life depends on it, yes! What do you suggest that I do, Captain Belcourt?"

"I do not know, but if I did not want to be on this ship I would not be here, if I did not want to marry Falco I would not marry him, and if I did not want to bribe innocent men onto this boat then I would not do that either! No matter what the consequences were!" Burke vented.

"Oh yeah? Well, as far as I know you do not want to be on this ship either but you are. So I am not the only coward in this room." Cori did not know how hard her statement hit Burke.

When she said that he realized how right she was. He did not want to be on the ship but he was, and he did not want to marry Odelia but he was going to. He did not want to give up his career but that was something else he had agreed to do. Burke was not a person to give up so easily and he determined himself to not let it happen. No one would stop him from sailing, not even Odelia. If he had to marry her, so be it, but she would never see her husband because Burke refused to give up his career if he ever earned it back.

He calmed his voice, "Why do you work for them? I understand that you have to be on this ship for now, but why do you trap others here as well?"

Cori looked at Burke with sadness in her eyes; she did not want to help the pirates. "Do you not understand that I have no choice? It is what they tell me to do. I do what I am told because they could kill me just as easily as they could anyone else. I am nothing special on this boat."

"But you are the captain's daughter and the Quartermaster's fiancé, you should be treated well," he reasoned.

"If my father loved me, then perhaps I would be. But he does not; now leave me alone, please." She whispered in agony.

"No," Burke refused, "Why do you say your father dislikes you? Surely you are his world! Does he have no other children with Sharlene?"

"Sharlene has a scar across her stomach from a complicated delivery long before she met my father. She says she had a son who died at birth and that she can no longer have children. He would have been nine or ten years older than me. I am my father's only child. I am not a son, like he hoped for," Cori stated dejectedly.

"Surely your father cannot dislike you only because you are a girl," Burke argued.

Cori looked Burke in the eyes, "He hates me because I killed my mother, okay?"

Burke was silent. He tried to understand what she had just told him. "You did what? You killed your mother?" He finally asked. *I have been rooming with a murderer!* He screamed inside his head.

"She died during childbirth. She was small and I was her first child. If she had been on land she probably would have been fine, but she was not. She did not have a midwife, only Novia, and no proper treatment or care," Cori explained, putting an end to Burke's shock.

"Oh, Cori, I am sorry." He apologized. Burke understood the emotional wall between Cori and her father now. However, he could not comprehend why Marin blamed Cori for it. It was nothing that could be helped, and Cori was not at fault.

"My father married Sharlene when I was five. She hates me worse than my father does. They do not give me any choice in the jobs they assign me to do. Luring ships in is one of them," she clarified.

"What if you just refused? What if you demanded respect for yourself, Cori? You cannot let them run your life for you. Tell them 'No'! Put them in their place. You seem so strong, so unstoppable. Why do you not show that side of yourself to them?" Burke implored with irritation. He was furious that they treated her so callously.

"They shall kill me!" She wailed.

Burke shook his head in disbelief, "No they will not! Just take charge…"

His sentence was cut short when loud feet were heard running down the long, below deck hallway. "What is going on?" He asked.

"Oh no," Cori whispered. Her door was thrown open and Marin stood in the portal, "A ship is coming this way, girl! Get out here."

"Who is it?" Burke asked, hoping that it would be his own ship.

"I do not know yet, but it is coming towards us from the direction of Europe, so probably other pirates or buccaneers. Get out here Cori!"

Burke knew if it was coming from that direction it would not be his own boat. Disheartened, he turned toward Cori who was still standing in place.

"No." She only spoke one word, but it provoked a big reaction from her father.

Marin stared at her incredulously, "What did you say, girl? Get your outfit on and get to the deck."

Cori held her chin high, "I said *no*. I will not do it anymore. I have begged you to let me stop that horrible job. I am not coldhearted like you. I shall not do it."

By that time Sharlene was in the doorway and so was Falco. "This is his fault, Captain!" Falco yelled. "He has given Cori this attitude problem."

"No, he has not. You know I have always hated this job, do you not, Sharlene?" Cori argued.

"Corisanda, you will mind your father. Get out here and do your job or face the consequences," Sharlene demanded.

Cori looked her in the eyes bravely, "No."

Within seconds, Sharlene and Falco grabbed Cori and drug her out of the room kicking and screaming. The door was slammed in Burke's face before he could stop them and the bolt was slid out, locking him in the room. He screamed, "Let her go! Do not hurt her! Please, punish me but leave her alone! I put her up to it. It was me! Leave her alone. Cori! Cori, are you okay? Cori!"

Nothing worked and he pounded the door until his fists bled. The sound of loud cannons filled the air and the ship rocked from side to side. It sounded like a war was raging right outside the door. The same thing continued for over an hour. Hundreds of shots were fired. Burke's ears rang with the sound. The ship took several hard blows and Burke wondered how the old boat was still floating. He wondered what he would do if the ship began to sink. Being locked in the room made Burke claustrophobic.

Finally, silence was heard. No one came for another hour. He wondered what was going on but no one came with information. When Burke had given up hope, the door flew open. Guillermo and Novia rushed in with Cori in Guillermo's arms. He laid her down gently on her bed and tucked the covers around her. "Is she okay?" Burke asked in a panic.

"She shall be fine; this is nothing new to her." Guillermo answered sadly.

Burke leaned over the bed and looked at her. She was wearing another skimpy nightgown like she had a couple nights before when Burke was her target. She was beautiful in the silky gown. It showed her long, tan legs and her feminine figure. Moving his eyes up her body he spotted big bruises already forming on her arms and across her chest. He gasped in shock. "What happened to her?" he asked incredulously.

"If she does not do what she is told to do, Sharlene punishes her. She has refused to work for them hundreds of times and we all thought she finally wised up and decided to do what they told her. They will kill her one day, and she is just lucky it was not today." Guillermo explained.

Novia shook her head in distress, "They have ordered that she does not eat for the next few days. You shall not either. I'm sorry. They blame you for her defiance. If we can sneak you any food then we will, but they will be watching us closely to make sure we are not helping you. Take care of her, and call if you need help."

With that, the two Hispanic servants left the room and locked the bolt behind them. Burke stood over Cori's bed and ran his fingers through her long black hair. He covered her up with blankets and pushed his chair closer to be by her side. The Count of Calais ran his fingers over the pirate princess's bruised skin. He woke up to check on her many times through the night, feeling an overwhelming guilt for causing her to be treated so badly. Burke understood why she had no choice and he hated the pirates for her harsh treatment. He vowed to help her escape, one way or another.

During the night he felt the pull of the ship and realized that it was turning around. He wondered why they were headed back towards Hispaniola but no one came to inform him of anything. It would take another two or three days to get back to the island and he hoped that *The Heart of Calais* would rescue him by then. When morning finally came and Burke's night of restless slumber ended he awoke to find Cori painfully turning over in bed. As she opened her eyes she gasped and jumped up in agony. "I am late for work!" she screeched.

"Shhh, shhh, it is okay! I think you will be locked here for a few days..." Burke consoled.

Remembrance of the night before flashed through her mind and she sorely lay back down, "Oh yeah."

"Cori, I am so sorry. I apologize from the bottom of my heart. I truly did not know anything like this would happen to you. Are you alright?" Burke asked.

"Yes, I shall be fine. Do not worry about it. I hope you are not hungry," Cori sighed as she stood from the bed, wrapped in her sheet. She knew Burke had been in her room and saw her skimpy gown but she did not want to subject herself to any extra indecency. Walking carefully to the far side of the room, she pushed her dresser away from the wall, stood behind it, and changed into her long, covering nightgown.

Burke smiled and answered her as she changed, "Nah, I can make it if you can. For some reason I think we are headed back to Hispaniola."

Cori nodded her head and walked back to her bed, "We won the battle last night but they really took a fierce toll on our ship. Zeeman can fix it but we need more supplies. We cannot make it all the way to Africa as we are so I am sure we are going back to Hispaniola to make the repairs before trying again."

"My ship should be following; we will probably run right into them! They shall take down *The Beloved Loss* effortlessly. I will not leave without you, Cori. You may come along and I promise to take you wherever you want to go. I must arrest your father and his crew, but I shall set you free somewhere along the way. Name anywhere you want to live and I will take you there."

Cori understood that if Burke's ship took *The Beloved Loss* down then they would arrest her father to make an example out of him for the rest of the pirates around. That Burke had been searching out *The Beloved Loss* for the sole purpose of arresting them in the name of the King of France was something Cori would not know or fully understand for quite a long time. Pondering her options, she replied "My Aunt and Uncle, Novia and Guillermo, they are from Cuba. Can you free them, too?" She asked, as always thinking of others before herself.

"Yes, anything you wish. I shall take them back to Cuba. Is that where you want to go also?" He asked, strangely hoping she would choose somewhere closer to France.

"No. I want to go somewhere that I do not have to ever deal with pirates again. Where should I go?" She asked.

"France, England, the Netherlands. Pirates tend to stay away from Europe," he suggested.

Burke surely knows where pirates like to avoid, since he is a pirate himself, she silently considered. "Falco is from the Netherlands so I do not want to go there. My father is French, I will go there. Maybe I have family I can find."

"That sounds perfect. I am from France, as well. I can show you around," he agreed.

"Alright," Cori whispered. Her arms were black and blue and she was in a lot of pain. They always tried to leave her face unmarred, so she would remain attractive enough to bring in enemy ships.

It took all the restraint Burke could muster to not pet the girl lying next to his chair. She was absolutely beautiful and he felt so sorry for her and the pain he had inadvertently caused her. Her tired body stilled and she drifted back to sleep. Burke could not take his eyes off of her. *She is everything a man could want for a bride,* Burke reasoned. He did not ever want to get married but even he could imagine how blessed a man would be to have her as a wife.

Now that she was sleeping again, Burke let himself run his fingers across her bruised arms and brush through her long hair. He wondered what kind of life she would have if she married Falco, what her life might be like if she married someone loving, kind, and generous in France, and if she would be happy married to someone like himself. That thought made him wonder what Odelia was doing and how she was taking his absence. It hurt him to the core that someone as sweet and honest as Cori might be forced into a horrible life with a man like Falco, when someone deceitful and vicious like Odelia would inherit a life of ease with a man that she only used as a bank account.

Burke knew he had to help Cori get away. He had to make this mission as successful as possible, bringing the crew of *The Beloved Loss* back to King Louis XIV. The plan was more important than ever. *Even if it means I must marry Odelia sooner than I wanted to, it shall be worth it to just get Cori to safety.*

Maybe Odelia will go back to France before I am found. It would be wonderful if she thought I was dead and set her sights on some other poor soul. When I returned it would be too late, she would be married, and I would be free. If that happened, he wondered, *would Cori consider someone like me for a husband?*

Burke could not believe what he was saying to himself. He had always wanted freedom, not a life tied down at home with a boring woman. *No, I must find a way to get her to safety. She shall marry someone who can keep her satisfied and I will have my career back,* he decided. He could not understand why that resolution seemed so unlikeable.

The morning ticked slowly by and Burke still sat by Cori's side, waiting for her to wake back up. When she finally did, it was close to noon. "Are you feeling alright?" He asked caringly.

She sat up in bed as carefully as she could, "Yes, I am fine. Have you been sitting here beside me all morning?"

"Yes, and all night too. I am just worried about you," he explained.

"I will be fine, this is not the worst I have had," she said with a forced laugh.

"I do not even want to hear about it," Burke stated angrily. "You do not deserve this."

"Life is not fair. Maybe my new life shall be so wonderful when we escape that it will make up for it, right?" She asked optimistically.

"Yes, I hope so."

"How long have you been sailing?" She asked, wondering if he had been born into pirating like she had been or if he chose it later in life.

"I bought my first ship when I was eighteen, your age. I am thirty now, so about twelve years," he answered.

Curiously, she replied, "Really? What is life like on land?"

"Stable. Safe. It is sometimes quite boring," he chuckled. "The best life, in my opinion, is one like I have. I can go back and forth between my home on land and my home on the water."

"That would be exciting!" Cori liked the ocean and knew no other home, "I just do not want to deal with pirates anymore, no offense."

"Oh, none taken! I do not want to either." He answered. Burke wondered why she might think he would take offense to that; he was no pirate, after all. She had visited with Falco for over an hour the day before and Burke had noticed several glares in his direction, so he knew their conversation had been about him. *Surely Falco explained to her that I am not a pirate, which is why she felt especially bad for luring me in.*

Cori, on the other hand, wondered what Burke meant when he said he did not want anything to do with pirates either. *Does he dislike his life as a pirate, like I do?* If he gave up his illegal pirating career it would put him in a whole new league of men. That league is one with men who Cori would happily consider for marriage.

SIX

Without notice their conversation was interrupted. No knock was heard but the loud bolt on the outside of the door was noisily unlocked. Burke's quick thinking gave him time to move his chair several feet away from Cori's bed. Without a moment to spare, he plopped back into his seat and closed his eyes, as if sleeping. The door opened and Falco entered dominatingly. "*Mevrouw*, how are you feeling?"

"I am alive, no thanks to you, Falco." She answered.

Falco sat down on the bed beside her and she scooted as far from him as she could. He reached out and laid a hand on her leg as he explained, "You deserved punishment. You cannot expect to act so defiantly and get

165

away with it, you are a woman nonetheless. Your job is to be submissive, why can you not learn that the easy way?"

"Maybe I believe that marriage should be about love. If I respected you I would want to listen to your words. If you appreciated me *minding* you, you would only ask me to do things that are *fair*. You do not appreciate me, respect me, or even love me. Why should I bow down to you? Give me a reason to be submissive and maybe I will do it, Falco," she retorted, staring him in the eyes.

"Listen, you have a chance to redeem yourself and get out of trouble. Do you want to eat again, my *Mevrouw*?" He questioned, staring at Burke's suspiciously sleeping form. "Why does he sleep during the day like this?"

"Um, well, *he is probably bored.* Since we are locked in this room and not trusted to speak to each other," Cori lied.

Falco shrugged, "Well at least he is obeying my orders. Now, do you want to redeem yourself or not?"

Cori watched Burke's purposely limp form stiffen in his chair, cringing at the thought of obeying anyone. Trying to keep Falco's attention off of Burke, she replied dryly "Depends, what is it?"

"A ship is coming toward us from the direction of Hispaniola," he began. Cori was listening to his words but staring at Burke. When Falco mentioned that a ship was coming towards *The Beloved Loss,* Burke's foot twitched, Cori caught his sign and hoped Falco did not. "Your father believes it may be *The Heart of Calais*, Captain Belcourt's ship. If that is the case we can expect a fight. We will leave him locked in this room; if we go down he is going down with us. I need you to get dressed and do your job. No complaints this time, do you hear me?"

Cori did not know what to say but wanted to be alone with Burke so he could give her appropriate instructions. "Yes, just leave me in peace for a few minutes to get dressed, alright?"

"Take your time, they are still a distance from us and we are not even positive that it is *The Heart of Calais* yet. Just get ready and I shall return for you within the hour," he commanded.

Feigning submissiveness, Cori replied "Yes, Sir."

As soon as the door was closed and the bolt sounded, locking them back in, Burke jumped to life in his chair. Cori leaped from her bed and raced to his side. "What should I do?" she asked with a rush of excitement. *This could be my big chance to escape!*

"He plans to leave me locked in here. I know Acel, he is my First Mate, best friend and cousin. He could blow this ship to pieces but he will not risk harming me. My men shall wave a surrender flag and pull right up to the boat, as if to give it away. Your father is smart enough not to fall for that but let's hope he does not start firing at a distance. When Acel comes to you to demand my release you need to give him a message without anyone from your ship being able to hear. Can you do that?" He asked.

With her nod, he continued. "Tell him I am okay and locked in your room. You must tell him to distract Marin and Falco while you sneak to get me. When they come to the deck to talk to Acel, you run down and unlock this door for me. I'll figure out what to do from there, but when we get safely to *The Heart of Calais* we will attack *The Beloved Loss*, understand?" Burke's plan was decisive and Cori could not see any flaw.

"Yes, that sounds good. Close your eyes while I change clothes," she commanded.

Closing his eyes, he let her change with respectable privacy. He wondered in those moments, not about the upcoming battle, but about what it would be like to be Cori's husband and be the only man to see her in see-through nightgowns.

When she was finished dressing she paced the room nervously. It was only minutes later that Falco burst back into the room. Burke, feigning sleep again, did not seem like a threat to Falco. "*Mevrouw*, are you ready?" he asked with something large weighing on his mind.

"Yes, I am. I thought you said it would be awhile?" she questioned in confusion.

He looked at Cori in fear, "Your father just confirmed that it is *The Heart of Calais*, but it is not alone. There is another ship following behind it. We must assume that Burke's crew brought back-up. We cannot afford a battle right now; our ship is already in a poor state due to last night's fight. Finish getting ready, I shall be back in a few minutes."

When Falco was out of the room again, Burke looked at Cori. She was smiling and he was not. "Did you hear that, Burke? Your ship brought reinforcements; we will have no problem taking *The Beloved Loss* down!"

"No, Cori. We know no one from Hispaniola, and they are all loyal to your father. I highly doubt that my crew could have found help," he replied cautiously.

Cori was nervous as well but she was too excited to be negative, "Surely they did. Maybe they found help from an island not loyal to my father, like Cuba!"

"Let's hope so," Burke sighed doubtingly.

"Are you going to behave now, Corisanda?" Sharlene asked as Cori anxiously walked to her usual position on the ship.

"Yes, Sharlene." Cori looked into the distance and could easily make out the two ships coming toward *The Beloved Loss*. The big, elegant ship that belonged to Burke was getting closer quickly. The other ship was still a ways into the distance but definitely following *The Heart of Calais*.

The minutes seemed to drag by for Cori as she paced the deck of her father's boat. They went by in the same manner for Burke as he waited impatiently in Cori's quarters.

"Cori!" Marin yelled from the helm. "Get up here!"

"Yes, sir?" Cori asked as she reached him.

Marin glanced at his daughter, scanning his eyes across her bruised arms. "You are alright, I presume."

"Yes. I am fine," she replied. For a moment Cori felt bad. She knew she would not miss her father, but she loved him more than she had ever been able to tell him. Burke would undoubtedly arrest Marin, Sharlene, and Falco. Cori did not resent that, but she pitied her father for his loneliness.

"Cori, I do not know what is about to happen. I will need your help, do you understand?" He questioned, looking his daughter in the eyes.

She tried to seem as innocent as possible, "Yes, Sir. It is *The Heart of Calais* coming after their captain, right?"

"Yes, that is Captain Belcourt's ship in the front. There is a ship following though, and I have reason to believe it is not *with* Burke's ship. Falco believes Burke's crew found a ship for back-up and they are all against us.

That could be true, and if both team up against us then we shall easily be taken. If it is not with *The Heart of Calais*, then it could attack either one of us, who knows!" He answered.

Cautiously, Cori asked "Why do you not think it is with Bur… I mean, Captain Belcourt's ship?"

"It is following at a strange distance." Marin pointed out, "If it was with Captain Belcourt's ship it would be close to it to help immediately with a battle or it would be far enough behind that we still cannot see it, like a surprise attack. However, it looks as if it is trying to catch Burke's ship and being cautious about ours as well. Perhaps it is not on either side. If that is so, it could be neutral. It might sail by as we wage war with *The Heart of Calais*. Or it could attack either ship."

"Oh, I see," Cori whispered, becoming even more nervous.

"Just do your part, lure *The Heart of Calais* in and ask the First Mate to come aboard. Tell him we shall give Burke to them if he comes on the ship, do whatever you have to in order to make their ship as weak as possible. We cannot take many blows right now. That is why we are not going to fire at them until they are in close proximity. Our ship is in desperate need of repair as it is and if we are close enough to reach out and touch them it will be a gun fight, not a cannon fight. However, if a fight breaks lose, help Laron, Yvet, Klaas, Zeeman, Falco, whoever needs you," he dismissed.

Cori nodded her head and answered with a shaky, "Yes, Sir."

Moments later *The Heart of Calais* was pulling up side by side to *The Beloved Loss*, as Cori waved her white flag beckoningly. A man who looked much like Burke walked to the side of the ship, only a few yards from Cori. The man was definitely younger but not much. Just like

Burke, the man was noticeably taken with Cori's supreme beauty. "Acel Belcourt, Mademoiselle. I am here after our captain," he said hostily.

"Yes, *Ace*." Cori addressed Acel with the nickname Burke used for him, letting him know that she was on their side. "Listen, I must talk quickly and quietly so no one hears. My father is the captain of this ship and has Burke held hostage. He and I have been locked in my quarters since he was detained. My father wants me to talk you into coming aboard the ship to further weaken *The Heart of Calais* so we can wage war, so whatever you do, do not come aboard! Burke wanted me to tell you to call my father, Marin, and my fiancé, Falco. You must hold their attention while I find a way to release Burke. The two of us will try to escape to *The Heart of Calais* then you can blow this piece-of-trash pirate ship to shreds. Understand?"

"Um, yes Mademoiselle. Alright. That could work," Acel stuttered in confusion. "What should I do to distract them?"

"Just yell their names, I shall run away and leave them standing here. Ask them for Burke back, or whatever you can think of to get their attention off of me. Okay?" Cori asked decisively.

Acel glanced at the rear of Burke's ship at the other vessel coming quickly behind. "Okay, hurry!" he whispered to her, then turning to face the helm of *The Beloved Loss*, Acel screamed "Captain Marin St. Aubin, I need a word with you and your Quartermaster immediately! I will not talk to this girl. I'm sending her away! Come immediately or I'll prepare my cannon."

Falco raised up from behind the barrels where he was hiding and Marin walked a few feet away from the helm, "What does he want, Cori?" Marin asked.

"He will not speak to me, Sir. He demands to talk to you and Falco about Captain Belcourt's release. *No funny business*, he says, he just *wants to talk to you both,*" she shrugged convincingly.

"Stupid girl, you cannot ever do anything by yourself, can you?" Falco yelled. He reached Cori's side right before Marin did and harshly shoved her out of their way. Acel witnessed it from a distance. As soon as Marin and Falco stood ready to talk to Acel, Cori ran from the deck to her quarters.

Burke heard the locks moving and stood ready, waiting for whatever was to come. When the door burst open, Cori shakily waved him forward. The two of them rushed up the stairs and toward the armory. Luckily, everyone's attention was dead centered on Burke's ship so they did not see the two pirate prisoners sneak to the large gun chest. Acel, on the other hand, did see them. He held his breath and hoped his cousin's plan worked. Ace was not sure what part the girl played in Burke's grand arrangement but he was trying to trust the plan.

They threw the lid off of the chest and grabbed a couple loaded guns off the top of the pile. "Captain!" Klaas screamed as he noticed Burke and Cori.

Marin whirled around and saw his daughter. "You traitor!" He yelled. Burke already had his pistol pointed at the pirate captain, quieting any further words.

"Just let Cori and me off of this ship and safely onto *The Heart of Calais* and we shall call it even, Marin. We shall not attack you; we will let you go peaceably. Just let the two of us off this ship, if you refuse I shall shoot you," Burke yelled in a voice that allowed no argument.

"*You* can go, but you cannot have my *Mevrouw*!" Falco screamed irately.

"She does not like being called that, you disrespectful imbecile. No, I will not go without her," Burke defended. Cori's palms were sweating and her heart was beating rapidly. She was terrified.

They were almost to the middle of the deck and Acel was already preparing a ladder to throw across to help the two in. All of the sudden, an extremely loud blast sounded through the air and *The Heart of Calais* shook violently, sending waves right in between the two boats. It separated them a few more yards, enough that a ladder would not be long enough for them to cross.

"IT IS THE OTHER SHIP," Falco screamed. "They are opening fire on us!"

"No, boy. They are not! They are attacking *The Heart of Calais*! This is our chance to get away without a fight. Hurry!" Marin yelled as he ran back to the helm.

Acel was barking orders at Burke's crew and turned back around to access the situation with *The Beloved Loss*. Marin already had the ship in motion and Acel, thinking as quickly as he could, threw a rope across. It was barely long enough to reach *The Beloved Loss* but Burke grabbed it. "It's not long enough for you both, Burke!" Acel yelled. "Just grab it and get over here. We'll save the girl when we take down *The Beloved Loss*. Please, just come now!" he pleaded.

"No, Ace. I cannot leave her. Just go. Meet me at Hispaniola. I shall find you somehow; just take care of my boat! Why is that ship waging war on you?" Burke asked.

"They are undoubtedly the most ignorant buccaneers I've ever come in contact with. Their ship is old and worthless, why would they even try to bring us down?" Acel questioned in irritation. "It won't be a problem, Burke."

Burke nodded, "Just take care of my ship, see you later."

That was as much as could be said, Marin was sailing away and Falco was sprinting toward Burke and Cori. A hard punch to Burke's stomach was the first thing that introduced Falco's presence. "WHAT DID I TELL YOU ABOUT LEAVING MY *MEVROUW* ALONE?" Falco screamed.

"She does not want to marry you! All she wants is to get away from here. I have not touched her, you moron! She is too good for you and this ship," Burke said, returning a jab into Falco's eye.

A fist fight broke lose as Cori screamed for the two to separate. "Stop, stop! Please stop, Falco, do not hurt him!" She wailed.

Then, to her surprise, she realized that it was not Falco doing the damage. She had never seen her fiancé taken down in a fight, but Burke was teaching him a lesson he would not soon forget. Falco was screaming and trying to crawl away as Burke viciously pounded the Quartermaster's head into the boat dock.

Within seconds, Laron and Yvet raced to the scene, breaking the two men apart. Yvet grabbed Falco and shoved him away; Laron grabbed Cori's hand and pushed her towards the stairway. "Both of you, run! Go to your room, Cori, and stay there, okay? Burke, you too! Just go, we can calm Falco down. Run!" he demanded.

Cori did not need anymore coaxing; she started to run, stopping when she reached the stairs. Burke was not behind her. He refused to give in. Shrugging Laron away he punched Falco another time, then another, before anyone could tear him off. Cori ran to Burke's side. "Stop, Burke! Come on!" she yelled.

Burke seemed not to hear her. She did not know what to do to get his attention. Then, it hit her. There was only one thing she knew to do to make him forget about Falco. She rushed between the two men, grabbed Burke's chin in her small hands, and kissed him on the lips. Burke jumped back in surprise, distancing himself from Falco inadvertently. His mouth dropped open and he stared at Cori in shock, "Now run!" She screamed.

Cori grabbed Burke's hand and flew across the deck, back to the stairs. She could hear Falco screaming curse words behind her but she did not slow down. Cori rushed Burke into her room and slammed the door behind her. Pushing her partner-in-crime out of the way she grabbed her heavy trunk and pushed it up against the door, blocking anyone's entrance. That was not good enough, she decided, and she heaved her heavy armoire up against the door as well. Burke still stood motionless with his mouth gaped open. Out of breath, Cori slumped to her bed.

"Did you just kiss me?" Burke asked in confused astonishment.

Cori rolled her eyes sarcastically, "Yes, Burke! I didn't know what else to do to get you away from him and down here to safety!"

"You just kissed me," Burke repeated again, trying to grasp what had happened. "And I really enjoyed it, despite the situation."

Cori scoffed dramatically. "Our plan fell through, Burke. We're both dead. You know that right? We'll never make it to Hispaniola. As soon as we get a safe distance from your ship my father is going to feed you to the sharks. Sharlene shall beat me and do the same thing if I'm still breathing."

"What are we going to do?" Burke asked, trying to think of a plan.

"There's nothing we can do! We're still at least one or two days away from Hispaniola," she cried.

Burke slumped to his chair, "How long will this trunk and armoire hold them?"

"Not long if they really want in," Cori explained.

Burke could not think of any plan that would save them until they reached Hispaniola. "We shall just have to wait and see what happens. Hopefully *The Heart of Calais* will stay on their tail and keep them busy."

The pair waited, and waited, and waited. To Cori's surprise, no one ever came. They each slept restlessly through the night, rising at every sound. Finally, the morning came and a light rapping sounded on Cori's door. "Who is it?" she asked quietly through the chest and armoire.

The door slightly bulged showing a small crack. Novia stuck her skinny fingers through the door in a waving motion. "Oh, Aunt Novia!" Cori wailed.

She slid the armoire out of the way, then the chest. Novia slid through the portal and hugged her niece tightly. "Oh! I was so worried about you!"

"I know, I was scared too. I kept expecting someone to come get me for punishment but no one has. What is going on?" Cori begged.

"Marin is nervous about getting the ship to Hispaniola. That is all he is focusing on for now. He demanded that Sharlene leave you both alone until we get to land. Falco has been in his bed since Captain Belcourt socked him! He is nursing his cuts and bruises, complaining that his *handsome face* is *destroyed*." Novia explained.

Burke turned to the Hispanic maid, "Novia, as soon as we get to Hispaniola I am getting away from this ship and bringing Cori with me. I am concerned for her safety and shall do anything in my power to save her from Falco. You and Guillermo are welcome to flee with us, if you would like. My ship is meeting me there and I will gladly drop you off at Cuba or wherever you would like to go. Do you agree to come with us?"

"*Si*, I shall speak to Guillermo about it. When we get to Hispaniola and everyone else is busy I will try to unlock your door. Do whatever you can to save my niece, with or without Guillermo and me. I must go," she whispered. With that, Novia turned and ran out the door.

Burke helped Cori move the chest and armoire back against the doorway. When they both sat down again, Burke flashed a bright, white smile to Cori. His blue eyes twinkled and she stared at the crooked scar on his cheek, "What are you so happy about?" Cori asked. "We have not made it there yet! My father could easily change his mind and we may never reach Hispaniola!"

"I am not smiling about that. I am still shocked that you kissed me," he chuckled.

"Oh, it is not like I enjoyed it or anything!" she said, blushing deeply.

Burke leaned back in the uncomfortable cranberry chair. He propped his feet up on the small table and smiled ruefully at Cori, shaking his head. The dark haired beauty smiled back and rolled her eyes in response, cuddling into her little bed. Burke closed his eyes, wondering why his hands became sweaty whenever Cori was around.

Teasing Cori about her purpose-driven kiss seemed natural, like something he did not have any choice but to joke about. What surprised him was the fact that he could not get the kiss off of his mind. It felt right, comforting, intriguing, and once again he felt as if she was luring him in. For what this time, he did not know.

Cori squeezed her eyes shut, hoping to block out anymore of Burke's mocking. *Yes, I kissed him! So what!* She silently scoffed. *The worst part is, Burke is not the only one who shall make a big deal about it. Falco, Sharlene, and my father are surely livid. If I do not get away from here soon, I will never live this down, if I live at all.* Cori told herself over and over that it was no big deal; kissing Burke was the only thing she could think to do to get him off of Falco.

It was supposed to mean nothing, but for some reason the way his soft lips felt against hers and the masculine scent of his skin sent shivers down her spine. She could not stop thinking about the brief kiss they shared. Since Cori had never kissed a man before she did not know if her emotions were normal or not. *Do all kisses feel so*

*wonderful or was something about his kiss exceptionally
special?* She wondered.

"We are sound and stable again, Acel." Karoly
informed the First Mate confidently.

"Thank Heavens," Acel replied in relief. "Burke
would have killed me if he returned to *The Heart of Calais*
and it was torn to pieces. No damage was severe, I
suppose?"

Quain smiled, joining the two. "Nah, everything
looks fine now that Karoly made a few minor repairs. Do
not worry; Burke will be happy when he gets back! I just
finished in the cargo room and those buccaneers who
attacked us had a ship full of goods from the America
coast! Burke shall like all of our new cargo from America.
Besides, that will save us some time traveling there after
taking down *The Beloved Loss*."

"I do not know if Burke wants time to be saved or not. Odie is still in her room sulking and pouting about Burke being gone. She has been questioning me about who his wealth shall be left to if he dies! I am just disappointed that we could not get Burke off that boat," Acel huffed.

"Calm down, boy!" Karoly soothed, "You know the captain, nothing can keep him down! He shall be fine; you just worry about this ship and let him take care of himself."

"I cannot understand why he would not just leave that woman there! She is a *pirate*, why is he trying to help her?" Quain asked.

Karoly smiled, "Let me tell you both something you may or may not know about our tough, brutal, unstoppable captain. Hidden deep in that thick chest of his is a heart. It is a big, beating, soft heart. He does not want anyone to know it is there, but rest assured, it is! Something tells me he wants to save that girl, rescue her. Maybe she is in danger, or maybe Burke just thinks she is pretty and wants to take her home."

"Sure, she is gorgeous," Acel agreed, "but why does that make any difference? It is not like he can marry her or anything! Not with Odie around!"

"Perhaps he wants her as a mistress?" Quain questioned.

"We will just have to ask him when he gets back on board," Garner surmised as he joined the rest of the crew.

"Everything alright in your department, Garn?"

The Gunner smiled, "Good as gold! I wish we had attacks more often."

"Do not wish that upon us until Burke is back!" Acel chuckled to the trigger-happy Gunner. "Okay, men. Let's get back to work. They are several hours ahead of us and we need to make a speedy arrival at Hispaniola. I do not know if they shall be able to escape the pirates or if we shall have to fight for their release. Since we are not too popular there anyway, we better be prepared."

SEVEN

The room was getting darker and Cori lit a few candles. Everything had been quiet and no one bothered to come for punishment. No one had come with food either. "I am starving," Burke complained.

"Yeah, I am too," Cori answered. Loud footsteps were heard down the hallway and quickly passed Cori's door. More were heard every few moments. The footsteps were sometimes walking quickly, sometimes running, but always in a hurry. "When do you think we will be getting close to Hispaniola?" She asked knowingly.

"Well, the way it sounds out there with people staying so busy it may be soon. Do you think they have spotted land?" he asked.

"Perhaps!" Cori answered. A light knock was heard on the door and Guillermo shuffled in.

"Cori," he said in broken English, "the captain has spotted Hispaniola in the distance. Novia said that you shall try to leave. We will escape this ship one day but we cannot go with you now. No one can take a chance on you being seen. Okay?"

"Okay," Cori agreed, hugging her uncle. "Thank you for everything, I hope we are soon reunited."

"Me too, child." He sighed as he left the room.

It was late into the night when *The Beloved Loss* made it to Hispaniola. Cargo remained on the boat since they planned to fix the ship and leave again for Africa. Burke had no belongings with him aboard *The Beloved Loss*. All he had was the clothes he was wearing. He advised Cori to pack a very small, easily hidden bag with her necessities in it, "Once we attack *The Beloved Loss* and take your father as prisoner, then it shall be safe to get all the rest of your things. For now, just get what you have to have."

Cori packed her hair brush first and folded a set of clothes into it. She picked up one thing, shook her head and put it back into the dresser drawer, then another and another, trying to decide what all to bring A moment later her small bag was stuffed totally full. Suddenly, a knock sounded on the door but it was not the timid, cautious one of Guillermo or Novia. She barely had time to stuff the bag under her pillow and sit down inauspiciously when Falco threw the door open and barged in. He scowled fiercely at his fiancé, "We have arrived at Hispaniola, *Mevrouw*."

She was too afraid to answer. *I will be punished and killed before I get a chance to escape!* She silently cried. He glared at Burke with his lip curled, "I do not know what kind of man you think you are, Captain Belcourt, but I can assure you that a bullet could kill you just like everyone else. Marin has given me his permission to kill you, due to

197

that stunt you tried to pull with my *Mevrouw*. Your time is short."

"You may try if you please, Falco. A bullet would kill me, the problem you shall have is hitting me with one," Burke shrugged.

Falco stared at Burke in rage, stomped out of the room, and slammed the door behind him. The bolts were clicked, ensuring their captivity. "We have to hurry, Burke!" Cori exclaimed quietly.

"Would you be upset if he killed me?" He questioned.

Cori faced him in surprise, "Burke! What kind of question is that? Of course I would be upset! I would be devastated!"

Burke stared at the floor, "Why?"

"I do not want you to die, especially because of me!"

"Would you be sad that your escape plan was ruined?"

Cori could not understand his reason for the depressing questions, but she answered honestly. "Of course I would be sad that we could not get away but I would mainly be upset that something bad happened to you. I do not know why you work in the career that you do, but I know you are the nicest man I have ever met in your job field. You do not deserve to be killed."

He did not know what she meant about his career. However, Burke believed she was compassionate and truly did care about his life. Cori was much more loving than Odelia Vadeboncour. Although Cori did not love Burke she would still have more compassion than Odelia. *The dark haired princess is certainly not a normal pirate,* Burke thought to himself as Cori finished packing her bags. *She cares little for money, jewels, or crime. She is not hateful or malicious. Cori wants a normal life, legal and fair. I wonder what husband she will choose for herself when she is free.*

The thought crossed Burke's mind that Cori might fall in love with Acel. He was not sure why, but the idea irritated him. His cousin was a great man, romantic, handsome, and kind. He would make a wonderful husband to Cori. But for some reason Burke did not want to picture Cori marrying any man. Burke played a list of Dukes, Knights, Counts, Marquises, and Princes through his mind and none of them seemed good enough. They were too weak or to strong, to nice or to mean, to proud or to timid. *Well who would be good enough, then?* He questioned himself in a foul mood. *Me? Yeah, if she wanted to marry a married man! Or a sailor!*

"I am ready!" she squealed in delight.

"Okay, here is the plan. Novia will unlock our door so we can sneak off the boat. Hopefully we get away unnoticed. Pull your hair up so it is not noticeable. Change your dress into something as unflattering as possible. Do you have any pants?"

"Pants? Like, for men?" She asked in awe.

"Yes." He answered without explanation.

"Well, I think there is one pair in here somewhere that I wear to bed in the winter," she replied.

Burke nodded his head, "Put them on."

Minutes went by and then hours. Novia never came and the ship grew quiet. "Burke, something is wrong. Aunt Novia would have come by now to at least tell us what is going on. They must have locked her and Uncle Guillermo in for the night."

"When shall they release them?" He questioned in discouragement.

"They might in the morning. They usually never lock them in anymore, but maybe they were concerned about *The Heart of Calais* and decided not to take any chances on us getting away," Cori surmised.

Burke took a deep breath and stood up from the uncomfortable chair, "Well, we cannot wait until morning. We must find our own way off of this ship. Do you have anything in here that we could use to loosen the hinges on the door?"

"I have a knife, but it is little," Cori shrugged.

"That will have to do," he answered as she pulled the small weapon out of her empty jewelry box.

Burke scooted the trunk and the armoire out of the way. He worked at the door hinges for what seemed like hours. Finally the bottom was loose as well as the middle. Burke twisted at the top latch until it finally came undone as well. Since the door was bolted against the wall on the other side of the door, the portal barely opened even with all three hinges off. "Can you squeeze through?" he asked.

"Yes, but can you?" Cori inquired.

Burke smiled shyly, "I shall make it. At least this way the door does not look like it has been messed with. The locks will keep it standing straight and it shall not look tampered with until they unlock it. Then it will probably fall on whoever opens it!"

Very quietly Burke peered through the cracked door. "No one is in the hall, Cori. Go ahead and sneak through but stay against the wall in case someone comes."

The thin girl squeezed through effortlessly, but it took a little more pushing and pulling to get her tall, muscular partner through the door. When both were together again they crept slowly down the hallway to the bottom of the stairs. Snores were heard coming from Klaas and Yvet's rooms. Falco's quarters were silent, as well as Marin and Sharlene's. Burke climbed up the stairs on hands and knees to get a better look onto the deck. Marin, as always, was standing at the helm. Sharlene was by his side overlooking the ocean, searching for any sign of *The Heart of Calais*.

"Let's go," Burke whispered to Cori. "Stay up against the wall and low to the ground. They are looking toward the ocean and not toward us. Try not to be noticed."

The pair crept along the far side of the ship. It was early in the morning and the sun was barely visible as it began rising in the sky. Cori and Burke scooted quickly and silently. They finally reached the edge of the boat, preparing to jump off the side and land on the beach. Burke glanced down quickly with Cori at his side, "There's Falco and Zeeman. We need to get back across to the other side."

Sure enough, Cori could see Zeeman replacing boards at the bottom of the boat. Her despicable fiancé stood by the Carpenter, barking orders and supervising the repairs. Cori gasped, pushing her back firmly against the wall. Burke rubbed her arm quickly, urging her to go. The pair snuck back the way they came, passed the stairs, and to the other side of the ship. Burke froze, squeezing Cori's arm. Sharlene had heard something and she scanned the ship's deck with her eyes. He pulled her down with him to a crouching position behind a couple tall black cannons and waited for her to return her attention to the sea.

When finally she gave up on the noise, they looked for a quick shelter on the ground to run for. After a long stretch of beach with no covering at all, there was a large clump of trees hiding the village. Burke took a swift leap off of the boat and landed with a slight thud on the ground. Cori remained against the wall, hoping no one but she had heard the sound. Burke motioned for her to jump and held out his arms to catch her. She scrunched her eyebrows together and then rolled her eyes at him, giving him a shooing motion with her hands until he shrugged and backed a short distance away.

Cori jumped, landing silently in the sand without Burke's help. "Quiet," he whispered as they snuck along the bottom of the boat. "We have to make it out of eyesight before Falco, Zeeman, Sharlene or your father spot us. Then, we have to get to the village and into a safe hiding place before they notice we are gone."

The pair tiptoed through the sand to put a little distance between themselves and *The Beloved Loss*. A few yards from the boat, they froze again and peered upward knowing that if they crept any further they would be in clear eyesight to their pirate enemies. "On the count of three, run for the trees. Okay?" Cori asked, taking charge.

"Okay," Burke answered with a devilish grin.

"THREE!" She whispered enthusiastically,

throwing Burke off guard. He ran as fast as he could but the

long legged vixen by his side easily outran him. When they

reached the edge of the palm trees they peered behind them

to see if anyone had followed. No one seemed to suspect a

thing and Cori took a deep breath of relief.

"Where did you learn to run so fast?" Burke

questioned with a smile.

Cori smiled, thinking of the many pranks she pulled

on Zeeman and Klaas over the past several years. "Practice,

practice, practice!"

They made it to the village before the sun was much

higher in the sky and the inhabitants were beginning to

shuffle around. One hut sat in the middle of the village,

larger than most and all alone. It had palm leafs covering

the doorway and large cracks for windows. "This must be

their storehouse," Burke whispered sneaking closer to it. "Let us gather up some food before we find a hiding spot."

"I shall stand here and keep guard. If anyone comes, I'll alert you. Grab something quickly," Cori ordered anxiously.

Burke nodded and walked into the hut where he picked up several large oranges, a bag of fish, a few yellow bananas, and a pineapple. He shuffled them around in his arms until he had a decent grip and slipped back out the portal to Cori. "Hurry," she whispered as he handed her a few things to help carry. "No one has been out of their huts yet but I've heard voices coming from several. They shall surely be out soon."

They crept back to the wood line between the beach and the village, "We need to hide somewhere close to the sea so my crew can find us when they arrive. On the other hand, we cannot stay close to *The Beloved Loss*. Let's sneak around toward the forested part of the island."

Cori stopped in her tracks and looked at Burke in fear, "The land is a rainforest, Burke. If we keep walking this direction we will get deeper and deeper into the swampy part of the island. It would be a great place to hide because of the dense tree cover, and many caves right off of the beach but it's extremely dangerous. There are enormous snakes that the natives call Boa Constrictors. When the Spaniards first claimed this land they died by the thousands. Not only are there man-eating snakes, but alligators, poisonous spiders, giant beetles, and disease carrying mosquitoes. Plus, it is easy to get lost in the bog before we reach the sea again. Are you sure we should try?"

"That's our best option, Cori. Who are you more afraid of, snakes or your father?" Burke shrugged. "Are you capable of trying?"

"Me?" She scoffed. "Oh, I am fine. I was just worried about you," she answered with her chin held high.

"That's what I figured," Burke chuckled. "Let's eat first."

The pair sat down in the covering of trees, hidden temporarily from *The Beloved Loss*. However, they were close enough to hear a loud crash when Cori's door fell away from the locks. Burke and Cori both gasped aloud, meeting eyes as they realized what the source of the noise was. Then, to reaffirm their silent question, Falco screamed clearly and unmistakably, "*MEVROUW*!"

"Off we go!" Burke commanded with a smile on his face. They grabbed the remainder of the fish and fruit, throwing it into Cori's small bag. Burke threw her bag over his shoulder and they raced ahead into the dangerous surroundings.

After over thirty minutes of running into the rainforest, Burke had to sit down and rest. "How can you possibly not be tired?" He asked between breaths.

Cori giggled, "I am just tougher than you, Burke Belcourt! Come on, let's at least keep walking. I do not want them to catch up!"

"Surely they will not look this direction for us. They shall search the village first," Burke shrugged, standing back up.

"If they cannot find me there they shall look here. They will search Hispaniola from side to side," she whispered in fear.

Burke elbowed Cori playfully, "Then we better find a good hiding spot."

They walked through the rainforest for hours, trying to stay close enough to the shore that they could hear the waves crashing. The last thing either of them wanted was to wind up lost in an extremely deadly environment. Later into the afternoon the sound of distant cannons erupting were heard. "What's that?" Cori questioned.

"Cannons. I've heard enough of those in my day to know. It's coming from behind us, where we left *The Beloved Loss*. If I was a betting man, I would say that *The Heart of Calais* just showed up," Burke said in relief.

More distant crashes were heard as Cori replied, "Why do you sound so calm about it? They are waging war back there!"

"I'm calm because *The Beloved Loss* is no concern for my crew. Acel will bring down your father's ship, then do all the arresting required, realize we're not onboard, and come looking for us. No problem, right?" He surmised.

Cori shook her head at him, "Oh, you think it shall be that easy, huh? Keep in mind, you might be the most feared *buccaneer* on the sea but my father is the most

feared *pirate* on the sea. I hope you are right and it is truly

that easy to bring them down, but I am not going to breathe

until it happens and I am safe and free in France!"

"I am no buccaneer! Silly girl," he chuckled, "But

do not worry about them. Let's just worry about finding our

way to a good hiding spot before it gets dark."

If he is not a buccaneer for France, I guess he is a

pirate. Then why does he have a home in France? How can

he live on land and on the sea both? Is he not afraid of

being caught? Cori wondered. She opened her mouth to ask

him her questions but her shrill scream came out instead.

"SNAKE!"

Not an inch in front of Burke's face was a tall tree,

full of leaves and vines. One of the vines he was about to

grab was no vine at all. It lunged toward them as Cori

screamed. The Boa Constrictor tried to wrap his giant

mouth around Burke's hand but thanks to Cori's warning he jerked his arm away with less than a second to spare. Burke stumbled backward and landed right on top of Cori. They both lay on the moist ground for a few moments, laughing at themselves as the snake slithered away. "Get off of me!" Cori giggled, "I am going to get bit by some horrible bug and die!"

Burke grabbed Cori's hand and helped her to her feet. "I do not like snakes, but it's sure beautiful out here, is it not?" He asked, still holding Cori's hand in his own.

"Yes, it is." She agreed, blushing and dropping her hand to her side.

The rainforest was filled with tall trees, towering so high above the couple that they could not see the sky. Each tree was covered in weaving vines and lush greenery. Exotic flowers bloomed all around them and the peaceful sounds of distant waves crashing on the beach, small animals communicating, and the light rain falling on the trees above filled their senses. "Yes," Cori repeated again, "The forest is stunning."

"It is," Burke concurred, "but the rainforest is not what I was talking about."

Cori looked at him in confusion for a moment until she understood his compliment, "Oh," she whispered quietly.

"Come on, beautiful. Let's keep going. It's probably early evening by now and we still need to get several miles further from *The Beloved Loss* before making our way to the beach," Burke planned, changing the subject.

Cori did not answer, she just followed his lead. She wondered to herself what life would be like married to such a man as the *pirate* captain, Burke Belcourt. Trying to avoid that subject though, she wondered about the men she would meet in France. She remembered Burke telling her a few nights back that she was beautiful enough to marry royalty. She did not care about titles, as long as he was an honest man who had no affiliation with pirates!

She wondered what the men of France were like. *Are any of them as handsome as Burke? Do they smell as good as Burke? Are they as charming and funny as Burke? Are any as smart as Burke?* She did not deny Burke's hold on her senses. He was an amazing man, attractive and kind. She would never allow herself to fall for a pirate though. *Never, never, never*, she silently vowed.

"When we find a good location to spend the night we will eat the rest of our food, alright?" Burke suggested.

"Sure."

Burke pondered the beautiful woman following behind him, "Why have you been so quiet lately?"

"Just trying to think, I guess. I have a lot on my mind."

"Like what?"

"Like what could be happening with *The Beloved Loss* and *The Heart of Calais.* I don't hear any more cannons but that could be because we are so far from them now, not necessarily because the battle is over. And even if your crew wins, the natives of Hispaniola are loyal to my father. Your crew better not try to waltz off their boat like they have been invited because it would be a disaster. They should just sail around the island until they spot us!" Cori began.

Burke felt a tender spot in his heart for the caring girl, "Acel's smart, Cori. He shall figure that out. Do not worry about them!"

"I am also worried about finding a suitable hiding spot. A beach cave would be ideal, but alligators probably agree. Then, assuming we even make it to France alive, where will I stay? How shall I live from day to day? I have never thought about money, housing, or a real job before," Cori distressed.

Burke decided that this was a good enough moment to tell her something he had been pondering on for the past couple days, "Well, you are welcome to stay at my home in Calais for a while until you decide what you want to do or where you want to go. And do not worry about money. I plan to sell *The Beloved Loss* and all the goods on it. All the money I earn from that will be yours. Deal?"

"Oh, Burke, no." She shook her head in denial, "I cannot stay at your home and burden you."

"It would only have to be for a few days, Cori. I will not be home much anyway. I shall be in Versailles handing your father and his crew over to the custody of King Louis. By the time I get back to my home in Calais, you will have had time to gather your wits and decide what you want to do with your life. You shall have plenty of money to live on until you get married," he convincingly suggested.

Cori smiled politely, "We will see, Burke. I shall consider all my options, even that one. Besides, why do you think anyone, besides the occasional pirate, wants to marry me? I am a pirate's daughter. People probably will not consider that I have the potential to be a good wife!"

"You are beautiful, kind, caring, intelligent, and young. Trust me; you shall be much sought after. Moreover, your father may be a pirate but I have come to realize that you are no pirate at all!"

"You really think so?" Cori asked hopefully.

"Definitely. I am sure it will not take long at all to find a man for you," Burke replied with a damper in his tone. He really did not enjoy planning Cori's courting experience. Once again, making him wonder why he even cared! *Yes, I shall give her the credit of being breathtakingly gorgeous, intelligent, mature, caring and kind, but no matter if she was a saint I could not marry her, I already have one marriage on my hands!* He inwardly huffed.

"Now who is being *quiet*?" Cori inquired sarcastically.

Burke chuckled at her humor. *She is funny also,* he added to his silent list of compliments. "Yeah, yeah! Maybe I have a lot on my mind too!"

"Like what, Mr. Confident?" she teased.

"Like all the snakes in this world!"

"Oh gracious, Burke! We will be out of the rainforest and safely to the beach in an hour or two!"

"No, I do not mean on this *island*, Cori! I mean all the snakes in this *world*. You know, bad men out there who shall fall for you and will not be worthy."

Cori scoffed out loud, rolled her eyes, stomped one foot, and put her hands on her hips. "I have you know, Captain Belcourt, that I am a grown woman! I have been around men all my life and I think I am a pretty decent judge of character!"

"You have been around seven or eight men in your whole life and the whole time you were under the protection and provision of your father. Yes, he is a pretty mean fellow, but he would not have allowed you to be harmed. Out of the thousands of men you might meet in France, how will you know which ones are honest and which ones are not?" Burke reasoned.

"Well," Cori tried to begin. "I shall figure it out! How do all the other women in France pick a respectable husband?"

"Women of prominence and men of esteem are raised around each other from an early age. If a lady meets a man who claims royalty or affluence that she had never heard of before, her father will surely know him or his family and can make a judgment. It could be that he is from a distant region of France or even has a title in a different country! Many times, women are paired with men of their father's choosing," he explained.

That was one thing Cori understood easily, "Then it is not so different from a pirate ship!"

"Why did your father choose Falco for you? Why not Laron or Yvet?" Burke questioned.

Cori shrugged with an over exaggerated sigh, "He likes Yvet to much to burden him with me. And Laron is the black sheep of *The Beloved Loss*. He works hard and does a great job but distances himself from everyone else. Falco asked my father for my hand in marriage four years ago. They have been waiting on me to turn eighteen so I could be *given* to him. I do not care if I ever marry or not! I just do not want to marry Falco."

"Most women obsess over marriage," he stated, thinking of Odelia's life-changing plans.

"Most probably do," Cori agreed. "All I want is happiness! If I found a man who made me happy then I would gladly marry him. No matter if he was titled, prominent, wealthy, or not! All I shall refuse to marry is a pirate." She felt truly saddened as she said the last sentence. Cori hoped it did not hurt Burke's feelings or insult his career. The young beauty thought Burke was an amazing man and would marry him in a heartbeat if he had a respectable job. She just wanted to make sure he knew not to fall for her. It was hard enough on Cori not to have feelings for Burke. It would be impossible if he was interested in return!

To Cori's surprise, Burke seemed to agree completely with her comment, "That is quite understandable. I would certainly not want you marrying a pirate." Then, under his breath he mumbled, "At least I would be better for you than Falco, if only by careers alone!"

Cori heard his mumbled words but did not understand his meaning. *What kind of strange captain is he? He says he is no pirate then he says he is no buccaneer! Yet, he travels the sea striking deals with pirates, trading with islanders and taking prisoners?*

Cori knew that buccaneers and pirates were almost the same thing, but used different terms to classify themselves. *Burke must be something related to pirates and buccaneers, with some small variation, and claims a different title.* She did not want to look stupid by asking

him what exact categorization of illegal thieving criminal

he fit into. *Regardless of what he wants to call it, a pirate is*

a pirate to me!

EIGHT

"We do not even have your captain, you blood thirsty pigs!" Sharlene screamed irately at Acel, Quain and Karoly.

Acel scoffed loudly, "Sure you do! Now hand him over or I shall blow another piece of your ship away."

"No, unfortunately we truly do not," Captain Marin St. Aubin argued. "That is why we were not aboard *The Beloved Loss* when you arrived. You had no problem wreaking havoc on my ship because there was no one to defend it but two of my men, you ignorant *children*."

"You did not release them, so where are they?" Quain insisted.

Marin sighed in resignation, "We are not positive. They were locked in my daughter's quarters last night when we spotted land. This morning when Falco went to retrieve them they were gone. That is truly all we know."

"Is he being serious?" Acel whispered to Karoly.

Karoly replied with a sharp elbow into Acel's ribs, "Never trust a pirate."

The older man continued the interview with Marin, "You truly have no idea where they are?"

"This is the only place we stopped, so they must be on this island somewhere. Since we arrived *The Beloved Loss* and *The Heart of Calais* are the only two ships that have been here. If you do not have them, and I do not have them, then they are somewhere in Hispaniola," Marin explained.

Falco stepped in before Acel could retort, "We have a deal to make with you fellows. Corisanda is my fiancé. I need her back on this ship immediately. If you work with us we will work with you. We take Cori with us and you take your captain. No hard feelings and no harm done. *Ja?*"

The three temporary leaders of *The Heart of Calais* answered in unison, "We do not make deals with pirates!"

With that statement they forcefully boarded *The Beloved Loss* and searched it from top to bottom. After thirty consecutive minutes of exploration, the three men met at the helm. "There is no sign of them," Quain whispered.

"Yes, Burke is definitely gone." Acel sighed.

Quain shook his head negatively, "No, I mean there is no sign of Captain St. Aubin or his crew. While we were searching their ship they all disappeared. I suppose one of us should have stayed back and watched them, huh?"

Acel slapped his forehead in disgust at himself, "Burke would have known that. He'd kill me right now, if he was here."

"Don't feel bad," Quain shrugged. "We can't go on the island looking for them though. The natives have made that clear already."

Acel sighed in irritation, "I guess I fell right into that one."

"Stop whining! Burke named you First Mate for a reason. You have this under control," Karoly comforted the best way he knew how.

Acel nodded his head confidently, "So, they could be telling the truth and Burke could have escaped with their girl, or they could be hiding them both somewhere until we give up and go home."

"Well, I do not think they are hiding them anywhere. If that was the case, the one they call Falco would not have offered a deal, Burke for Corisanda. Right?" Karoly reasoned.

Acel chuckled, "Are you not the one who said never to trust a pirate?"

"Yeah, yeah, but we cannot waste any time. So what do you want to do?" He asked the First and Second Mates.

"Let's do a search of the coastline. *The Beloved Loss* is a little torn up, it will be at least a day or two before they are up and running enough to leave." Quain suggested.

Acel put the plan in progress by saying, "I agree."

When they boarded *The Heart of Calais* they faced a foe much more intimidating than the pirate crew they argued with an hour before. "WHERE IS MY COUNT?" Odelia demanded.

"Now Odie, Calm down! We shall find him," Acel soothed.

"I shall NOT calm down! I want to know where he is! I heard that pirate say something about a woman!" Odelia huffed.

Acel patted Odelia's head as if she was a puppy, "Yes, well, Burke shall have to give you the details on that. We are not truly sure why their captain's daughter escaped with Burke. She was supposedly engaged to their Quartermaster. I am sure it is nothing to worry about, Odie. After all, Burke *loves you until death do you part*. Right?"

"Do not mock me, Acel Belcourt! I shall be in my quarters; I fear my stomach is already growing weak again. Find my fiancé, kill whatever woman he is associating with, and let us return to France where I belong!" She screamed as she stomped back to her bed.

Acel rolled his eyes at Quain who was hiding fearfully behind a pole. "You coward," he chastised.

"Sorry, Acel! Put me up against *The Beloved Loss* or feed me to the sharks! Odelia is scarier than either one," Quain answered with a shiver, looking over his shoulder to make sure he was safe.

"It is getting really dark, Burke. Do you not think we should make it back to the beach?" Cori advised.

Burke replied as he glanced over his shoulder at the long legged beauty behind him, "Yes, just a little further. You see that small clearing ahead?"

"Yes, I see it." She answered.

"I believe it is the swamp. If we follow that a little way it shall lead us straight to the ocean," he clarified.

"You can't be serious right now! Do you know what animals live in the swamp, Burke? Alligators! And infectious mosquitoes! And more snakes! No way, I am not going anywhere near that swamp. Let's turn now," Cori pleaded.

Burke stopped and turned toward her, "The trees are too thick to turn into them now, Cori. We shall get lost for sure. They're too dark to see through already. If we just follow the swamp line we will be to the beach within an hour at the very most!"

"Oh Burke, no."

"Do you trust me at all, Cori?"

"Well, yes, I suppose I do."

"Okay then, just trust me with this and I will keep you safe. Alright?"

"Oh, for Heaven's sake! You just worry about yourself, I shall keep myself safe!" She consented with an irritated grin.

Burke smiled back. "Fine, as long as you trust me."

The swamp was overgrown with bugs buzzing consistently. Cori stared at the logs floating through the marshy water. Upon a second glance, half of them were not logs at all. Snakes hung from every tree, casually dropping off into the water and slithering through the water getting angry snaps from the log-disguised Alligators. Burke held Cori's hand and walked briskly but carefully along the edge.

Cori's heart pounded in her chest and Burke's hand was moist with sweat. The ground under their feet was muddy and posed a constant question as to where they should step. After an hour of walking they came to a tall tree growing sideways in the marsh. Since it was not growing straight up, but slumping inward toward the swamp, it blocked their path completely. Burke assessed their situation, "Okay, we have three options, Cori."

"What are our choices?" She asked, hoping for a safe answer.

Burke took a deep breath, "We could go into the woods and around this tree. If we do that we shall be completely emerged in blackness. Look how dense those trees are, we will not be able to see a single thing for several minutes while we get around this Pine and back to the water's edge."

Cori shook her head negatively, "That does not sound good, what is next?"

"We could go through the swamp. That is our quickest route and we would be in bright moonlight the whole time," he started.

She snorted, "Oh, right! And take a chance on thirty snakes dragging us under the water or an alligator eating us! No, next please."

Burke shrugged his shoulders, "Well, the third option is that we could go over this log."

"What is the downside to that one?" Cori asked positively.

"Well, you see that light brown stripe across the top of the tree?" he pointed.

"Yes, is the bark chipped away there, or what?" Cori asked squinting for a better look in the darkness.

Burke shrugged, "Watch it for a moment."

She focused on the discolored stripe until it seemed to move before her eyes, "Did the line just move?"

Burke answered casually, "That line, my dear, is another snake."

"Oh!" Cori squealed jumping backwards into Burke's arms.

He chuckled, "Alright. We really have no choice but to go over the log but let's try to get rid of its slithering resident first, alright?"

Cori nodded her head, "Deal, you do it!"

Burke glanced carefully at a nearby tree. Making sure it was a real limb he was grabbing, he broke the stick off and poked the snake harshly with it.

That earned a loud hiss from the long, light brown stripe. Burke gave it one more shove and the snake fell off the tree and landed with a splash in the water. "Okay, I am going across first Cori. There may be one hundred more on the other side that I cannot see from here. Wish me luck," Burke bravely whispered.

"Oh, Burke! Be careful!" Cori whined grabbing his hand in hers.

He smiled teasingly, "Well, if I had known I could get that much attention from you I would have decided to go over the log in the first place!"

Cori rolled her eyes and gave him a flirtatious push. "Just do not get hurt!"

He crossed the tree with ease and reached one hand over for Cori, "Come along, beautiful."

She bounded over the giant, tree and into Burke's arms on the other side. He put her down without a comment and continued on their march for the seashore. Only a few minutes later they were breaking free of the swampy rainforest and safely on the beach again. "Oh! Thank you, Lord!" Cori squealed in delight.

Burke agreed, "Amen! Let's find a place to rest. The beach gets really rocky over there, Cori. I bet there are some small caves. Plus, we shall be higher off the beach and less visible to *The Beloved Loss*. As long as we are watching for *The Heart of Calais* we should be fine."

Cori led Burke up the steep set of rocks until a small shelter was found. "This would be perfect, Burke. It's not a big cave, just a small formation, but the location is ideal. We can see clearly along the beach on both sides to watch for anyone coming by land. It also overlooks the sea majestically. If your crew comes by way of the sea we will see them in plenty of time."

Burke agreed with a positive nod of his head and sat down in the small cave. It was barely big enough for both of them to lie down and still be covered by the rock overhead. He began pulling the rest of the fruit and fish out of Cori's bag for them to eat. "Could you not have picked a more comfortable rock than this to sleep on?" Burke chuckled kiddingly as he nestled into the uncomfortable rocks. "I feel like I am sleeping in that cranberry chair in your quarters again!"

She giggled, feeling bad for making him sleep in the scratchy chair. "Well, I might be a pirate's daughter but I still believe in sleeping alone until marriage!"

Burke smiled, "You are the most ladylike pirate I have ever met. You will make a wonderful wife to a very lucky man."

"You do not have any legal, land-loving brothers do you?" Cori asked playfully.

He rolled his eyes, "No brothers! I have one handsome cousin, but you already met him. Besides, he loves the sea as much as I do."

"I love the sea as well; it shall be hard to give it up. It's the only home I have ever known," Cori sighed.

"Then why give it up?"

"I want nothing to do with pirates, Burke."

"You might run into pirates occasionally on the ocean, but you do not have to work for them anymore. Maybe you should buy a ship, sail around and be your own captain!"

Cori laughed as her eyes blinked uncontrollably, "One of us should get some sleep. The other needs to keep watch. We can take shifts, what do you think?"

"You go to sleep, Cori. I will wake you in a few hours, alright?" Burke asked. Hearing no response from his partner in crime, he turned toward her. She was already asleep on the hard rock slab they were using as a floor and bed. Burke shook his head and smiled at the black haired pirate princess. He whispered quietly enough to ensure she did not hear his words, "Goodnight, my love."

Burke's watch proved dull and motionless. He was beginning to wonder if *The Heart of Calais* was coming for him or not. *Maybe they were damaged by The Beloved Loss? Or maybe they already sailed by here once while we were still in the rainforest?* Finally, close to dawn, Burke could keep his eyes open no longer and woke Cori to take a vigilant turn.

He nestled down in the warm spot where Cori had been lying and fell asleep immediately. Corisanda St. Aubin stared at the handsome man sleeping next to her. *If only you were not a pirate,* she silently thought. She watched the sun rise into the sky over the tranquil blue water. By the time half of the sun was visible over the distant water's edge, Cori noticed a small black dot advancing along the coastline. "Burke, Burke, wake up!"

"Cori, I have only been asleep an hour or two at the most!" He complained wearily.

"I see a ship!" She squealed.

"A ship?" Burke asked jumping up alertly.

Cori pointed at the distant boat, "Yes, do you see it?"

"Yes, I do. I cannot tell if it's *The Heart of Calais* or *The Beloved Loss*. It's too far away," he stated, scurrying out of the cave for a better look.

"What should we do?" His companion asked.

"Well, I suppose we should just stay here until we know who it is. If that's *The Beloved Loss* we shall just hide until they pass, but if it's my crew and my ship we need to get onto the beach so they will see us." Burke answered anxiously.

Minutes passed that seemed like hours and finally the ship was in clear enough view to tell that it certainly was the large, elegant, stylish vessel that Burke designed himself a couple years before. The pair dashed down the rocks and onto the sandy beach below. They waved their arms over their heads until loud whoops and hollers were heard from the advancing ship. "We've been saved," Cori squealed in excitement.

"You were safe with me all along, Cori." Burke chastised as he chased her around the beach.

"Help, help!" She hollered in playful laughter as she ran from Burke.

The large vessel finally came to a stop and Acel threw a rope ladder down for his cousin to climb up. Cori went up first and Burke followed closely behind, watching her derriere the whole way from the beach to the deck. Acel, Karoly, Quain, Garner, Davet, Leala, and Miette met them as they boarded and hugged Burke lovingly. They each shook hands curiously with the girl he brought aboard. Acel was jabbering quickly to Burke about the victory with the buccaneer vessel and the small battle with *The Beloved Loss*. Ruining the reunion, a hateful voice cried, "Burke, *my darling*."

"*Odelia*," Burke whispered under his breath, realizing he had not even mentioned his fiancé to Cori.

The conniving blonde squeezed herself between Cori and Burke, falling into Burke's arms dramatically. "I have been worried sick, *dearest*. Where have you been?"

"Really, Odelia? I hoped you would not *concern* yourself over me. This is Corisanda St. Aubin," he introduced placing one arm lovingly around Cori's shoulders.

Odelia glared at the taller, younger, prettier girl and snidely answered, "I am *Lady* Odelia Vadeboncour, Burke's *fiancé*, but I am sure he has told you all about me."

Cori stared at her in shock, trying not to show her embarrassment, "Actually no, he told me very *little* about himself. Congratulations on your engagement."

Purposely ignoring Cori, Odelia grabbed Burke's hand and drug him toward the ornately designed dining area, "Come, Burke! Let's catch up on all the time we've lost in the past few days."

Burke, not knowing how to get away from his future wife, shot a glance back toward Cori as he paused to whisper to his crew quietly enough that Odelia could not hear. "Quain, will you show Cori to her quarters? You may give her mine, it is the most comfortable. I shall be spending most of my time at the helm anyway. Acel, turn us around and get us back to *The Beloved Loss*. I will be back momentarily."

Burke accompanied Odelia to the large table and pulled a chair out for her to sit down. She sat politely and turned toward him, "How kind of you, Burke. You must have missed me indeed."

Odelia's voice made Burke's stomach turn. He winced at her phony version of flirting. "Is that your impression?" He asked dryly, scooting her chair toward the table for her.

She smirked and turned toward his chair to wait on him to sit. "Well, aren't you going to..." She began as she turned to see Burke abruptly walking away instead of taking the chair next to hers. "Where on Earth are you going, Burke?"

"I have important matters to attend to right now, Odelia. I have not had a proper bath in days, I have been wearing these same clothes since I last saw you, and I need to prepare my men for the upcoming battle with Cori's father. You've *missed* me this long; perhaps you won't mind missing me just a little longer. I know *I* shall have no problem with it. You will excuse me, *right*?" He asked, giving her no time to object.

Odelia glared at him through squinted eyes, "What do you mean by 'Cori'? I thought the lowly piece-of-garbage pirate was named 'Corisanda'?"

"ODELIA!" He snapped loudly, marching back to point his finger in her face. "Do not ever let me hear you say another hateful word about her! Do you understand? You might become my wife and I may be stuck with you until death but if you do not watch your tongue when addressing Cori your death shall come much sooner than you expect!"

Odelia watched him storm through the dining room door as she silently planned her revenge against Burke and the dark haired sea nymph he brought with him.

"That did not take long, Captain." Quain stated as Burke walked down the corridor leading to his spacious quarters.

Burke nodded impatiently, "Did Cori seem satisfied with her room?"

"Yes, she was fine with it. She is such a beautiful girl, is she not? Not to mention, agreeable and so friendly!" He answered.

Burke grunted, realizing that men would be dropping for Cori like flies from that point forward. "Yeah, she is pretty special, I guess."

He dismissed Quain and knocked softly on his own master doorway. "Cori, can I come in?"

Burke heard a few shuffling footsteps then a hesitant, irritated reply, "It is your room, is it not?"

He pushed the door open slowly and smiled, "How do you like living in a space with a lock on the inside of the room instead of the outside?"

Cori did not bother with small talk or joking, "Why did you not tell me you were engaged?"

"Ah, Cori, it is a strained situation," Burke began, closing the door behind him. "You see, it's not a very happy union."

"She sure seemed happy about it to me!" Cori quarreled.

Burke nodded, "She is. I'm not."

"Then why are you marrying her?"

"She is a wealthy French Earl's daughter and he does not plan to give me any choice in the matter. Odelia claimed a few untruths and I am the one paying the price," he explained vaguely.

"That does not seem right at all. Why would an Earl want his daughter marrying a sea-faring man who will never be home?" Cori prompted.

"It is a long story and I shall tell you about it soon. I must go help Acel. If we attack *The Beloved Loss* I want you to stay in this room with the door locked, alright? I will take no chances on losing you to them again. Plus, if it gets rough you do not need to see that violence. Farewell," he whispered, leaving her alone in the large room again.

NINE

"What are the plans, boss?" Acel asked Burke, giving his cousin another pat on the back.

Burke chuckled and hugged his best friend tightly, "I think you missed me a little."

Acel scoffed, and punched Burke playfully in the arm. "I was a little worried. I did not know if I was capable of finding you or not. You know, if it had been me missing, I would have had faith that you would rescue me in no time. I just did not know if I could do the same for you! I'm relieved."

"Oh, little Ace! I had faith in you, I had no doubt you would find me. Ask Cori, I kept telling her not to worry about anything. I knew you would handle it. I taught you well," Burke teased.

Acel grew silent for a moment, "So, what is the deal with the girl?"

"She needed off that ship, Ace. She is not like them," he explained in a whisper.

"Yeah, but Burke, is it really safe to feel sorry for a pirate? She tricked us once; this whole thing could be another ploy for the pirates to get to us or something. Who knows?" Acel reasoned nervously.

"I know she is being honest. I just know it in my heart. She needed away from *The Beloved Loss*. I am helping her get to safety somewhere to start her own life. She is a sweet girl with a loving heart."

Acel believed Burke about Cori, but that made him even more afraid. "Speaking of hearts, is saving hers worth breaking yours?"

"What do you mean by that?" Burke asked in confusion.

"I know you. You're my cousin. You are my best friend. You were there for me when no one else was. I know you, and I know that you brought that girl here for more than just pity. I think you're in love with her," he said, laying it all out on the table.

"What? Me? In love? No way! I just want to help her have a normal life, Ace! That's all. She deserves happiness, freedom, a good man." Burke grumbled in denial.

"And do you want to be that good man?" Acel argued stubbornly. Burke was silent for a moment. If it was anyone but Acel Belcourt fighting with him he could have easily lied and gotten away with it. No one had to know about Burke's strange infatuation, but Acel knew Burke too well for lies or secrets.

He sighed exasperatedly, there was no way to lie to his cousin and be believed, "Okay, maybe a little bit. However, I know what you are going to say, so spare me! I am marrying Odelia, like it or not. I have no choice! And Cori is a good girl. She would never agree to be my mistress; I have already thought of that and ruled it out. So, all I am going to do is free her from Marin and Falco. They are horrible to her, Ace. I am just going to release her so she can live her own life and be happy. Then, I will marry Odelia as planned. Alright?"

"Well, I do not think you should marry Odie without a fight. I think you should keep looking for a way out of the union with her. I just think you should be careful trusting Corisanda, alright?" Acel begged.

"I'm not stupid, Ace."

"Just promise you shall be careful."

"I promise, happy?"

Acel smiled roguishly, "Yes, Captain, I am happy."

Burke shook his head dramatically, "Since all your fears have been confronted, can we make some plans for attacking *The Beloved Loss*?"

"When we searched their ship yesterday evening they hid from us. They disappeared. The Hispaniola inhabitants are loyal to them, so we can trust no one for help. However, we did some damage to their vessel so they should still be making repairs. The only way they could be gone already is if they worked through the night. Even if they did, they should not be far ahead of us," Acel considered.

Burke stood at the helm and steered his adored ship with ease, "If they are afraid of us Marin shall get them away. He is pretty wise for a pirate. However, I doubt they would give up on Cori that quickly. Falco really wants her."

"How many men will we have to arrest for King Louis?" Quain asked as he joined the group.

"Marin, Falco, Sharlene, Klaas, and Zeeman. There are two Spanish servants, Guillermo and Novia, to be freed in Cuba. There are also two other pirates, Yvet and Laron, who we are pardoning as well. They deserve freedom with a warning that if I ever catch them pirating again I shall turn them in immediately. Those two, along with Cori will be released when we reach France. There are also a slew of children on that boat, Quain. They were all kidnapped from Argentina. Falco was going to sell them on the Barbary Coast of Africa as slaves. We must return them to their families."

Quain scribbled down Burke's answer on an aging piece of paper. It was his job, as Second Mate, to work one on one with Garner and the other French Naval gunmen when they invaded *The Beloved Loss*. "Alright, we are arresting five, freeing five, and rescuing a boat load of traumatized children. We were once fearsome sea voyagers but we have recently become policemen, judges, and babysitters. I better go inform the men," Quain shrugged as he walked away.

Cori sat in Burke's spacious quarters trying not to cry. *Why am I so upset?* She wondered. *It is none of my business whether Burke is engaged or not. I have no plans of marrying him, he's a pirate. So why does it bother me?* Someone knocking lightly on the wide, mahogany door jarred Cori out of her tiresome thoughts. "Come in," she called.

The two maids she met a few minutes earlier bustled in. The older one, Leala, gave Cori a curious stare while the younger maid, Miette, smiled shyly. "Do you want a warm bath, Mademoiselle?" Leala questioned courteously.

"Yes, if it is not too much trouble. A bath would be wonderful. I can heat my own water though if you will just show me where everything is," Cori answered politely. She was used to acting as a ship's maid just as Leala and Miette were.

Leala was confused at the pretty woman's offer. Odelia would have never offered to do anything for herself, "No, Mademoiselle. That is our job, we shall be happy to help you."

"Oh, I really do not feel right letting you help me. I am no privileged Lady, as Burke's fiancé is. I have been a ship maid since I was five years old," she informed them.

"Really?" Miette gasped. "Burke said you were a *pirate princess!*"

Leala scowled darkly at Miette but Cori only giggled, "Oh, did he? Well, that may be his term for me because I'm a pirate captain's daughter. However, I was a burden to him, not special like most daughters are to their father. My stepmother put me to work as soon as she married my father. I am no princess of any kind."

This time it was Leala who seemed surprised, "You poor girl! You are no longer a pirate! You are now a guest aboard *The Heart of Calais* and we will treat you as such. Just get comfortable and we shall be right back with warm bath water and scented soaps."

"Are you sure you do not mind?" Cori asked.

Leala did not answer; she just hurried out of the room on a mission. Miette lingered for a moment with another shy grin. "You are very beautiful, Mademoiselle!"

"Oh, thank you, Miette. You are too, but you may call me by my name," she replied.

"Okay, *Corisanda!*" Miette whispered as she rushed from the room to help her mother.

Minutes later, Cori was relaxing in a large bathtub for the first time in her life, soaking in luxurious vanilla scented soap. Miette washed Cori's long black hair and combed through it until it was glossy and straight. "This is so much nicer than a little bucket of cold water and a scratchy bar of soap!" Cori sighed, sinking deeper into the warm water and closing her eyes.

"Mother says that Burke looks at you like he never does with any woman," Miette whispered.

Cori's eyes popped open, "No, she must be mistaken. Burke does not care about me."

"Yes, he must! Mother has known Burke since he was a young boy! My father has too! I heard Daddy tell my mother that Burke was smitten with you and she actually agreed with him! They never agree on anything," Miette rattled.

Cori felt her heart beat speed up momentarily and a light blush come to her cheeks. "Burke and I are only friends. We helped each other escape and that is all. He is marrying Lady Odelia, right?"

"Right, but he does not want to marry her. He cannot stand Lady Odelia! She's hateful and mean, no one likes her. Mother is preparing Lady Odelia's bath right now. She takes two baths a day in lavender oil, eats all of her meals in her quarters, and rarely leaves her bed! She gets seasick," Miette whispered nervously.

"How is she going to handle marriage to a captain then? If she ever plans to see Burke she will have to travel with him. Surely she shall not choose to stay home alone," Cori prompted curiously.

"Well, I heard my father saying that Burke plans to give up his career as a captain to stay home in France with her. He does not want to and seems sick about it! I think he will keep all of his ships and own his company, he shall only handle the business end and let Acel take care of sailing," Miette explained sadly.

Cori was in complete shock that Burke would give up something he enjoyed so much. "What do you mean by *his company* or the *business end*?" She asked.

Miette tried to remember the explanation her father had given her before about Burke's career, "Well, Burke is a trader, you know. He trades goods from Japan to Africa, France to America! The only place we do not deal with often is here, the Caribbean! He says that this is controlled by to many pirates and buccaneers to interfere with. Anyway, people place orders all over the world and Burke collects the merchandise they request, whether it is rugs, spices, or jewels. Then we bring it to them! That takes a lot of work."

Cori nodded her head in amusement, "I see." *Burke is not a normal pirate; he is a very good one! How does he trade and make orders like that without being caught or arrested? People actually trust Burke to steal things they request and bring it to them reliably! What strange behavior for a sea-criminal.*

The two sat in silence for several minutes until Miette finally spoke up, "Well, Mother probably needs my help. She said we were getting closer to *The Beloved Loss* and that we would be waging war with them. I will have to help with anything they need. Just call when you are ready to get out and I shall help you dry off!"

Cori sat still in the tub until Miette walked out, closing the door behind her. She quickly stood up, wrapped herself in the towel and dressed in the spare outfit she brought in her bag. *There is no way I could relax when Burke is attacking my father's ship! Besides, I like to dry myself off.* Cori thought hurriedly.

Cori paced the room, too afraid to leave but too nervous to sit. She was being bombarded with thoughts and felt unable to sort any of them out. *Are we close to The Beloved Loss? My father could be killed! What if Burke loses? Falco will kill me! Burke's engaged! We shall no longer even be allowed to speak. If Burke planned to give up pirating for Odelia, would he give it up for someone like me?*

Forcing herself to sit and calm down, Cori leaned back in Burke's bed. It was the only one she had ever laid in besides her own aboard *The Beloved Loss*. Burke's bed was nearly three times the size of her meager bunk. It was much more comfortable too! His pillows were soft and fluffy instead of hard and flat. His sheets and covers were soft and expensive instead of old and scratchy. *I could get used to this lifestyle,* she considered dreamily.

As content as she was, even the newfound comfort was not enough to make Cori relax. Bounding off the bed, she made her way to the grand door. Cori paused for a moment, took a deep breath, swung the door open, closed it behind her and bounded down the elegant hallway to the ornate set of stairs that led to the main deck of Burke's grand ship. She walked cautiously up the stairs and peeked meekly onto the deck.

Burke was at the helm, proudly looking over the bright blue Caribbean Sea. Acel stood smiling at Burke's side, animatedly unfolding some lavish story he was telling with the use of his arms, legs and feet. Quain, Burke's redheaded Second Mate, was discussing battle plans with Garner and Karoly, Miette's father.

Garner is handsome, Cori consented to herself. *Although he is not as masculine and breathtaking as Burke, there is something about Garner that seems mysterious, gentle, and easy to be around. He will make some lucky woman a fine husband, but I do not want him to be mine.*

She shook her head, wondering why Burke came to mind every time she thought about marriage, love or romance.

Davet, the French cook Cori had been introduced to an hour earlier, was bringing samples of food around from person to person. Cori did not understand why everyone politely declined a sample of Davet's snacks but after agreeing to taste one of his appetizers she had a clear understanding of the carefree man's lack of cooking skills.

Continuing onto the deck, Cori walked bravely to one side of the ship and sat down on a long, intricately designed, ivory bench. Overlooking the sea was nothing new to Cori but seeing it for the beauty, freedom, and happiness it now symbolized was something she was not accustomed to. For as long as she could remember, the sea had been her prison and *The Beloved Loss* was her barred cell. Now, it seemed tranquil and inviting, as if washing away Cori's past and opening up countless doors for her to open and explore.

"Excuse me, Mademoiselle." A familiar voice called strongly from the helm.

Cori looked toward the powerful wheel and the captain who controlled it with a smile. She rose from her seat and left her thoughts behind as she walked across the mahogany covered deck, up a sturdy set of stairs, stopping when she reached Burke's side. "Do you need something from me, Captain Belcourt?" Cori asked with a shy smile.

Burke could see pain, fear, and confusion behind Cori's big brown eyes. He wanted so badly to hold her in his arms, tell her all would be fine soon, and promise her a long, happy, carefree life to make up for the one she had been cheated of so far. "Are you alright?"

"Yes, Burke. I'm just a little nervous. Any sign of *The Beloved Loss*?" She asked.

He chuckled at her concern, "We are almost back to the beach where your father's ship sat the last time we saw it. Can you believe that we were sneaking through the village, stealing fruit and fish this time yesterday morning?"

She shook her head negatively, "No, it all feels like a dream."

"Well, it's not. We're here, safe and sound. Speaking of dreams, it would be best for you to go lay down for a while. We should be closing in on that part of the island any minute now. I'm not sure what to expect, but do you remember what I asked you to do?" Burke prompted gently.

Cori knew exactly what he was talking about, "I shall go lock myself in. I just wanted to see what was going on first."

"Rest for a while. Try to take a nap, alright?"

"Alright, Burke."

Acel stood with his arms folded across his chest, "I do not understand, Burke. They were right here! I'm telling you, we damaged *The Beloved Loss* pretty bad. There is no way they could have fixed all of that overnight. By the time we left to look for you last night it was already getting dark. It's not even noon yet! Where could they have gone?"

"I'm not sure, Ace." Burke answered skeptically, "But I know someone who knows their captain better than any of us."

"You really think Corisanda will help you search for her father's ship? I cannot imagine her wanting them harmed, Burke. There is something wrong with that picture," Ace said dismally.

Burke nodded his head, "Nah, Cori does not want them harmed. She wants them arrested but not hurt. Cori has not said any of that but I know it's how she feels."

"She's not a beginner on the subject of ship attacks. Corisanda must know that a harmless detainment may not even be possible. Her father is not going to surrender without a fight. What if he's killed, Burke? Will she hate us for it later? More importantly, could she hate *you* for it later?" Acel questioned, rattling at high speed again.

"No, I think she's prepared for the worst." Burke paused momentarily, wondering how to explain Cori. He barely even knew her, yet considered himself her closest companion. "Cori has had an unbelievably hard life and her father hates her. She does not want him killed but I think Cori shall pay any cost for freedom."

"I guess we should call her. Let's see if she knows anything," Acel suggested.

"She seemed tired, I told her to go rest. Can we not let her sleep a little while?" Burke mumbled tenderly.

"Burke Landis Belcourt! We are in the middle of a mission for King Louis XIV and you want to put everything on pause, while our enemies escape into the unknown, so that *your girlfriend* can sleep a little while?" Acel asked incredulously, this was not the Burke he knew!

"She is not my girlfriend, Ace! She is just, well, she is my friend, okay? And she just happens to be a girl. That does not make her my girlfriend, it's not like I'm courting her or anything!" Burke scolded.

"Okay, am I allowed to court her then?"

"No!"

"So she is a girl, she is your friend, and no one is allowed to court her. That sounds like she's your girlfriend. What's your plan with all of this, Burke? Are you going to ditch Odelia, marry Corisanda and live happily ever after, or what?" Acel asked in indignation.

"No, I told you that already." Burke snapped wearily, then lowering his voice he calmly continued, "I do not plan to do anything. I plan to marry Odelia, free Corisanda, and never think of her or my own happiness again! It's that simple!"

The First Mate of *The Heart of Calais* sighed, "It is not like you to just resign yourself to something you do not have to do. That is not the Burke I know."

"What choice do I have? If I refuse to marry Odelia then Lord Orson will take the matter to King Louis who shall strip me of my title and arrest me for *raping* Odelia. I would have to flee before Odelia found out she had been jilted, give up my life as the Count of Calais, and live by sea permanently to escape a prison sentence! What kind of life would that be for Cori? She has lived that way her whole life and hates it." He said, shaking his head sadly.

Acel took a deep breath, "Look, I do not know what you should do. All I know is that we are on a mission and I am your First Mate. It's my duty to keep you on track, *Captain*. Are you going to ask Corisanda where her father is or are we just going to let him go and sail around hoping to run into him somewhere?"

"Yes, I'll go talk to her. Take care of my ship and if you spot *The Beloved Loss* just yell for me," Burke mumbled.

"Cori? Are you awake?" Burke asked in a whisper as he cracked open his door.

"Yes, here I am." The lovely brunette answered from Burke's lavish wardrobe closet. "I was admiring all your clothes; you must be very good at your career to afford all you have." Cori had never seen a pirate who wore stainless, pressed designer suits.

Burke smiled at her enthusiasm, "When we get to France we shall buy you some gowns befitting your beauty. I will take you to the best shops Calais has to offer. If you would like, you could go with me to Versailles or Paris and have dresses made for you by the same tailor who assists the Queen. How would you like that?"

"Oh," Cori whispered with a smile. "I do not know! That would be wonderful, but I shall need to be careful with my spending until I find a stable job."

The thought of Cori working as a servant somewhere or in a merchant shop crossed Burke's mind and made him shiver violently. Cori deserved a title. She deserved nobility and a life of privilege and ease. He was sure she would marry a titled Lord and not need to worry about finances, once again prompting his own feelings for her. Trying to focus on the present situation, he changed the subject. "Cori, I need to ask you a very important question about your father."

Cori was startled by his abruptness but she nodded her head in agreement. "What is it?"

"*The Beloved Loss* is not where it was when we left it yesterday morning. It was there last night when Acel left to find us, but it's gone now. Acel claims there was quite a bit of damage done to the ship so it should still be in the repair process. Could they be hiding somewhere here on the island?" He asked patiently, hoping she would have information.

Cori pondered his question for a moment then shrugged her shoulders in confusion, "My father is popular here in Hispaniola. This is where he feels safe to dock on the shore and not be in any hurry to leave. He must be somewhere on this island."

"There are other islands close, Cori. Jamaica and Ponce Puerto Rico are not far. What about Cuba?" Burke prompted.

"No! He is terrified of Cuba and blames the island for all the pain he has felt in the last eighteen years. The people of Ponce Puerto Rico do not like my father because of a trading agreement that went wrong years ago. He could be in Jamaica, but that's a risky travel with a damaged ship. It was already in bad shape after the attack at sea. They must still be here," Cori insisted.

Burke was apprehensive but decided to trust her, "Alright, and you have no idea where they might be hiding on this island?"

Cori motioned for Burke to follow as she walked out of the captain's quarters, through the long hallway, up the stairs, and onto the deck. "We are in Port -au- Prince. And as you said, this is where we last saw *The Beloved Loss*. When *The Heart of Calais* located us this morning we were on the other side of Santa Domingo, close to La Romana. My father's Hispaniola allies are in three cities, Port –au- Prince, Saint Marc, and Puerto Plata. Obviously they are no longer in Port –au- Prince. They must be in Saint Marc or Puerto Plata. I have no doubt."

Burke questioned her decision worriedly, "Cori, we really cannot afford to waste any time."

"Believe me, I know. It pains me to betray my father, but I know it must be done. You do something wrong and you'll have to pay the price, right? Saint Marc is only a few hours north," she assured.

"Where is Puerto Plata?"

"It's a full day journey from here with my father's ship but with your faster vessel we could probably reach it sometime tonight. They have a head start on us so we need to get going. If we are lucky we can catch up before they reach their destination. If *The Beloved Loss* is damaged they will be forced to sail slower than usual," she explained as she walked toward the Helm. Burke was following her as a puppy would its master.

When Cori reached the massive wheel where Acel stood waiting, she pointed her finger north. "We are going to Saint Marc, Sir. We are in a hurry! Can you handle the ship?" She asked courteously.

"Yes, Mademoiselle Corisanda," Acel agreed as he whistled at Burke's lingering crew to get busy. The ship rolled into action and they were suddenly in attack-mode. Chasing *The Beloved Loss* would be no easy feat, even though it was in need of repair.

"Burke, I shall be here with Acel. You are exhausted and filthy. Please, help yourself to your room that you so kindly let me share. Bathe, nap! We will be fine and I shall call you if we are in need of your assistance, alright?" Cori posed her proposition as a question but in a tone that demanded no negative reply. She shooed him across the deck and toward the stairs.

"Are you sure you do not need me?" He questioned in reluctance.

"Yes, I'm positive. Now go!"

As Burke consented and made his way to the luxurious bath awaiting him he marveled at Cori's leadership, intelligence, and care. *She has every quality a man could need or want. Please Lord,* he prayed silently as he slipped his foot into the steaming bathwater, *just let Odelia fall off the ship unnoticed.*

Unfortunately for Burke, Odelia was not that easy to get rid of. She sat on the deck urging her seasickness to pass. The wealthy woman stared at the dark haired, dark skinned, dark eyed, long legged, slender, seductive woman who was drawing a smile from every man aboard *The Heart of Calais*. She was talking quietly to Acel and Quain, both seeming to agree with every word she spoke.

"Mademoiselle Corisanda is a lovely girl. Would you not agree, Lady Odelia?" Leala asked as she returned with Odelia's snack.

"No! She is despicable," Odelia barked. "Why would you ask me that?"

"Oh, I do apologize for your anger. She seems so kind and loving. I assumed you would concur," Leala mischievously said.

"Ha! She is just a sea pirate! I am sure she shall be imprisoned by King Louis as soon as she is taken to France. She annoys Burke, I can tell," Odelia spitefully suggested.

Leala knew she should not continue, but could not resist one last jibe. "Really? He seems quite taken with her to me."

"HE IS NOT TAKEN WITH HER! He shall marry me, do you understand? No one can change that!" Odelia screeched.

"Of course, Lady Odelia. It would be awful for you if he found a way out of your master plan. You would have to find some new arrangement to trick him with," Leala snidely replied.

She could feel Odelia's hateful glares as she walked away to help Davet with dinner. Leala cared very little for Odelia's approval. She disliked the bratty Lady for deceiving Burke and snaring him with her conniving ruse. *It would be wonderful for a good man like Burke to marry Mademoiselle Corisanda. She would be a suitable wife, not Odelia!*

TEN

"Just a little way further, Acel. Do you see that stretch of white beach up ahead?" Cori asked.

Acel smiled broadly, "Yes, I do. Is that Saint Marc, Mademoiselle Corisanda?"

"Sure is! I do not see any sign of *The Beloved Loss* but when we get a little closer we might. I will go wake Burke," she replied giddily as she raced from the helm to the deck.

Odelia was still sitting in the same place she had been for the past few hours, glaring at Cori rudely. There was no denying the blonde haired Lady's disapproval of Cori, and she was quite sure it was because of Burke's attention. Cori nodded politely at Odelia as she walked by. Odelia just rolled her eyes and raced toward Acel.

"Acel! What on Earth was she up here doing with you all this time? Why is Burke letting her take part on this mission? Did she talk about him?" Odelia demanded.

"No, Odie! Mademoiselle Corisanda did not speak about Burke. We discussed *The Beloved Loss*. She told me about her father and his upcoming trip to Africa, if we do not catch him first. Then we talked about her job on the ship and why she wanted to leave her father's vessel. Besides, Burke is not simply *letting* her help, Odelia. Burke has *begged* her to help! Who could know Captain Marin St. Aubin better than Corisanda St. Aubin?" He answered assuredly.

Odelia prattled on irately but Acel lost himself in his own thoughts. In only a few short hours, Acel had gone from being unsure and skeptical of Cori to being absolutely crazy about her. He considered her a saint. *She is the smartest, bravest, most beautiful woman to ever walk across The Heart of Calais, to be sure.* He decided silently.

Burke would be blessed to marry Mademoiselle Corisanda!
She's a woman befitting of him. I have a feeling that if he
can get rid of Odelia then he will be marrying our little
pirate princess... and if he does not, he needs to lose his
feelings for her so I can!

"I shall kill her if she lays one finger on my fiancé. And where did she go now, anyway?" Odelia was insisting as Acel tuned back into her.

"She went to Burke's quarters, to wake him up."

"That tramp has no business being in any man's quarters, it is not proper! Besides, she definitely has no right being in my fiancé's cabin!"

"Well she has to get used to that, since it's her quarters too."

"I am sorry, what did you just say?" Odelia asked as her blood pressure began to soar.

"We do not have any spare rooms on *The Heart of Calais* right now; we are fully stocked with cargo. She shall be sleeping in the captain's quarters. Don't panic though, Odie. Burke plans to sail the ship through the night so Cori can sleep in peace. Then, in the morning when Cori wakes, she shall help me at the helm and Burke will rest. No need for you to concern yourself." Acel shrugged nonchalantly. He knew she would be livid over the prospect of Cori and Burke sharing a room and he loved to see her anger.

Odelia's face turned red and her lips quivered, ready to exhale a violent scream. She balled up her fist and stormed across the deck.

"Are you sure you have napped long enough, Burke?" Cori asked considerately.

"Yes, that was a wonderful nap. So, you cannot see *The Beloved Loss* near Saint Marc?" He questioned in concern.

Cori sighed in disappointment, "No, but once we get closer we may see them up ahead. If not, they may be further ahead of us than we had hoped. They could be almost to Puerto Plata by..."

The door flew open and banged brutally against the wall, cutting Cori's sentence in half. "WHAT DO YOU THINK YOU ARE DOING IN HERE, YOU TRASHY LITTLE PIRATE?" Odelia screamed irately.

Cori met eyes with Odelia instantly and began explaining, "Lady Odelia, I beg your pardon. I was only..."

"No! I want to hear no excuses from you! Burke is my fiancé, whether you like it or not. He is marrying me! Not you! And you have no right to be anywhere near him, do you understand that or are you too uneducated? You are not to speak one more word to him or I shall have you

thrown off this ship!" Odelia screeched as seasickness over

took her again. Turning white she slumped to a chair in

Burke's room and held her stomach queasily.

"Good, I'm glad you're sitting, Odelia!" Burke

raged as he shook his finger in her face. "What did I tell

you about your behavior toward Cori?"

Odelia just glared. Cori stood by the door, trying to

hide her tears. Burke spoke sternly, wanting no confusion

about his feelings, "Yes, I am marrying you but let there be

no misunderstanding! I absolutely despise you. You sicken

me and make me miserable. If it was my choice I would not

be marrying you. The only reason I am is because you lied

to your father and to the King, saying I took your

innocence. You know well that I did not! Cori is helping

me with this mission, and you are hindering me. I have

been instructed by our King to arrest Marin St. Aubin and

turn him in. She is helping me find him, so I shall talk to

her as much as I please through this journey. You have no strength over me until we reach France, Odelia."

"Oh, just shut up and leave me alone!" Odelia barked. "Send someone in here to carry me to my room, I have grown weak and frail listening to your abhorrent disrespect! I need to rest in peace."

"I will send Leala to help you to your own quarters and it would be wise of you to stay there until we get back to France. Your father can protect you there, but he cannot here. I hope you understand what I mean by that, Odelia. There are a lot of sharks in the sea and I would *hate* for you to have an accident," Burke threatened as he took Cori's arm delicately in his own and escorted her from the room.

Once the door was closed behind them, Cori's tears fell freely from her eyes. "Oh Burke, I am so sorry to get you in trouble," she wailed.

Burke held her in his arms and dried her tears with his handkerchief. "It's alright, Cori. You did not do anything wrong so don't let her make you think you did!"

"Yes, I did. I would not want any woman in a room alone with my fiancé either. She had a right to be angry at me. I shall stay away from you," Cori sniffed.

"No! I need your help and I want to be near you, Cori. I have grown *attached* to you in the past several days. We need each other," he consoled.

Cori shook her head, "That doesn't matter, Burke. We will never see each other again once we get to France anyway. You shall marry Odelia and I will go my own way, remember?"

"It's strange. I have known you for less than a week but I cannot imagine never seeing you again," he whispered, feeling a strange emotion.

"I agree," Cori agreed solemnly, "but it's a concept we must become acquainted with. There is nothing that can be done about it."

"Well, if I do not marry Odelia then *we could...* I mean, I might still see you some." Burke choked, wondering what on Earth he was doing.

Cori nodded. She did not want him to change his whole life, including his agreement to marry Odelia in order to be her friend. She could not hide the fact that she was attracted to Burke, and her feelings were growing stronger every day. Her heart began beating fast when he came around, her hands grew clammy, and she sometimes lost her breath when he smiled.

Cori refused to admit that she was falling in love with him, but it was impossible to imagine being pulled from his side. Trying to end the awkward conversation and banish the thoughts from her mind, she shrugged. "Yes, I suppose we could still be *friends*. That is, when you are in France between trips on the sea, of course. However, you must marry Odelia, you have already given your word."

"I have been trying to find a way out of my wedding since it was brought up, Cori. Even before I met you I was searching for proof that I am not to blame for Odelia's loss of virtue," he explained as they walked across the deck. *The Beloved Loss* was nowhere in sight but a large group of villagers were standing on the sandy beach watching *The Heart of Calias* pass. No one seemed ready to run into the water to try to take down the massive ship or anything ridiculous but they certainly didn't look happy and they loudly grumbled amongst themselves.

"Let's just take things one step at a time, alright?" She continued, hoping to put an end to the uncomfortable conversation. Then, hoping she didn't sound awkward or overly serious, she explained further. "We will find my father, attack his ship, take him and his crew as prisoners, return to France, turn them over to the King, establish my freedom, get you out of your marriage, then you can return to sailing and we shall remain friends when you are in town, alright?"

They were arriving at Acel's side so there was no room for Burke's rebuttal. He swallowed his response along with his pride. "Any sign of them?" She asked Acel.

"No," the younger Belcourt cousin answered. "Mademoiselle Corisanda, do you know Spanish?"

"Yes, my uncle and aunt taught me. Why?"

"Listen to them. Do you understand what they're saying?"

Although the residents of Saint Marc grumbled fervently their words were barely recognizable across the distance from the beach to the ship. "The only thing I can really discern are a few phrases. I know I heard someone say 'La Perdida de Amado' and 'El Corazon de Calais,' so that could be a good sign that my father's ship has passed through."

With both men raising their eyebrows at her questioningly, Cori took a breath and continued with her clarification. "*La Perdida de Amado* is *The Beloved Loss*. My mother's name was *Amad*a, meaning *Beloved*. That is how my father's ship earned its name. *El Corazon de Calais* is *The Heart of Calais.* The strange thing is, however, that the people of Hispaniola only speak Spanish and none of them can read in English."

Both men seemed to silently question her, not understanding what the significance of the islanders' language was. When she noticed they were still befuddled, she explained further. "The name, *The Heart of Calais,* is written in English across the vessel. The Hispaniola natives cannot read in English. Therefore, my father must have been here and told them that *The Heart of Calais* is chasing him. You see?"

Realization dawned on the handsome cousins as they understood what Cori meant. The revelation renewed their excitement to catch *The Beloved Loss* and gave them confidence that they were on the right track. Burke took the giant wooden wheel, Acel rushed to update Quain, who in return informed the rest of the crew. Cori revisited her ornate mahogany bench on the deck to stare at the sea until further needed.

It was hard for her to understand the emotions she was experiencing. *How did this happen?* She wondered. *These feelings snuck up on me out of nowhere and now I feel so entranced by them that they cannot be shaken away. I cannot imagine never seeing Burke again, standing by his side, or talking to him. If he marries Odelia she will truly never let him speak to me again. To be fair, I understand why she would not.*

If he does not marry her then he shall be sailing for months at a time, possibly even years before returning. Then, he will be in France for a few short days and if I see him at all it shall be momentarily. The only way I could go with him is if I married him! I cannot marry a pirate, even one as amazing and kind as Burke. I absolutely cannot allow myself to live like a criminal anymore. I want children one day, a real family, and a pirate ship is no place for that! Besides, I'm assuming Burke means much more than he does. He does not want to marry anyone, especially Odelia or me. He just wants us to continue being friends.

Thoughts raced through her head for hours. She wondered why Burke planned to take Marin and his crew back to France for King Louis. It seemed risky for a pirate captain to be anywhere near a King. Cori first assumed that Burke was taking Marin prisoner to make a point to the other pirates to leave him alone, but he mentioned turning them over to King Louis when he spoke to Odelia minutes before.

The notion confused her, but she assumed he knew what he was doing. Cori remembered first meeting Burke, when he climbed from *The Heart of Calais* and onto *The Beloved Loss* the evening her father threw him into her room. He mentioned then that the King of France had sent him in search of Marin, but until then it had never really dawned on her.

The sun was setting in the sky, casting a warm orange glow on the crew of *The Heart of Calais*. Davet called the sailors for dinner but most ate quickly and returned to their positions. Cori knew that they would reach their destination, Puerto Plata, late into the night. It would be a very dangerous situation. The islanders living in the village of Puerto Plata were extremely violent, irrational, and fierce. Not to mention that *The Heart of Calais* would be arriving in the middle of the night when the darkness could hide unknown perils.

Cori's heart thumped loudly in her chest as she contemplated the situation. Tears formed in her eyes as she thought about her father and his fate. She loved Marin, despite his cruel treatment of her. The thought of helping him crossed her mind but she knew that it was impossible. Sharlene deserved imprisonment for the crimes committed long before becoming a pirate, not to mention her illegal lifestyle the past thirteen years. Cori wondered if losing her son at birth was what caused Sharlene to turn so hateful and malicious.

Falco deserved to be incarcerated as well. He was a danger to society. Cori was not sure what his life had been like as a child. She knew he was raised in The Netherlands and claimed to have no living relatives besides his mother who apparently abandoned him as a young boy. He rarely spoke of his mother and seemed extremely uncomfortable when anyone questioned him about her. It made Cori sad but she felt no pity for him.

The sun was no longer visible in the sky when Burke approached Cori and interrupted her nervous thoughts. "Cori, we are getting close to Puerto Plata, are we not?" He asked.

Cori nodded solemnly, "Yes, we should be there within an hour."

"It's going to be dangerous arriving during the night," he stated as he sat down next to her on the bench.

"I have been thinking about that Burke. I think we should construct a plan. Just sailing up to them expectedly will not work in our favor," she whispered.

Burke smiled at her, "You are probably right, Cori. I had not thought of that. What should we do?"

"Well, I have a few ideas. Maybe we should call a meeting?" Cori suggested.

He contemplated her idea for a moment, "Why would we do that?"

Cori gave him her opinions openly, accepting his answer regardless, "So we could get your crew's opinions. They all seem smart and capable. You must trust them or else you would not have them working for you, correct?"

"Yes, you are exactly right Cori. I agree that we should call a meeting. You have great leadership abilities, did you know that?" He questioned, trusting her outlook.

"No, I have never led anything in my life! Would you like us to meet at the helm?" Cori asked.

Burke nodded enthusiastically, "Yes, that's perfect. Who should we involve?"

"Everyone."

"Everyone?"

"Yes. Everyone."

"Do you not think that might cause the ladies to fret?"

"Oh, Burke! We are not normal ladies if we sail around in ships facing men like you and my father every day, are we?"

"No, certainly not. *You* can handle anything, I am sure. Leala and Miette probably can as well. Odelia is a different story entirely," Burke sighed.

"Yes, she may not be up for the challenge of helping. However, if we call a meeting to include everyone on the ship but her it shall hurt her feelings. I certainly would not want to do that. Burke," Cori said with true consideration, "I know you are not crazy about Odelia. I know you do not necessarily want to marry her. But you need to understand that she has a heart and I am sure she gets her feelings hurt. She must love you dearly to want a relationship so badly and I'm sure your words earlier crushed her. Please give her a chance. She may prove you wrong, and your life may be amazing with her by your side. Will you invite her to the meeting?"

Burke felt his eyes moisten a little. His emotions were not for Odelia or his harsh words earlier in the day, but for Cori and how kind, loving, and honest she was. He worried that Odelia would only hurt Cori worse as the mission continued, but he did not have the heart to deny any request she made. "If you want me to invite her, I shall do it."

"Thank you, Burke. I'm sure she shall like that. I will gather up Quain, Karoly, Davet, Leala, Miette, Garner, the Naval Gunners, and Acel!" Cori said decisively as she raced away to do her part.

"LEALA! I TOLD YOU I DID NOT WANT TO BE DISTRUBED!" Odelia screamed hatefully as she swung open the door. Finding Burke instead of Leala changed her attitude entirely, "Burke! My darling, come in and let's talk. I know you want to apologize for the hateful things you said to me earlier. You don't even have to tell me you were wrong, I know you were. And I know you are extremely sorry, so I shall try to forgive you. Just do not talk to her again! As a matter of fact, we should probably tie her up in a storage room with her father. That would be proper punishment for her misplaced adoration of you, right?"

Burke wanted to yell but he took a deep breath instead, cooling his temper. "No, Odelia. I am not here to apologize to you. I meant every word I said." Odelia's mouth dropped open and she was beginning to protest but Burke held one hand up to silence her, "Cori is an angel, as far as I'm concerned and you are nothing more than a thorn in my side. However, I'm doing what's right by you until I figure out a way to prove your lies. What I came down here to tell you is that we are about to attack *The Beloved Loss*. It's extremely dangerous and we need everyone's input on a strategy. I voted to leave you out of it completely, but Cori wanted you to feel included. Now, are you going to come help or not?"

Odelia sniffed with her nose high in the air, "I do not know if I shall come or not, Burke. You have hurt me to the core!"

"Oh well, I invited you..." He said with a nonchalant shrug as he started to walk away.

"Wait!" She hissed, "I shall be there. Just let me powder my nose!"

Burke rolled his eyes, feeling sick to his stomach at the sight of her. He returned to the deck and made his way toward the helm where everyone stood waiting. "Is Odie coming?" Ace asked with a mischievous grin.

Burke snorted, "She says she is. I truly hope she gets lost."

"Boys! You should be ashamed," Cori scolded playfully.

The laughter was cut short as Odelia stormed across the deck, ready to make her grand appearance. When she reached the helm, Burke cleared his throat and began. "Before embarking on this mission I knew a few things with certainty. One of these things was that Marin St. Aubin was one of the most feared pirates on the ocean. I also knew that this task would be a dangerous one. Meeting Cori was a surprise, but it helped me realize just how fearsome Marin truly is." He paused for a moment, glancing at Cori. Hoping he had not embarrassed her.

With her smile, he continued. "Now, we could not have chosen a more hazardous setting than the one we are in right now. Do not make light of the situation, this is not going to be an easy battle. We will be arriving in the middle of the night, and as you can see it's as dark as coal out here. We cannot see what's looming around us or what's ahead. Second, we're all in a land we barely know, with the exception of Cori. Marin, on the other hand, knows this land like the back of his hand. We are definitely at a disadvantage."

He nodded to Cori, hoping she would begin where he left off. "Burke's right; my father has the upper hand right now. He didn't choose to sail here by coincidence. This is where he knew he would have the best chance to defeat us. However, I have several ideas and I'm sure you all do as well. I think we can use our disadvantages to our favor. Would you like to hear what I think?"

Everyone nodded, except Odelia, so Cori began. "As Burke mentioned, it's so dark we cannot see around us. However, neither can the enemy. If we darken the ship by snuffing out all candles and oil lamps, no one should be able to see us coming until we are directly on top of them."

Burke was smiling proudly, Acel and Quain were nodding enthusiastically, and the rest of the crewmembers were listening as if Cori was a genius. Odelia sat with her nose in the air, "Next..." Cori began.

Odelia stopped her abruptly with a huff, "Am I really needed here? This is a man's business and I am a *Lady*. Keep in mind that I am the only *Lady* aboard this ship! Can I return to my quarters? I would like another bath."

"Go, Odelia. That's just fine! Your assistance is not needed. I'm quite sure you have no valuable thoughts, especially not about anything important. Enjoy your bath," Burke dismissed coldly.

She stomped across the deck and almost to the stairs leading to the under deck quarters when she called over her shoulder, at Leala. "Are you not coming to prepare my bath?"

Leala sighed in exasperation and started toward Odelia when Burke reached out one arm to stop her, "No, she's not coming, Odelia. Leala's insight is needed, she may have good ideas. Help yourself to a bath if you want one."

Odelia stormed down the stairs to her private quarters in a rage, slamming the door behind her. "Please continue, Cori. I apologize for Odelia's evil heart," Burke expressed.

"That's fine, she is only tired. It's been a long day for her as well as everyone else. Anyway, if we snuff out all the lights they shall not be able to see us coming. If we

sail extremely slow and quiet, they should not hear us

coming either. Next, if we sail a distance from the island,

angling in toward it, we should accomplish two things.

First, the islanders will not see us coming up the shoreline

and warn my father. Second, we would be blocking my

father between us and the island, so he should not get

passed us and make haste into the sea. That would give us

the advantage of a surprise attack. They shall never know

we're coming until we are right on top of them firing our

cannons."

"That's an amazing idea, Cori! It's exactly what we

needed to succeed. Does anyone else have anything to

add?" Acel whooped with glee.

Burke added his approval, "All of that sounds

perfect to me. What we need to worry about is if Marin is

not aboard *The Beloved Loss*. We cannot take any chance

of fighting on the island. They'll get away and we shall not be able to find them. Plus, the islanders will be helping them if they are on the land. What can we do to ensure that they shall be on *The Beloved Loss* instead of on the land?"

"I have an idea for that too," Cori said with a sound of resignation in her voice. "It's not something I adore doing, but I think it will work. Let's sneak up on them, as planned. Once we are there, fire a shot into the sea for warning. We should be positioned close enough to *The Beloved Loss* to reach it with cannon fire, yet far enough away not to alert them that we're there before we're ready. Just leave that part of the plan up to me. If they are in their quarters they shall race onto the deck, prepared to battle with us or follow us away. If they are on the island, they will board quickly with the same thing in mind. Then you shall surprise them by open firing."

"Are you sure your idea is that irresistible to them, Cori? It will make them risk everything and board the boat?" Burke asked doubtfully.

She sighed sadly, shaking her head from side to side. "Unfortunately, yes. I know it is absolutely that *irresistible*. I shall be in your quarters, Burke. Please send Leala or Miette to fetch me when we find my father's ship, become perfectly positioned, and come to a halt."

Burke nodded wonderingly, "Alright, Cori. I'll trust you."

ELEVEN

Several hours later *The Heart of Calais* crept to a stop a short distance from *The Beloved Loss*. The pirate ship sat half in the water and half onto the beach for repairs. It was deathly silent and still. No one seemed to be aboard, and if they were, they slept. "Call for Cori," Burke whispered to Miette.

The young girl tip toed quietly across the deck of Burke's elegant ship, down the stairs to the narrow corridor leading to all the rooms, then raced to the large captain's cabin at the end. She knocked so quietly that Cori barely heard it from inside. "Is it time?" Cori asked as she cracked open the door.

"Yes, Mademoiselle Corisanda. Burke has called for you," Miette whispered in a panicked voice.

"Tell him to get all the men to their stations and ready. I shall be out immediately," Cori confidently ordered.

Miette rushed away to do the lovely woman's bidding. Everything on the ship was pitch black. Cori had to feel her way across the ship trying not to bump into anything until she reached the mahogany bench. Minutes later, Cori lit one small candle from her seat. The tiny light on the deck was Garner's signal from Cori that she was ready for him to fire one round into the sea with the hefty cannon. The cannon sounded and a deafening BOOM shook the silent night.

With the aid of the darkness they had successfully snuck up on *The Beloved Loss* but now light was needed and silence was no possibility. At the sound of the canon, Miette, Leala, Davet, and Karoly began lighting kerosene lamps and candles to provide the crew with luminosity for the battle at hand.

From Burke's position at the helm, he saw Cori standing on the bench. He realized immediately what her plan was and why it would be so irresistible to the members of *The Beloved Loss,* especially Falco. The Quartermaster of the vessel would doubtlessly risk everything he had to chase *The Heart of Calais* into the sea, the depths of hell, or anywhere in between. Cori was wearing nothing but the tight fitting, black, lacey, transparent night gown that she had been forced to wear so many times before. Cori knew her plan was irresistible to Falco. He would race after her at any cost.

"No," Burke whispered in fear as he realized that Cori was in danger. He was about to forget his position at the helm and race onto the deck to prevent any harm befalling Cori when the members of *The Beloved Loss* raced across the sandy beach.

Falco's scream could be heard from miles around as he saw his *Mevrouw* and *The Heart of Calais*. He raced frantically aboard *The Beloved Loss*, barking orders at everyone, including Marin. The ship was rolling off of the beach and into the sea toward his fiance before the pirate crew could get to their positions. The plan was going exactly as Cori had hoped it would.

When *The Beloved Loss* was a few yards from the shoreline, Garner began blazing his cannon. Yvet returned fire and both ships were jumping with life. Garner shot another cannon at the smaller vessel, blowing part of one side away. The crew of *The Beloved Loss* had been lured, so Cori's job was done. She raced to Burke's side at the helm, "What can I do to help?"

"Go to our quarters and lock the door. Do not open it for anyone but me. Will you go?" He asked.

Cori shook her head, "Yes, Burke, but..."

"No! Just go, Cori! Listen to me; I do not want you harmed. Will you go?" He repeated.

"Yes, Burke. If that's what you want."

"It is," he sternly barked. She immediately turned around to obey Burke's order but he reached out and grabbed her arm. He pulled her to him and hugged her forcefully. Shocked at his display of affection, she met his eyes with her own. "Go Cori, just be careful... and for the love of everything holy, please put some clothes on before this whole ship loses their mind. I love you."

Her eyes widened and her heart felt like it fell through her chest, landing at her feet. Cannons were exploding around them but she could not move. The emotion in his eyes, his deep voice, warm arms, and tender words made Cori feel something she could not describe. It was as if, in that moment, her heart and his attached themselves together, unable to ever part.

Another cannon exploded from *The Beloved Loss*, nipping the side of *The Heart of Calais*. Burke and Cori stared at the deck in shock. The bench Cori was standing on only a couple minutes before was nothing but dust and splinters. "GO!" Burke shouted at Cori with extreme emotion in his voice.

She ran from the deck as fast as she could go and did not stop until she was safely in Burke's room with the door bolted behind her. Cori slumped to the bed, trying to catch her breath. There was a war going on around her involving every single person she knew, but all she could think about was Burke's words. *He loves me. Burke Belcourt loves me. Do I return his love?* She knew the answer to her question without any doubt. *With all of my heart, I love him too.*

Cori could not sit still; she paced from side to side in the spacious quarters. She quickly realized that pacing seemed to be better therapy than merely sitting. Thoughts flew through her mind and her hands shook uncontrollably. Her heart throbbed loudly in her chest and her breathing was short and sporadic. Hours went by with Cori completely unaware of her surroundings. She thought of Burke Belcourt and his beautiful blue eyes. His shaggy dark hair, the small scar on his cheek and his perfect smile made Cori's heart beat even faster.

A million scenarios played through her mind. *What shall happen if my father wins? What will happen if Burke wins? Will the King put my father to death? Worse, shall Falco have Burke fed to the sharks? What if both ships sink? What if Burke, my father, and Falco all die? They could all be dead already! Why has no one come to tell me what is happening?*

Cori constantly heard people running across the deck over her head. Men yelled every now and then, sometimes she could hear Acel or Quain but nothing from Burke in hours. Burke had two large storage rooms on the ship. Both had locks on the outside of the door that could only be opened with a key. Burke kept one of the keys with him constantly, and the only spare key was kept a secret, hidden at the helm for Acel and Karoly. She knew the storage rooms were where he planned to keep her father's crew on the trip to France. The thought crossed her mind that Falco might escape and kill her during the night. *That is, if they ever catch him!* Cori mused.

Oh Burke, Burke, be careful! She silently begged him as she slumped back to the bed. *I doubt I ever see you after we return to France. I know you shall marry someone far better than me, like Odelia, who accepts your criminal lifestyle. I cannot imagine life without you, although it will soon be a reality. If you die because of me I shall never, ever forgive myself. Please, please, be careful.*

The door swung open without warning and Burke came flying in. He did not greet Cori, he just began digging through a large armoire. "What's going on?" Cori questioned in confusion.

"We have won. *The Beloved Loss* is sinking and we have drifted to far from the island for them to swim back before we catch them. I'm going to cross to their ship and arrest them. I need to find ropes to tie them with. I know I have some in this armoire somewhere! When they are tied well I'm bringing them back with me. Stay here until they are securely locked in the storage room, alright? I don't want to take any chances on you getting hurt," he explained quickly, shoving the ropes in his pockets.

"Alright, Burke. Please be careful, I... I just cannot... I do not want anything to happen to you..." She choked, fighting tears.

Burke was at her side, making her his number one priority in an instant, "I'll be fine, Cori. This is part of my job, remember? Knowing you care means the world to me. Just don't worry, I won't be gone long."

Just as quickly as he had entered, he exited. Cori sprawled across Burke's bed, trying to calm her nerves. It did not work.

Burke didn't even need to use a ladder to cross from *The Heart of Calais* to *The Beloved Loss*. The two ships were close enough that they were almost touching. He jumped across with Quain, Karoly, and Garner following suit. Acel watched from *The Heart of Calais*, prepared to take action if anything went wrong. The jobs aboard *The Heart of Calais* were equally as important, with every person knowing what duties were theirs to perform. Davet, Leala, and Miette boiled water, cut clothes for bandages, and began cooking a celebration breakfast.

The sun was beginning to rise in the dark sky. Quain, Karoly, Garner, and Burke stood on one side of the deck, advancing toward Falco, Yvet, Zeeman, Klaas, and

Laron. *The Beloved Loss* was sinking fast and the fate of its crew was to surrender and hope for mercy or sink with the ship. Swords were drawn, pistols were pointed, and the ship rocked uneasily. "Surrender!" Burke yelled.

Guillermo, Novia, and the children from Argentina crossed to Burke's ship with ease and Acel helped them all aboard gently. "I am warning you now, Falco! You better surrender," Burke bellowed.

"Never!" Falco cried back. Two small clanking thumps were heard as Yvet and Laron dropped their weapons to the deck behind him, holding their hands in the air. Falco barked, "You cowards!" but it did not matter.

Quain quickly helped them cross to *The Heart of Calais*, turning them over to Acel's custody. Falco and Klaas held strong, shaking their weapons at the four men advancing toward them. Zeeman still stood but he was obviously afraid, tip-toeing slowly backward trying to get away. "Surrender now, Zeeman!" Burke offered loudly, "You shall be treated fine on *The Heart of Calais*. Although a prisoner, you will be fed and bathed. The King shall treat you mercifully if I tell him you caused no problems. But if you give me trouble…"

The threat was not needed. Zeeman threw his sword down and raced toward Burke with his hands held high. "Please do not feed me to the sharks," the large man wailed. Quain dutifully tied his arms and transferred him into Acel's custody as well. When he finished, the four men advanced slowly toward the remaining two men.

"Where is Marin?" Burke barked at Falco.

Falco screamed several words in Dutch, and followed by yelling, "He is no coward! You will not get him to surrender. He will go down with the ship!"

Burke picked up the pace, "This is your last chance to surrender!"

"No," Falco screamed, turning to jump off the boat. Klaas stood in place, not knowing what to do and was quickly grabbed by Karoly and Garner. Burke caught Falco by the shoulder and spun him around to fight. Both men were tall, muscled, and young. Falco, two years Burke's junior, had blood and dirt streaked through his yellow hair. It was a struggle but between Burke and Quain, Falco finally gave up his fight.

"Take these fellows to *The Heart of Calais* and make sure they are tied tight, hands and feet, and locked securely in the storage room." Burke ordered.

"What are you doing, Sir?" Garner asked in concern.

"I still have to find Marin and Sharlene," Burke said with a sigh.

Quain shook his head, "Not alone, we shall go to!"

"Burke, do not be stubborn. We will help," Garner agreed.

"I just need you to handle the prisoners. When you have them properly incarcerated you can come back to help me. I shall be fine until then," Burke compromised, walking with his head held high to the helm of *The Beloved Loss*.

"Captain St. Aubin," he addressed as he met eyes with Cori's father standing behind the wheel of the sinking ship.

"Yes, Captain Belcourt?" Marin asked wearily.

"Surrender, Sir. You shall be shown much mercy, maybe more than you deserve," Burke stated solemnly.

"I will go down with this ship, boy." Marin replied with a heartfelt smile. "My one and only love, Amada, awaits me and I want to go to her. This ship is all I have, I shall go down with it."

"What about your daughter? What about your wife?" Burke asked.

"I have never loved Sharlene. The only reason I remarried was out of hope that it would make me forget my beloved Amada, but nothing ever will. Cori reminds me of her daily, Burke. She is identical to her only lighter skinned," Marin said with a tired chuckle.

"Why do you hate her so, then?" Burke questioned defensively. "I know Cori reminds you of her, but it was not her fault your wife died. You are blessed that Cori survived. You should have worshiped Cori for the reminder."

"I know it was not Cori's fault. There was no one else I could blame for the pain I felt. I hate myself for hurting Cori. There was just nothing I felt I could do to change it," Marin agreed.

Burke sighed, "Sir, I have to arrest you. This is your last chance to come peaceably."

"Just let me die here, alone."

Burke reached out, taking Marin's limp arms from the powerful wheel. The prisoner's eyes were distant, misty, and forlorn. Burke tied him up without a fight in time to see Karoly and Garner dragging Sharlene's kicking, screaming, thrashing body from the captain's quarters. With the last two prisoners tied they made their way back to *The Heart of Calais*.

Cori stood at the door with it cracked open barely wide enough to see and hear. Miette raced down the hallway to Cori's side with a broad grin on her small face, "We won, we won!"

"Is Burke back?" Cori asked in fear.

"Yes, they are taking the last two prisoners to the storage room right now!" She squealed.

Cori opened the door, assuming it was safe to leave.. She emerged onto the deck just in time to see her father and Sharlene being escorted to the locked room that would be their prison for the next couple months. She lost her strength and sagged wearily to the deck. Cori heard the sound of the storage room swinging open as they entered, then a loud yell from Quain and a scream from Burke. She jumped to her feet as Falco flew out of the storage room and toward Cori with a knife in his hand. Cori screamed in shock, not knowing what to do. Burke was a few inches behind Falco and tackled him barely one second before he reached Cori.

The knife rolled across the floor and Karoly quickly assisted Burke by kicking Falco's head hard enough to snap a normal man's neck. Quain helped Karoly by searching Falco for anymore hidden weapons before throwing him brutally into the storage room, bolting it loudly behind them. Cori raced to Burke's side. Blood stained his shirt and was leaking brightly onto the deck, "HELP!" She screamed.

Novia, Leala, Miette, and Acel heard Cori's panicked voice and raced toward Burke. "Falco…" Burke muttered, holding his side.

"He has been cut," Cori whispered in alarm. "We must get him to his bed."

Acel screamed at Davet to get the water and bandages ready as Karoly returned to heave Burke into his arms. Cori took charge, racing to their shared quarters. Burke moaned in pain as they gently lowered him to the bed. "He's bleeding badly," Karoly said as Davet and Quain rushed to his side.

"Will he be alright?" Davet asked Quain.

"I think so," the ship's Surgeon and Second Mate whispered in relief. "He is losing a lot of blood and shall be weak for days, but I don't think Falco punctured any of Burke's organs. That is the most important thing."

Over an hour was spent trying to stop Burke's loss of blood, cleaning the wound, and bandaging it tightly. The captain of *The Heart of Calais* was in an impalpable amount of pain, vomiting from the throbbing sensation in his side. Cori stood right by Quain and Davet through the process, holding Burke's hand in her own.

When all was done that could be, Quain and Davet left, asking everyone but Cori to join them so that Burke could rest. "I shall gladly stay by his side and help him," Cori whispered through tears, "but Odelia must want to be the one to do it."

"I doubt it, Mademoiselle," Garner said shaking his head.

"Acel, please stay with your cousin for one more moment while I fetch her. If a woman loves a man she will do anything for him, this is something Odelia shall *want* to do for Burke," Cori sobbed. No one had any doubt that Cori was in love with Burke, even the half-conscious captain who was too exhausted to speak.

Cori reached Odelia's room and knocked boldly. "Come in!" Odelia answered from a full bathtub of water and soap.

"What on Earth are you doing bathing at a time like this?" Cori demanded in shock, "Did no one tell you that Burke has been injured? He's wounded. It's critical, Odelia. Perhaps even fatal!"

"Yeah, so what do you want me to do about it?" Odelia scoffed coldly.

"Someone is going to have to stand by Burke's side for the next several days, assuming he lives that long. It

331

will take him the next month of this journey to fully recover, if he does! Are you not going to be the one to take care of him?" Cori asked as calmly as she could.

Odelia rolled her eyes, "I was seasick all the way here and he never even checked on me. Why should I take care of him now? As long as he lives long enough to marry me then I am not concerned."

Cori's scream was loud enough to alert the whole crew who ran to watch. "THERE IS A DIFFERENCE BETWEEN SEASICKNESS AND A FATAL KNIFE WOUND, ODELIA!" Cori shrieked. "He is in horrible pain! You do not even care. Why? Why do you even want to marry Burke if you do not love him?"

"Why would I not? He's rich and titled. Love is not part of that. I deserve the best there is. You are nothing but a pirate- an uneducated, ignorant, insignificant commoner.

You do not think Burke loves *you*, do you?" Odelia lashed viciously.

"All I care about is him living, as you should." Cori replied, lowering her voice to barely more than a whisper. "Never mind, Odelia. I came to see if you wanted to help Burke. I suppose I'm glad that you don't care about him, because I do desire to be there for him in his time of need. You just gave me a chance to take care of the man I love."

With that, Cori turned on her heels and walked through the line of people watching. Odelia's door slammed behind her and she walked with her chin held high into Burke's room. Acel nodded at Cori trustingly, and patted her on the back. "He shall be alright, Corisanda. He's strong."

"Yes, I agree. I'm just worried about him," she said as tears spilled down her cheeks.

"I have to go. We will have Karoly working to fix *The Beloved Loss* and *The Heart of Calais*. Hopefully we can save your father's ship," he said with a sigh.

Cori dismissed him politely, "I understand. Whatever you need to do is fine; I shall take care of Burke."

When the door closed and Cori found herself alone with Burke once again she dropped her head to her hands in sobs. Burke lay on the bed appearing to sleep. He was awake, hearing her pain but too exhausted to open his eyes or speak. "Oh Burke," she cried. "I'm so sorry. Please be alright! Life will be hard to live without you once we reach France but at least I would have the hope of running into you occasionally. I don't know how I could live from day to day if something happened to you."

The sounds of her sobs lulled him to sleep. The pain was overwhelming but the love he felt from Cori gave him the strength to recover. All he could think of as he drifted into an unconscious state was that he had to find a way to make Corisanda St. Aubin his wife. The sun was high in the sky and it was time for breakfast but nothing could keep the handsome man from sleep or the woman taking care of him from his side.

Most of the crew took turns sleeping through the day. The repairs needed on *The Heart of Calais* were simple enough that Burke's crew could handle it without Karoly's expertise. Karoly and Miette spent the day attacking *The Beloved Loss* to keep it from sinking. By nightfall, he announced to the crew of *The Heart of Calais* that he would be able to save *The Beloved Loss* indeed. Acel came to inform Cori that her father's ship was in good hands but all she cared about was Burke.

Cori stayed with Burke all day. She funneled soup down his throat, changed his bandages, washed his hair and face with a wet sponge, and whispered to him gently. "Usted va a estar bien," Cori would sing softly, "Mi amor te salir adelante." Although she sung in Spanish and Burke only spoke English, he understood her perfectly. Her words were clear and beautiful to him, "You shall be fine. My love will pull you through."

TWELVE

By the next day, Burke was strong enough to prop himself up in bed and eat without Cori's help. She sat by his bed at all times, never leaving for a moment. He smiled at her through his pain and she could not help but cry with relief. Burke wanted to get back to work and being forced to stay still for another few days outraged him. "I have work to do!" He yelled at Acel from his bed.

"We are taking care of everything, you stubborn fool!" Acel screamed back. "Just be still and let Cori take care of you!"

Burke scoffed in irritation, "I'm fine!"

"Yes Burke, you shall be fine. But you aren't yet! Now listen to your cousin and let me take care of you," Cori scolded.

"Thank you for your help, Cori. If it was up to Odelia I would be left alone to die," he chuckled.

"I don't even want to talk about her," Cori fussed in anger.

Three days after the attack, *The Beloved Loss* was repaired enough to move and Burke Belcourt was standing at the helm of his ship again. "Argentina, here we come!" he whooped in joy.

"What are we doing after we return these children?" Karoly asked.

"We will swing back by Cuba and drop off Guillermo and Novia. Then we shall sail to France like a bolt of lightning. I hope to be back on French soil two months from today," he confidently challenged.

"Do you want me to sail *The Beloved Loss* behind you, Burke?" Acel asked in preparation.

"No. I think I will move Cori to *The Beloved Loss* with Novia and Guillermo so that they can feel comfortable. Plus, I want to keep Odelia's fangs out of Cori. I shall follow you in *The Beloved Loss*, you take care of my ship," Burke decided.

Within an hour the ships were sailing at high speed toward the beautiful land of Argentina. "Is it alright if I begin cleaning the boat?" Cori asked Burke from the helm.

"Why don't you let Novia..." he began, being cut off instantly.

"No, I have always cleaned this ship. Until we sell it, it is mine to take care of. Alright?" Cori begged.

"Alright, Mademoiselle. Anything you wish is my command." He chuckled in honesty.

The two spent every free moment together. They sat together at dinner, talked throughout the day, and danced together in the evenings. The week seemed to fly by joyously and they arrived in Argentina with time to spare. They waved a white flag of surrender all the way to the shore where angry parents stood screaming and waving swords. However, the weapons were thrown down immediately when their babies ran off the ship and into their mother's arms unharmed.

No eyes were dry aboard *The Beloved Loss* or *The Heart of Calais*, none except those of the prisoners who sat in a storage room fuming in anger. Likewise, Odelia only thought they were wasting time by not going straight to France. She most certainly didn't swell her beautiful eyes shut by crying.

The oversized crew was invited to stay for a meal in Argentina in appreciation for returning the children. The hosts sat everyone on the beach. Lucky for Karoly, Leala sat alone watching Miette talk to Cori a few yards away. He approached her sternly, not letting her shoo him away this time. "What do you want, you over-sized brute?" Leala demanded.

"You," was his short reply.

"Well, that is out of the question!" She denied.

Karoly rolled his eyes, "Let's get something straight between us, Leala. You have always meant the world to me. Yes, I might have flirted with a few girls years ago before I knew you were pregnant with Miette but you are the only one who has ever held my heart. I want you to marry me. Think about it."

He walked briskly away, leaving Leala with her mouth open. Several hours later the crew began boarding again. "Burke, I think we should trade ships for a few days," Acel said unexpectedly before leaving Argentina.

"Why?" Burke demanded in disagreement.

Acel shrugged, "There's something that seems to be wrong in the steering. Karoly says he can fix it but he needs you around to explain the problem and I don't know *The Heart of Calais* like you do. It shouldn't take more than a day or two, at the most."

Burke grunted in response but agreed that it had to be done. With Acel aboard *The Beloved Loss,* Cori was not nearly as giddy. "Don't worry, he'll be back soon!" Acel chuckled.

"Oh, it's fine," she tried to smile. "I need to get accustomed to being away from him. I keep reminding myself that I'll never see him again once we get to France!"

"Maybe you shall, Mademoiselle. Burke hates Odelia and will be trying to find a way out of the marriage unceasingly. He just doesn't have much time once we return. If he's able to cancel the union, would you marry him?" He asked in amusement.

Cori blushed, "Oh, I don't know. I think Burke cares about me, but not enough to marry me or anything. He would prefer to spend the rest of his life a bachelor, not married to someone like me. Besides, I want nothing to do with pirates after this trip."

Acel assumed she was talking about Burke running into pirates occasionally on his trade routes. He shrugged it off, wishing he could explain to her that the chance of meeting pirates was slim and when they did the pirates were typically too afraid of Burke to try and attack. Plus, if she was that scared of pirates she could always stay in Calais.

Acel knew that the woman who married Burke would be the Countess of Calais; plenty could keep her busy at home until Burke returned. *Burke loves the sea and his dream is to continue sailing as long as he can, but if he is willing to give it up for Odelia then he sure would for Cori!* He surmised.

Broaching the subject again, Acel prompted further. "If you don't like pirates you can stay in Calais. Burke has a huge home there; you shall love it. He might even give up the trading business altogether and stay home with you if you promise him a few children."

Cori giggled, "Children? Burke wants children?"

Acel chuckled in agreement, "Yes, he always said that he wanted to remain a bachelor for life because not many women were able to strike his fancy. Children, on the other hand, Burke loves."

"And how does he plan to have children without a wife to take care of them, pray tell?" Cori playfully asked with her hands on her hips.

"Who knows with Burke, but let me tell you something. When Burke Landis Belcourt sets his sights on something, *or someone*, he finds a way to get it. And he has his sights set on you, Mademoiselle Corisanda. He wanted to shoot me, his favorite cousin, for making him trade ships! Every second away from you is hard on him. I can tell that he loves you. Do you realize what a big deal that is?" Acel questioned protectively.

Cori sighed, "If Burke truly loves me then yes I do know that it is a big deal. I cannot think of one thing better in this world than to marry him, Acel."

"So you love him too?"

"Oh yes, with all of my heart. I just don't think there's anything that can be done about it. Odelia's going to marry Burke, whether we like it or not," Cori finished, feeling extremely sad again. "Please don't tell Burke how I feel though. It will just embarrass me worse when Odelia marries him. I'm going to get back to work."

"Burke, darling! I'm so glad you decided to come back to *The Heart of Calais* and make that commoner cousin of yours sail that old, beaten up pirate ship! I missed you," Odelia cooed.

"I didn't hope to be here. I would rather be there."

"But you love *The Heart of Calais*!"

"Yes, but I love a woman on *The Beloved Loss.*" Burke was not a person to lie or sugarcoat his answers. "I love Cori, Odelia. And I'm going to marry her. When we get back to France you need to tell your father that I'm not the man who took your innocence. You need to track down whoever did and marry him. Not me."

Odelia's face turned as red as blood, her mouth dropped open, her bottom lip quivered, and her hands formed into fists. She stood silent for a moment then turned and ran from the helm to her quarters below deck.

He is going to regret this. Oh, he is going to regret this. What can I do? She wondered, storming around the room. *I have to think of something that will teach them not to mess with Odelia Vadeboncour! That witch, Corisanda, needs to learn that she's nothing compared to me and Burke's title and money will be mine, whether he likes it or not!*

She paced around her small quarters, raging about Cori and Burke until she was blue in the face. Her door opened cautiously with a quiet squeak and Miette walked in meakly, "Lady Odelia?"

"WHAT?!" Odelia screamed violently.

"Mother wants me to ask if you need a bath now?" Miette asked in trepidation.

Odelia scoffed, "No! What I need is for Corisanda St. Aubin to marry some other man and leave mine alone!"

"Oh, Mademoiselle Corisanda is a very nice woman. She didn't deserve to be put through marrying someone she didn't love, like Falco. Mother says that Burke and Cori deserve each other." Miette said, bravely trying to protect Cori.

"Miette, you stupid girl! You make no sense. What are you talking about? Who on Earth is Falco?" Odelia said, rolling her eyes.

"Falco was the Quartermaster on *The Beloved Loss*. He was supposed to marry Mademoiselle Corisanda and inherit *The Beloved Loss* from Captain Marin. I saw them load him into the storage room with the others. He's very handsome, indeed. Did you see him too?" Miette asked.

"I don't think so. What does he look like?" Odelia questioned curiously.

"Oh, he's tall and broad like Monsieur Burke! He has short blond hair. Burke's longer, dark brown hair is more appealing in my opinion, but Falco is undeniably attractive. Something about him terrifies me though. It's definitely well that someone sweet and beautiful like Mademoiselle Corisanda shall not have to marry him!" Miette explained, as she laid out Odelia's night gown, hair brush, and lavender soap.

Odelia was silent for a long moment. "Hurry with my bathwater, but put away that night gown. Lay out the lavender lacey one instead."

"Alright, Lady Odelia. Call when you need me to dry you off," Miette answered.

"Before you leave, I have one more question." Odelia prattled.

"Yes, Lady Odelia?" Miette asked.

"How many prisoners do we have, total?"

Miette counted on her fingers for a moment, "We had seven, but Burke said that two of them are allowed to wander the boat and will be released in France. They get to sleep on the deck and aren't tied up in the storage room with the others, so I don't know if you would count them as prisoners or not. Laron and Yvet, *that's their names*, are both very nice. So I guess that leaves five prisoners. They're keeping the captain of *The Beloved Loss,* Marin St. Aubin, separate from the rest. The other four are in the first storage room. Why?"

"Just wondering," Odelia said with a smile.

Miette left quickly before Odelia could ask anything else. *Dealing with a crazy woman like Lady Odelia would drive any man insane!* Miette thought as she walked down the hallway, pitying Burke.

The night was dark and almost everyone slumbered soundly aboard both ships. One small woman with blonde hair, light blue eyes, pale skin, and a deceitful plan crept quietly from her own quarters to the captain's cabin at the end of the hallway. She knocked lightly, and Burke ordered sleepily for whoever it was to "Come in."

Odelia closed the door behind her and approached Burke in a tight fitting lavender colored night gown. "What do you want Odelia?"

"You, Burke. I want to marry you, you know that. Why do you not love me?" She asked seductively as she sat on the edge of his bed.

"Odelia, don't be silly. Leave me in peace, I'm tired." Burke scolded.

Odelia stood up and walked around Burke's room slowly, speaking to Burke in low tones. "I would make a good wife," she whispered as she ran her fingers over Burke's dresser. "Men would die to trade you places. I am beautiful, educated, classy…" she continued as she scanned the items in his chairs. She crossed to Burke's small luncheon table that he typically used for card games or meetings with his crew, "I would be on your arm at every social gathering and we would look grand together."

"What does that matter if I don't love you? And you don't love me, I am not stupid, Odelia. You love my money and my title. There are a few men in France wealthier than I, like King Louis XIV or his brother, Phillipe! He is the Duke of Orleans. Go after him," Burke begged.

"No, I shall not." She said determinedly, still looking around Burke's room as if on a treasure hunt.

"What on Earth are you looking for?" Burke finally asked.

"Nothing," she answered, "Only looking at all of your things. It helps me know my fiancé better."

She is so strange, Burke thought to himself. "Odelia, coming in my room is pointless. I do not love you, nor will I ever. And I shall not marry you either. Not unless you can prove that I am the man who took your virtue, which you cannot do because I did not take it."

Odelia was silent, pretending not to hear what he said as she rubbed her hands across Burke's armoire. Opening the mahogany doors, she ran her fingers across his clothes, his wallet, his watch, and everything else he carried in his pockets from day to day. "Burke, my darling! You are quite right. It's late and I really must be going. Goodnight," she called as she ran from his room, closing the door behind her. Burke lay back down on his bed, confused by Odelia's actions. *Oh well,* he thought, *at least she's gone now!*

Odelia walked quickly down the hallway, pausing at her door. Instead of entering, she walked up the stairs and onto the deck of the ship. She snuck quietly to the large storage rooms being used as prison cells. Fumbling with the key she stole from Burke's room, she unlocked the door quietly. Turning the door knob she peered inside. There were four hostages tied up in the first storage room.

She knew that the second storage room held only one prisoner, who she was not interested in. Each captive was tied at the wrist and ankles. All seven were sleeping uncomfortably in the floor and Odelia scanned each one until she picked out the handsome one with long legs, muscular shoulders, and blond hair.

Odelia crept to Falco de Vries quietly and when she was standing over him she realized he was awake. She bent down to him, and whispered "I am Lady Odelia Vadeboncour."

"I'm Falco de Vries. What do you want?" He answered suspiciously.

Odelia smiled flirtatiously, "I think we may be able to help each other if you shall shut up and listen to me, you worthless pirate."

"Oh, *ja*?" Falco asked, unamused.

Odelia traced her finger down Falco's face and ran her hand through his blond hair, "You must be real unhappy that Burke is stealing your fiancé, right?"

He growled in a low voice, "What does it matter to you?"

She grabbed his chin with force, "Because your tramp of a fiancé is trying to steal my man. Burke is supposed to marry me and I want him back. I'm not going to sit around doing nothing like you."

"What do you expect me to do? I'm tied up and locked in a storage room! Do you expect me to break these ropes and take my revenge?"

"You don't have to. What if I told you I had a very good plan that shall return your fiancé to you and my fiancé to me without ever being suspected?"

"How?" Falco asked in consideration.

Odelia smiled ruefully, "Let me tell you all about it…"

"All done, boss!" Karoly said with a sigh of relief the following day. "I tried to hurry so you could get back to *The Beloved Loss* with that woman of yours. She sure is a beauty!"

"I know, Karoly! She is as pretty as a picture and sweet as candy. Now if only I can get rid of Odelia so that I can marry Cori," Burke chuckled.

"There is no way to do that! You know Odelia will not confess," Karoly hissed.

"No, she probably won't. I'm not sure what I shall have to do to get out of her. I even thought about giving up my title as Count and sailing away with Cori, not caring what the King, Lord Orson or anyone else thought. But that would hurt the people I love, like my parents. They would be discredited. Besides, Cori deserves an easy life as a Countess. I cannot give that to her if I give it up," he said in a dreamy tone.

"Perhaps you shall find a way to get out of the marriage with Odelia and not have to suffer yourself. You can find the man who took her virtue," Karoly suggested.

"Oh, Karoly. I'm sure Lady Odelia has slept with a countless number of men but none of them would admit it now. They've heard what she has pulled on me and don't want a similar fate!" Burke rejected. Karoly didn't reply for a minute. He was staring onto the deck with an elated smile on his face. Burke tried to see what Karoly was staring at but the only person on deck looking toward them was Leala. She was cleaning the floor, often glancing up at Karoly. Burke wondered if the two of them were making progress but he decided not to interfere. Instead, he just grunted to get Karoly's attention back.

"Oh well, at least you can spend some time with Mademoiselle Corisanda now that your ship is repaired and we're closing in on Cuba!" The carpentering Boatswain finally consoled as he returned his concentration to Burke.

"Very true!" He chuckled. "Drop the sails, Karoly. I have to get this boat stopped."

An hour later he was aboard *The Beloved Loss*, gazing in awe at the woman he had fallen so hopelessly for. "Did you miss me, Cori?"

"Oh, of course. I had no one to dance with last night," Cori giggled.

"How did Acel treat you?" He asked with a smile, assured that Acel was a perfect gentleman.

"Acel is a sweetheart, Burke. It must run in the family. What am I ever going to do when we get to France? I don't know how I shall stand it when you get married and we can no longer be friends," she said with a dejected sigh. Cori had been trying to prepare herself for heartache but it seemed so impossible that Burke could be ripped from her.

"Perhaps we won't be separated," he cooed.

"Your fiancé begs to differ, Burke. You're going to have to get used to the idea, as I am. We are just not meant to be friends. All we have is this last voyage," she replied, feeling defeated. Before he could answer, Cori turned on her heels and walked away, feeling the sting of tears in her eyes.

Burke knew very little about Corisanda St. Aubin. He hadn't even known her for a month yet she consumed his thoughts, dreams, and plans. *What am I going to have to do to get you to love me, Cori?* He wondered as he stood at the helm of *The Beloved Loss. How things have changed lately! Before this voyage I never wanted to marry. I still don't, unless I can have Cori. There is no other like her. I would be such a happy man waking up next to her every morning.*

He couldn't imagine what it would take to convince her to fall in love with him. *She cares, I know she does. That was obvious with her concern for me after Falco stabbed me in the side. If she's in love with me or not is something I cannot know for sure, unless she tells me.* With his thoughts about love the memory dawned on him that he had told her he loved her on the night of the battle with *The Beloved Loss*. After being stabbed and struggling to heal, he had totally forgot that the concession had slipped from his lips.

What did she think? Does she think I'm crazy? Or does she love me too? I cannot believe I said that. I do love Cori, I know that. She's the only woman I have ever felt this way about. But that is typically something you tell someone after they agree to court you, possibly marry you! Not when you're trying to blow her father's ship to pieces and take him prisoner!

Thoughts about her opinion of him raced through his mind. *Her feelings were extremely hard to read or understand. One minute she laughs, smiles, blushes, and stares at me like I have her heart. The next minute she seems determined to let Odelia marry me and never see me again once we reach France.* He sighed, shaking his head from side to side as he watched her scrubbing the deck of *The Beloved Loss* vigorously on her hands and knees. Burke wished she would just quit and allow him to treat her like a proper lady of class and nobility.

Cori knew nothing about life off of a ship. She had never been to a city, never been in clothing shops or seen a French Mansion like the one Burke owned. Cori knew nothing about the lavish lifestyles a Count and Countess would share, or that maids were hired to clean… not the lady of the estate! *What can I do to convince her that I would do anything in the world to become her husband? Does she understand that I don't love Odelia? What can I do to show her my love?*

Cori sat on the floor that she had scrubbed time and time again. She felt bad for being irritable with Burke; she just didn't know any other way to become accustomed to the idea of being without each other but to banish their flirtatious gestures.

His words, *I love you*, played in her mind daily. *Did he really mean that or was he just in the excitement of battle and get carried away? Does he care about me like he seems to or is he just leading me on, thinking I am young and naïve? He is going to marry Odelia, maybe he just thinks of me as one last conquest before his wedding? Or, perhaps he led Odelia on and that put him in the predicament he is in now! If so, am I different or is he doing the same thing to me as he could have done to her?*

If he does love me, what does he expect to do? I will not be his mistress! If he marries Odelia I will no longer be a part of his life, not only because I shall not be his mistress but because his wife would not let him be my friend. If he found a way to break the union with Odelia then I would love to marry Burke. But I cannot marry a pirate captain. That is the one life I have dreamed of being out of since I knew what it was!

I want a legal husband, one who is dependable, credible, trustworthy, and honest! I care naught for titles, wealth, or a big house but I want a husband who doesn't run from prison! If he would give up his pirating career for Odelia, would he do the same for me? And if he does, what shall he do for income? How will he survive? Does he have enough saved to last him a lifetime or would he take another career? Could he even get a legal career without being arrested for a previous life of pirating?

Cori didn't know what he wanted from her and that was the hardest part of all. *Why will he not just come to me and tell me exactly what he wants so we can talk this out?* She sighed, realizing that she could do the same thing but would not. Cori didn't know exactly what her future held, but she vowed that she would try to let each day come and go.

She glanced up at the man who made her head spin. He was staring back. Cori felt the warm blush spread across her face as he looked her questioningly in the eyes. After several moments he opened his mouth as if to say something to her. He closed it back, not allowing himself to speak. Burke just smiled and shook his head at her. Cori could not help but to smile back. There was no way for her to resist his attention.

THIRTEEN

"How many days until we arrive at Cuba?" Cori asked Burke to break the awkward silence at the dinner table.

The pair sat alone waiting on Novia and Guillermo to finish cooking, "We should be there the day after tomorrow, if all goes well."

"I've been trying to spend as much time with them as I can," Cori sniffed, fighting back tears as she thought of her Aunt and Uncle. "They're the only family I have ever had, Burke. When my mother died, my father just handed me over to Novia's care. I don't know what would have happened to me without them."

"Do you want them to stay with you? They could move to France!" Burke suggested, trying to console the woman he worshiped.

"I have asked them to consider it, but they're both anxious to return to their homeland. They want to know what happened to their family. Uncle Guillermo and my mother were very close to their father, my grandfather. They're hopeful that he's still alive. Although I shall miss them both, I'm happy that they'll receive their life back," she said, trying to smile.

Burke rubbed her shoulders soothingly, "Maybe you will be able to visit them one day?"

"Perhaps, but that would require a ship, a captain, a crew, and a lot of money!" Cori giggled.

"You should marry a captain! Think about it, he would own a ship, have a crew, and be excited for you to sail with him!" Burke replied with a devilish grin.

Cori's giggle turned into roaring laughter, "Oh! You aren't fooling me, Burke Belcourt."

"Well, I thought it was a wonderful idea," he chuckled with a shrug of his shoulders. His blue eyes twinkled mischievously as he stared into Cori's dark brown ones.

Dinner was served and the four current members of *The Beloved Loss* ate together, enjoying their meal. "Out of curiosity, Captain Belcourt, Guillermo and I were wondering if your prisoners have said anything of interest since their arrest," Novia prompted timidly.

Burke shook his head, "I have only spoken with them once since then. At that time, I only talked to Yvet and Laron. I have not said anything to Marin. Karoly, my Boatswain is in charge of feeding them three times a day and helping them to the bathroom when needed. Why do you ask?"

Guillermo spoke up, scowling at his wife for bringing up the subject in front of their niece, "We were wondering if Marin has said anything about Cori or if he is worried about prison. Sharlene should be mortified since an escape from incarceration is what landed her on a pirate ship in the first place and we assume that Falco has been raising quite a fuss as well, especially over Cori."

"I'm interested to know as well. As soon as we reach Cuba I shall ask Karoly for any information he might have. Are you both excited to return home?" Burke asked.

"*Si*, we are. But we will miss Cori!" Novia answered.

"I shall miss you both also. And I know this seems strange, but I'm going to miss my father. If only there was something I could do to save him. All I have ever wanted was to be close to him and make him love me. He deserves to go to prison for his crimes but I hate to see him punished. Is that silly?" Cori questioned sadly.

"No, Mademoiselle. It's not silly. If my own father committed a crime that was prison worthy, I would still hate to see him go. I would do anything in my power to save him from it, if it was me," Burke comforted.

"There's nothing I could do though, Burke. You're the one arresting him," Cori laughed.

"Oh, I almost forgot," he said in confusion. *Why do I expect Cori to have any faith in me? Why do I expect her to fight for me when I'm the one sentencing her own father to prison?* "Cori, if there was anything I could do to get him out of this I would do it for you."

This time it was Cori who patted Burke on the back sympathetically, "I know you would, Burke. And I understand why you cannot! He arrested you, nonetheless. It's quite fitting for you to arrest him. If you were hired by the King to capture him then you are most certainly expected to do it."

The long day proved tiring to Cori and she retired as soon as dinner was over. Burke seemed forlorn about it, hoping to spend time with her. "I just need time to sleep and the morning light will bring answers or a better attitude," she explained.

However, when she snuggled into the covers it did not feel as soothing as she had hoped. Cori tossed and turned with many thoughts playing in her mind. She contemplated marriage and a nice home in France. She pictured children playing in the sand on a beach by the ocean. After hours went by and the comfort of sleep did not come, she decided to take a walk on the deck.

The night was dark but the stars shined brightly in the sky. The round orbs overhead reflected brightly on the crystal blue water surrounding her. No land could be seen in any direction. They had both ships floating a distance from any island to avoid other pirates. She lay down on the wooden deck, staring up at the breathtakingly beautiful night around her. "Quite a picture, is it not?" Burke said, startling a gasp out of Cori.

"You scared me!" She squealed. "Yes, it is certainly beautiful. Do you think this is as beautiful as the rainforest in Hispaniola?"

"It's a completely different atmosphere, but I'm more at ease on the sea. It's my home just as it has always been yours. I don't think I could live without it," Burke said.

"You would if you had to," she argued, thinking of Odelia.

Burke dropped to his knees and rolled onto his back, lying next to Cori. "True, but not happily!"

Cori laughed. "Are you going to miss me, Burke?"

"I don't want to have to miss you, Cori. I want you to be with me. If you married me, we could always be together. When you felt like staying on land we could settle in at my home in France. It's a big, beautiful home. You shall like it. And when you are ready for a mission on the sea, we could jump on *The Heart of Calais* and sail. Acel could handle the ship in my time off with you. Does that sound so bad?" He asked in hope.

Cori's heart was racing again. Any time that Burke mentioned marriage, love, or a life together she could not help but yearn for it. "It sounds wonderful. I just don't see a point in discussing it and dreaming about it when we both know it cannot happen. Besides, why would you want to marry me? I'm sure all the French women beg for your attention. Odelia proves that point."

"You know how Odelia is. She cares nothing about me, Cori. Only my money and the easy life I could provide for her. I have never offered it to her, but I would freely give it to you," Burke prompted.

"I cannot deny that I would love being with you. I just don't know how that makes any difference when you are bound to marriage with another woman."

"If I'm able to get out of the marriage, would you consider… a courtship?" He asked nervously.

"A courtship? What is that?" Cori asked.

Burke realized he had been speaking to her as if she was accustomed to the lavish balls and parties that introduced men and women to the prospect of marriage in Europe. "It's where a man and woman see each other exclusively. We would get to know each other and if it worked out, it could result in a marriage agreement," he explained.

"Besides the exclusivity part and the agreement to wed, is that not what we are already doing?" She asked in true speculation.

Burke chuckled, "Well, I suppose it is."

Cori smiled broadly, hoping she understood the subject. "Alright, if you don't marry Odelia we would be exclusive. Once we were exclusive and knew all about each other, marriage might or might not be an option. Yes, I agree to court you if you don't marry someone else."

Burke just smiled, staring at the beautiful stars. *It's no agreement to marry me, but at least it's in progress!* He silently decided. "Cori?"

"Yes, Burke?"

"Do you want to dance?"

"Right now? It's dark!"

"So what? Do you want to?"

"Yes."

Burke stood quickly, helping Cori to her feet. There was no music like there had been the few evenings when they danced in the dining room after dinner. All was silent as Burke began waltzing Cori elegantly around the deck. He started humming softly to keep the rhythm, and when Cori began laughing Burke turned his soft tune into a loud song. They floated around the boat, with Burke singing through Cori's laughter.

Several yards away on *The Heart of Calais*, Acel and Karoly stood at the helm watching the young couple's bliss. "If Burke marries Odelia and loses Cori it will break his heart. He shall not be the same man anymore," Karoly sighed solemnly, knowing all too well the feeling of heartache.

Acel nodded, "If there was anything I could do, I would!"

"Do you think Mademoiselle Corisanda is falling in love with the Captain?" Karoly questioned, knowing the answer.

Acel sighed, "Yes, I think she loves him just as deeply as he does her. I've never seen Burke smitten with anyone before, even as teenagers when everyone thought they were in love with someone! Burke never was. He undoubtedly is now. The question is, what are we going to do to keep him from regretting it?"

"We have to find some stupid man to testify against Odelia. If someone would speak up to the King, in front of Lord Orson, saying that Burke's not the one to blame for Odelia's indecent behavior then that's all King Louis would need to drop the charges on Burke. Right?" Karoly suggested.

Acel chuckled quietly, watching Burke spin Cori around a short distance away. "Where are we going to find any man stupid enough to risk marrying Odie?"

"It's getting late, Burke." Cori said as the dancing partners took a break.

"Yes, it is. Should I let you retire for the evening, again?" He asked.

Cori smiled, "Perhaps it would be best for us both."

"I'm quite glad you couldn't sleep earlier."

"Me too."

"Are you alright, Cori? You've seemed sad since we left Argentina." Burke pried.

"Yes, I'm alright. Burke, can I tell you something?"

He sat down, holding her hand in his own, "Anything."

"There are so many things on my mind that I can hardly think straight. I've been worried about my father. I love him, you know. Whether my father loves me or not, I've always wanted to be close to him. Now I know that there shall never be a chance. He will die in a prison cell and it's unlikely that I shall ever see him again. My father deserves that, but I don't. I don't deserve to never have that opportunity. Aunt Novia says that my father was an amazing man, happy, carefree, gentle and loving. When my mother died it broke his heart and pushed him into this life. *Can you imagine losing someone who meant the world to you? Would you give up everything you had and turn to a life of crime if your love was taken from you?*" She asked.

Burke knew she was speaking only of her father but it shocked him. He had mentioned to Karoly that morning that the only way to lose Odelia and keep Cori would mean to give up everything he owned, including his title, and turn to a life of crime, running from Lord Orson! "Yes, I understand his pain. When you love a woman, you would do anything for her."

She shook her head sadly, "I just know that I pity him. Whether I should or not, I do. And I pity myself! I always thought that one day he might grow to love me and now I have no hope."

"Cori, I believe your father does love you. He told me that he blamed you for your mother's death, although it wasn't your fault. Your father loves you, he just doesn't know how to show it," he comforted, hoping not to offend her.

Cori sat in silence, pondering Burke's words. "Regardless, we have no hope of ever having a decent father-daughter relationship. Life's not fair, right?" She asked jokingly, trying to seem strong. "Good night, Burke."

"Cori, wait. I... I just... I want to tell you that... Never mind, goodnight." Burke stuttered, not knowing what to say or do to relieve her pain.

She walked to her room with nothing else spoken between them. When the door was closed and her tired body slipped between the sheets on her small bed, Cori closed her eyes and cried.

The next day was spent in silence. Burke tried to talk to her, comfort her, or cheer her up but she only thought of her father and his imprisonment. Once Novia and Guillermo were in Cuba she would have no one left. An incarcerated father, a deceased mother, and distant relatives who live half a world away did not paint a pretty picture of a happy family. "What can I do to cheer you up?" Burke asked.

"Nothing, Burke. I'm just dreading telling my Uncle and Aunt good-bye. When they are gone I will only have my father, and that leaves me no hope at all," she refused.

She stayed in her room alone, even eating dinner there. Burke saw her very little that day and it broke his heart. *Being away from Cori for this long is horrid. How can I handle being away from her permanently? What can I do to show her my love? What can I do to make her love me back? What can I do to console her about the loss of her family and father? If only I could do something to help her!*

When Cori awoke the following morning, *The Beloved Loss* and *The Heart of Calais* were stopped on the shore of Cuba. It was the first time Cori had ever set foot on the island, and her Aunt and Uncle were home after an eighteen year journey.

Reality hit Cori the moment she saw the island. Spaniards were bustling around speaking to Burke in broken English. Novia and Guillermo were unloading the few belongings they owned. Each had large smiles on their faces, "Burke?" Cori asked in sudden anguish.

"Yes, my beauty?" He replied, coming to her side.

"Is this Cuba?" She bit her lip to keep from crying.

"Yes, this is your mother's home! I have someone you should meet. Follow me," he urged.

Cori walked behind Burke to a group of older individuals who sat on the beach, taking in the action. One man with graying hair stood up when he saw the pair approaching. He was handsome, and looked more like Cori than her own father did. "Governor Ricardo, this is Corisanda Aleene St. Aubin, your granddaughter."

Cori felt her knees buckle, and if not for Burke's strong grasp she would have fallen. "Oh my, you're so beautiful. You look just like your mother, my sweet Amada!" He said with a tear rolling down his face.

She reached out a hand to shake his, but he pulled her in for a gentle hug. "I don't know what to say," Cori shakily stated. "Aunt Novia and Uncle Guillermo told me you were most likely dead! They said that you were struck with Yellow Fever when it hit Cuba. How is it possible that you're alive and well?"

Cori's grandfather smiled, "I did have the fever, indeed. I was sick for weeks but I kept holding on. Finally, beating all of the odds, I recovered! It was a miracle. I'm so glad that I lived through it just so I could meet you now!"

"If only my mother could be here to see you. I understand that she loved you dearly," Cori replied, fighting back tears.

"Ah, I feel like my heart has been returned to me for the first time in eighteen years, since Amada left! I'm so sorry you never knew her," he whispered. Burke had been the one to break the news of his daughter's death less than an hour before. The man waited daily for *The Beloved Loss* to return with news of his daughter but it never came, until that day.

"I am too," she whispered. "Did Burke tell you what happened to her?"

"Yes, dear child. He did. Your father was wrong to blame you and if Captain Belcourt would let him off the ship I would chastise him properly! Then I would hug the boy, he loved your mother so much," Ricardo said mournfully.

Cori just sniffed back tears and held her grandfather's hand. Burke smoothed Cori's hair with his hand and patted Ricardo on the back, "Sir, I trust that Cori is safe with you for a few minutes. I must help Guillermo and Novia get settled in and start unloading the merchandise we're trading!"

"Yes, Captain Belcourt. Corisanda and I have a lot to catch up on!" He chuckled as Burke walked away.

"We're trading with you?" Cori asked in surprise.

Ricardo nodded animatedly, "Yes! We do not trade with bad people on this island, and those were the only ones around until now. Captain Belcourt does not normally trade with Cuba but says that if we are interested in a trade agreement that he would be willing to make Cuba part of his business route. I certainly hope we can, because you could come with him and I would be able to see you!"

"Oh, that would be wonderful! I could visit you, Aunt Novia and Uncle Guillermo!" Then, remembering Odelia, Cori added "Assuming Burke and I are able to remain in contact once we reach France."

Ricardo smiled, knowingly. "Dear girl, I know this is none of my business. However, I must tell you that I am a decent judge of character. It's obvious to me that Captain

Belcourt is a marvelous man, you would be quite wise to marry him!"

"Oh," Cori blushed. "Burke is very wonderful, indeed. But there's already a woman who plans to make him hers."

"Yes, he told me about his situation. He says you're prettier, sweeter, smarter, and much more suited for him though! That must count for something," Ricardo advised.

Cori shook her head solemnly, watching Burke work from a distance away. "It's out of Burke's hands though. Besides, how do you know Burke is such an upstanding man? He's not much different than all the other traders in this area, is he?"

"Goodness, yes! He is much better. All we have around this area are pirates and buccaneers! There's one thing you need to always remember about a good man, Corisanda. He has strong hands, good hands, capable hands. Even if something might seem out of his hands, or out of reach, you should not underestimate his grasp. You understand what I'm saying?" The aging governor questioned.

"You're saying that Burke might find a way out of the marriage with Odelia, if he tries. And if he does, I should marry him?" Cori questioned, understanding his view.

"If you love him you should. Do you love him?"

"I... Well... Yes, I do. But he doesn't know that."

"You should tell him. I think if Captain Belcourt knows you return his adoration then he would do anything it took to be your husband," Ricardo instructed.

"I'll consider it," Cori giggled.

When the work was finished and Governor Ricardo and Captain Burke Landis Belcourt reached a trading agreement, the family and friends relaxed on the beautiful sandy beach of Guantanamo, Cuba. Ricardo explained that his own home was in Cuba's Capitol, Havana. He was in Guantanamo for a few days visiting his brother's family. Cori was introduced to her cousin, Rosa, who was only a few months younger than herself. Rosa and Cori looked like twins, with the same dark brown hair, deep brown eyes, long legs, and slender body. The main difference was that Rosa was darker skinned, having a Spanish mother and father, instead of a Spanish mother and French father like Cori.

Rosa and Cori became fast friends and inseparable throughout the day. "You are quite blessed," Rosa squealed in delight. "The man who stares at you constantly is so very handsome! It's obvious Captain Belcourt worships you, Corisanda!"

"Thank you, Rosa. He's a wonderful man. You know, he has a cousin on this journey. Would you like to meet Acel?" Cori suggested, playing matchmaker.

"Oh, of course!" Rosa agreed with a twinkle in her eye.

At dinner that evening, Acel informed Burke that the ship was in tip-top shape, ready to leave the following morning. Rosa immediately caught Acel's eye, making him almost forget what he came to say, "Acel, this is my cousin, Rosa."

"Beauty must run in your family, Mademoiselle Corisanda." Acel complimented as he kissed Rosa's hand.

With a silent agreement to let the new acquaintances get to know each other better, Burke asked Cori for a walk around the beach with him.

When the pair was out of earshot, Cori giggled in glee. "Did you see the way they were looking at each other, Burke?"

"Yes, I think they make a fine couple!" He laughed.

"Where has Lady Odelia been all day?" Cori asked.

Burke rolled his eyes, "Karoly says that Odelia refuses to leave the ship. I was pleased to hear that, though."

Cori smiled, "Yes, she wouldn't fit in well here with her blond hair."

Burke held Cori's hand in his and they walked together down the beach. "Cuba's views are breathtaking."

"Yes, they are, including the one I'm viewing now." He smiled playfully as he stared at her, jabbing her gently with his elbow. "I knew you must be the product of an exceptionally beautiful place."

"Thank you, Burke. My grandfather seems to think you're an awfully special man," Cori added.

"He knows my feelings for his granddaughter."

Cori blushed, "Yes. He mentioned that."

Burke's blue eyes met Cori's brown ones momentarily, "Cori, I know you care about me. You were so gentle and kind when I was hurt. Tell me your feelings; am I wasting my time fighting for you?"

Cori did not know exactly what to say, but she took a deep breath. "I'm just afraid, Burke. I don't know what to expect. I don't want to be hurt when Odelia marries you and I'm left alone. There's not much more loss I can handle," she explained. "Besides, I know you say you care for me too. But how do I know you truly do? Odelia thinks you love her, as well."

"I do not love Odelia. I don't even like Odelia! Cori, whether you want to believe it or not, I love you. I love you with all of my heart, and I would do anything for you. Saying it is not enough, I *will* prove it to you. Just wait," he whispered. Burke let go of Cori's hand and left her standing. He rushed to the ship, trusting Cori to make it back alone. After much thought, it finally struck Burke what he could do to prove his love for Cori and pacify all of her fears. Burke knew what he had to do and a plan was forming in his mind.

Late into the night a pair of quiet, tip-toeing feet cracked open one of the large storage rooms. There was only one prisoner in the room, Marin St. Aubin. Marin met eyes with the quiet culprit sneaking in. "What can I do for you, Burke?" Marin asked.

"It's not about what you can do for me, Sir. It's about what I can do for Cori," Burke said as he untied Marin's feet and arms.

Marin looked at Burke in confusion, "What's going on?"

"I'm releasing you. Cori said you're bitter against all Cubans so this may not be much better for you than prison. However, it shall be better for Cori. She loves you and doesn't want to see you punished," Burke replied.

"She loves me?" He asked solemnly.

"Yes, I don't know why, but she does. She wants to be close to you one day and for her sake I hope that's possible. I am keeping my eyes on you though, Marin. No more pirating! Make yourself a home in Cuba and leave the thievery to someone else. Understand?"

Marin nodded his head in hope, "If you ever see me sailing the ocean, it will only be to check on my daughter. I love her too, Burke. Are you going to marry her?"

"If she shall let me," Burke answered honestly.

"You have my blessing. Goodbye," Marin replied as he hurried away from *The Heart of Calais*. He paused, staring at *The Beloved Loss* for a long moment. Taking a deep breath and feeling the sting of a warm tear falling down his cheek, he hurried into the village.

Cori cried for hours after saying goodbye to her newfound family, as well as Novia and Guillermo. She slept on the boat, knowing that when she awoke they would be sailing toward France. The day had been bittersweet. Meeting her relatives and easily loving each one gave her a sense of family for the first time in her life, but telling them goodbye was almost impossible. Cori considered staying in

Cuba, making it her permanent home. For some reason, the prospect of marrying Burke gave her enough hope that she couldn't stay behind.

When Cori did wake up the next morning it was not quiet and lonely as she expected. Instead, it was to the sound of flares exploding behind *The Beloved Loss*. She raced onto the deck to see what the commotion was all about. *The Heart of Calais* was summoning them to stop. *It must be an emergency!* Cori thought in extreme panic.

"What's going on?" Burke asked calmly as *The Heart of Calais* pulled next to *The Beloved Loss*.

"Burke!" Acel screeched, "One of our prisoners is missing! Captain Marin is gone! He's no longer in the storage room! Someone must have helped him escape in Cuba. We must go back!"

Cori's face turned white and she felt as if she was going to faint. "Acel," Burke mumbled, "Come across so we can speak... in private."

"But we have no time to waste!" Acel argued.

Burke glanced at Cori again, "Just come over here. Please."

Acel climbed across and Burke led him to the other side of the ship, a distance away from Cori. They spoke for several moments in what seemed like a heated argument. They both kept glancing at Cori, worrying her worse. Finally, Acel crossed back to *The Heart of Calais* without a word to her. She waited for the ships to turn around and make a speedy trail back to Cuba, but they continued in the same direction toward France. Finally, Cori could stand no more. She marched toward the helm to ask Burke what was going on.

"Captain Belcourt!" Cori demanded in an authoritative tone. "What happened? How did my father escape? Why are we not turning around?"

"Ah, Cori. Well, it's nothing really. No worries," Burke dismissed.

"What do you mean *no worries*?" She asked angrily.

Burke chuckled at her charisma, "I mean just what I said! No worries. It's true that your father is no longer a prisoner of mine. He's free somewhere in Cuba. We're going to France. We still have Sharlene, Falco, Klaas, and Zeeman to bring to the King."

Cori stared in silence for a few moments, trying to understand what had happened. "You're going to let my father get away, after he arrested you? Are you not concerned about how he escaped? Do you think someone let him go, like Yvet or Laron? Whoever released my father could release Falco tonight!"

"First of all, the King will not miss him. As long as the mission was successful and your father has been stopped from pirating then I did a good job. I could tell the King that Marin died in the battle if it came to it. Secondly, I don't think anyone will let Falco out. Don't worry," Burke shrugged casually.

"My father arrested you, worked you, and locked you in a room with me for days! Why are you not angry? Why do you not want him killed?" She demanded, stomping her right foot.

Laughing heartily, Burke waved her anger aside, "We all make mistakes. I'm sure that he's a good man underneath all of that. Besides, what harm can he do? He's jobless, crewless, and stranded on an island where there are no boats! My ship will be the only one they trade with or that commonly visits. I suppose it's possible that a passerby might stop at the island but it rarely happens. In France, most captains refuse to sail toward Cuba due to the danger. I know one man from Ireland who does, but his boat is so small and old that most pirates don't find it worthy to even bother him! Regardless, most likely Marin will be stuck there."

Cori didn't know whether to smile or cry. She was relieved that her father had escaped and wouldn't have to suffer in prison. She was elated that with his free status their paths may one day cross again, and when it did he wouldn't be in charge of her. Marin being in Cuba helped, because Cori hoped to travel there with Burke, *Odelia willing*! "Alright, I guess." She mumbled in confusion.

"Now, are those all of your questions, my beauty?" Burke asked.

"Yes. Wait, no it isn't! Why do you plan to release Yvet and Laron?" Cori probed.

The captain smiled again from the helm of *The Beloved Loss,* "Yvet and Laron helped me a lot when I was a prisoner of your father's ship. They also surrendered quite easily when I attacked them. Yvet was part of the French Navy as your father was and he never wanted to go into the life of pirating. He just felt like he had to stick by Marin's side, out of a sense of responsibility. By the way, how much do you know about Laron's life before joining *The Beloved Loss?*"

"I don't know, nothing I guess!" Cori dismissed, not seeing the point behind Burke's explanation. "All I know about Laron is that he loves women, all women! He cannot keep his hands off of anyone who glances at him. The only times Laron has ever been in trouble with my father is when we would get to an island or a country and he would just disappear! They would give him a time to be back and he would miss it. My father would have to go looking for him and drag him back from a brothel!"

Burke sat down, pulling her down next to him on the deck. "Well, let me tell you something about him. Laron was very poor. He worked hard for an income to support his family and they were still barely able to eat. He had a young wife, and although they were impoverished they were crazy about each other. Do you know what happened, Cori?"

Suddenly curious, Cori replied "No. I don't."

"A thief broke into their home one night while Laron was away working. He killed Laron's wife and took everything they had been working for. He was only twenty years old when his wife died. People tried to blame him for her death, saying that if he was home to protect her it wouldn't have happened. Others said that it was him who did it. Heartbroken, lonely, guilt ridden, with a ruined reputation, Laron joined your father's pirate crew. I believe his fascination with women is a defense mechanism to hide his pain for his late wife," Burke reasoned.

A tear slid from Cori's eye, "Burke, he has been on my father's ship for seven or eight years now and I never knew any of that! How did you find out?"

"When I was healing from Falco's attack, after the battle with your father, I went to the storage room to speak to the prisoners. I pulled Laron and Yvet aside separately and asked them to give me their history. Both did. After making sure that neither was wanted for other crimes or bad behavior, I told them both that they would be released once we reach France. They don't deserve prison, Cori." Burke finished.

"Thank you for being so kind. My grandfather was right about you, you're different than most!" Cori lovingly alleged.

"Your opinion of me is the only one that counts," he whispered.

"Let me leave you to your work, Burke. Dance after dinner?" She asked flirtatiously.

"I shall think of nothing else. You have made my day," he huskily replied. Cori winked teasingly and floated away, happy and in love. The Count of Calais felt his heart beat quicken in his chest and he sighed dreamily as he watched the woman who held his captivation drift away.

FOURTEEN

After the trip to Cuba, Burke and Cori spent every free moment together. They were the only two passengers aboard *The Beloved Loss.* Burke sailed the ship during the day, Cori cooked and cleaned. When she was not busy, he taught her to sail. When he was not busy, she taught him to clean. They danced every evening after dinner, and stayed up late into the night talking about everything under the sun.

Burke told her about his family in France. Since Burke considered his title a mute point, he purposely left out that information. For some reason, he felt though he just wasn't ready for her to know. So many women in Burke's life had been more interested in his title and wealth than him as a man. He just found it easier to talk to Cori as a captain... rather than a Count. Cori enlightened Burke about Falco's engagement request, her many failed escapes from *The Beloved Loss*, and Sharlene's hatred. One evening, Cori asked Burke how much longer it would be until they arrived in France.

"Probably another ten days," he answered nonchalantly.

"Only ten days?" Cori screeched, suddenly upset.

Burke did not understand her obviously unhappy reaction, "Yes, why? What is wrong?"

"It took my father nine or ten months to sail from Cuba to France when my mother was pregnant! I expected that we would have several more months together. Not just ten days!" She wailed, close to tears.

Burke wrapped one arm around her shoulders as he explained, "It was almost nineteen years ago when Marin made this trip with your mother. Back then, ships like *The*

Beloved Loss were built much slower than they are now. They were big, hefty and resistant, but they were not fast. Now, ships like *The Heart of Calais* can make the trip from Cuba to France in less than a month. Even after your father had *The Beloved Loss* updated into a speedier vessel after your mother's death, it is still slowing *The Heart of Calais* down by several weeks."

He shrugged, "Besides, we are traveling in the summer. If you were born in February, your father must have traveled all through the fall and winter. The winter months are a sailor's worst nightmare. Ice storms, snow storms, blizzards, so many things can happen to slow a ship down."

"Oh Burke, I am nowhere near prepared to arrive in France!" Cori cried in shock.

"What do you have left to do? The ship is in perfect shape to be sold, the prisoners are ready for judgment, and you will be staying at my home in Calais until you decide where to go from there. There's no hurry, I shall spend the first several days in Versailles and you'll have plenty of time to settle on a travel location!" He soothed.

Tears ran down Cori's cheeks, "No, I'm not ready to tell you goodbye. Let's face it, you shall probably marry Odelia while you are in Versailles turning the prisoners in. Her father will not wait much longer than that! When you come back, if I'm still at your home in Calais, Odelia shall be accompanying you. I must tell you goodbye forever within two weeks!"

"Cori, what can I do to show you that I'm going to find some way out of my marriage to Odelia? I don't want to marry her. Plus, you promised to let me court you if I can get out of the union," he said, shaking his head.

"Yes, Burke! If you can get out of a union I will still have you for a little while. I have yet to hear you tell me any plan that might make that work. What do you think you're going to do, get to France and have a clear ticket out? I doubt it happens like that," she said with her hands on her hips.

"What do you mean 'for a little while'?" He asked, changing the subject.

"I mean, if you decided to court me you would still be ready for another sea voyage soon. I won't be able to keep you in France and I'm still undecided with how I feel about remaining a pirate!" She stomped.

"Why do you keep calling me a pirate? I'm not a pirate, Cori. I'm a captain, a sea trader, a sailor, and a shipping company owner, but I am not a pirate!" He tried to remind her.

She still didn't understand that there was any difference, "Pirate, Buccaneer, Privateer, whatever you want to call it is fine with me. It's still an illegal career where men steal, kill, and attack to make a living. You run from the law, and receive a prison sentence if you get caught! I don't want to live like that. The rest of my life could have dignity if I chose to remain on land. I keep hearing how good you are and how you're not like everyone else. If I had my way I would see you every day for eternity, but I'm just not sure if I'm willing to give up my dream of being legal and respectable!"

With that, and the tears flooding her eyes, she ran to her quarters. Burke stood at the helm in complete confusion. *She thinks I'm a pirate. That's why she keeps saying that, because she doesn't understand that you can be a legal sea trader!* Burke took a few steps to follow her, planning to explain the situation. Then he changed his mind. *No, that's a good test. If Cori loves me enough she shall stay with me, no matter what my career is. Odelia only loves me for being a Count. Perhaps Cori will love me no matter what I am. If she loves me enough to stay with me thinking I'm a pirate, then she'll truly deserve to be a*

Count's wife.

A week later Burke and Acel traded ships again. This time, it was so that Burke could speak to the prisoners about their cooperation during the King's judgment. Falco sat on the far side of a room behind a tall stack of Persian rugs. Sharlene sat on the other side of the rugs, close enough that she could talk to Falco but not able to see him. Klaas and Zeeman sat together in the middle of the room where they were originally placed.

Shrugging off Falco's seclusion as a strange need for privacy, Burke began his speech. Falco and Sharlene glared at Burke with a wicked smile upon their faces. "We should reach Calais in the next few days. Once we arrive, I shall take you immediately to Versailles. King Louis is extremely forgiving but not patient at all. If you're smart you will be on your best behavior and ask him to take pity on you. If you do that, you may be forgiven of your crimes

411

and released quickly with fair treatment while you're in prison. If you annoy King Louis, I promise you shall never see daylight again. Understand?"

Sharlene and Falco still glared. Finally, Falco snarled his nose and spoke "I will not be incarcerated; I can assure you of that."

"Why do you think that?" Burke asked, not amused.

"I'm not at liberty to say. However, I shall give you a little hint. *The Beloved Loss* and Cori will both be mine soon. You shall have your hands quite full with a family of your own," he rattled, not making much sense to Burke.

"Whatever you want to think," Burke shrugged, walking out of the room and locking the door behind him.

Sharlene laughed derisively, "You and I will be free in no time, my boy."

"*Ja*, we will." Falco growled with clenched teeth.

Three days later, Burke woke Cori during the night. "Cori?" He asked, peeping through her door.

"Yes?" She asked from the bed, trying to cover herself in a ladylike fashion.

"I just spotted land. We shall be arriving in Calais in a couple hours at the most. You should get ready. Acel will escort you to my home in Calais, Quain shall be taking Odelia to Le Havre, Yvet and Laron will be released, I shall bring the captives to Versailles, and the rest of the crew will stay behind to unload the ship." Burke explained in haste.

"Just give me one moment," she politely commanded.

Burke nodded understandingly, "Sure, I shall see you on deck in a moment."

Acel, sailing *The Heart of Calais* directly behind *The Beloved Loss*, spotted France only moments after Burke did. He announced to the crew that they were almost home. Odelia was the happiest of all. She smiled from ear to ear with a mischievous grin that would have concerned anyone who saw her.

Her trip had been a successful one, in her opinion. Keeping Burke tangled in her web, refusing to let him slip away, was the whole purpose of going on the mission. Odelia was afraid that King Louis would pity Burke and let him out of the union if she stayed in France. However, going with him insured that her reputation was on the line. She had no doubt that she succeeded in snaring him even further into her grasp through this trip. The snotty blond packed her belongings quickly, hoping for a speedy departure to Le Havre.

When she was done and only a few minutes from the shore, she grabbed the small silver key hidden under her pillow. The precious little object was her answer to every locked door, trunk or case on the ship. It was also to thank for creating her *ingenious* plan to keep Burke. Odelia crept up the stairs and across the deck. She knew before *The Heart of Calais* docked that there was one person she needed to say *farewell* to, and one small favor she promised to carry out.

Several minutes later Cori appeared in front of Burke at the helm of *The Beloved Loss*. "Our journey is at an end, I suppose." Cori said solemnly.

"Yes, our first journey. I hope we have several more," Burke cheered positively, hoping that King Louis had decided to relieve Burke of his forced union to Odelia.

"I do too," She whispered inaudibly.

"When you leave the ship, follow Acel closely. I will have Karoly helping me with the prisoners, but I don't want to risk Falco getting lose and trying to harm you. When I spoke to them a few days ago, he seemed over confident about his freedom. I'm sure he's just bluffing but I don't want to risk your safety," he said with a soft shrug.

"Alright, Burke. How long might it be until I see you again?" She asked.

"Probably only two or three days if all goes well!" He said. "I'm hoping that the King will pardon me from my marriage as a gift for this successful trip. If that's true, we shall be spending plenty of time together soon. You still plan to let me court you, correct?" Burke questioned hopefully.

Cori giggled, turning red. "Yes, I suppose."

Soon, the ship was docking in Calais and although dark, Cori was amazed at the beauty of the country. Odelia ran off of *The Heart of Calais*, jumping for joy when she reached the ground. That proved too much for the poor girl and she doubled over in sickness again. "She shall be fine," Burke whispered to Cori in amusement. "Her stomach is just weak from the trip. Sailing most certainly isn't the life for her."

Quain rushed behind Odelia, hoping to avoid her wrath by taking her to Le Havre immediately. Odelia rushed to Burke's side, squeezing between him and Cori. "I shall see you soon, *darling*. The wedding is only days away, nonetheless." She cooed sarcastically, glaring at Cori. Odelia held Burke's key to the storage room in her hand, rolling it around in her palm, hidden from everyone's view.

Burke just rolled his eyes. "Good luck to you, Corisanda. You're going to need it," Odelia chuckled meanly as she threw a small, silver object into the water.

Burke wondered what she had thrown, but dismissed it as nothing of importance.

"Be careful," Burke whispered as he patted Cori on the back. She hugged him goodbye and rushed to follow Acel to Burke's home. Burke waited several minutes, wanting Cori a safe distance away before he dealt with the prisoners. However, she lagged behind several times, fascinated by the different world she was in. There were stores and shops everywhere! Enormous, beautiful homes sat all over the town. Not just huts, or ship quarters, but giant houses! She was amazed and could not keep up with Acel. After him urging and urging, Cori was barely off of the dock when she heard shouts behind her. Recognizing Burke's voice, she turned around to run back to him.

Cori soon regretted her decision. Falco was lose and running straight toward her. He grabbed her arm forcefully as he reached her and threw her over his shoulder, running toward town. He pulled a gun out of his pants pocket and aimed it straight at Burke. "She's mine!" he screamed irately.

"PUT HER DOWN!" Burke yelled, unable to contain his fear and anger. Acel raced behind and stood a distance behind Cori and Falco, waiting for any signal Burke gave him.

Falco chuckled, "You want her a lot, huh? She shall be punished for playing a tease with you. Let me go or I *will* shoot her. Don't chase us either. I demand for my crew to be returned to me! *The Beloved Loss* is mine now. Let us pass or Corisanda gets a bullet."

Cori was ghostly white, scared to death. Her heart pounded in her chest and she didn't know what to do. She worried about Burke, knowing that Falco wouldn't board *The Beloved Loss* until he had his revenge on the dark haired man. Burke worried for Cori. He couldn't let Falco take her but he couldn't let him shoot her either. "Let me speak to my men," Burke pleaded.

"No, just let us go!" Falco demanded.

"We have your crew in our custody, let me order their release and we will let you go," he suggested, hoping to sound honest.

"Hurry up," Falco grumbled, shaking Cori roughly in his arms.

Burke turned to Davet and Karoly in a gruff whisper, "How did he get a gun?"

Karoly shook his head in confusion, "Someone left the gun-trunk open. He must have known it because he rushed straight for it when he slipped out of my grasp. Someone must have left it open for him."

"That's impossible. No one has been in contact with him but you and me. Oh well, we shall worry about that later. When I grab Cori, you grab Falco. Just go along with me," Burke decided.

No one but Burke was sure of the plan, but it had to work! Burke hoped he sounded honest, "Alright, we will let you go. We don't want to be outnumbered for our own safety, so we shall let you pass with Cori. When you get on the boat we'll release Sharlene, Klaas, and Zeeman."

Falco pointed the gun at him as he walked slowly toward them, then in a dead sprint he ran between the three men. Ignoring the gun, Burke grabbed Cori's arm and jerked her toward him. Falco spun on his heels, trying to regain his balance and tighten his hold on Cori. It was too late; Karoly grabbed him by the back and tackled the man into the water. The brawl was fierce but Acel and Davet jumped in and helped Karoly fight Falco back onto the dock. Burke hugged Cori tightly, glad she was safe. "YOU ARE STUPID!" Falco screamed at Burke. "You don't realize what has happened right under your nose, you fool!

But you will soon, don't worry. I shall be free, Corisanda will be mine, and you will be miserable. This part of my plan may not have gone perfectly but the rest of my wrath is still to come. It won't fail! Believe me! You're doomed, and so are you *Mevrouw*. You can be sure of that!"

Acel looked at Burke questioningly, and Burke swallowed hard, hoping that Falco was lying. He seemed assured, and that was terrifying. "Change of plans," Burke whispered to Acel as Karoly tied Falco's arms behind his back again. "I shall take Cori home. You take the prisoners to Versailles and I will meet you there tomorrow."

Acel quickly nodded, knowing that Burke needed to protect Cori from whatever plan Falco had devised. The couple ran through the streets, not allowing Cori to dawdle. She stared at the houses as they ran, soaking in the beauty of each one. Finally, they reached a long, country lane. Assuming they were taking a side route to get away, Cori followed closely. The long lane was flowing, turning back and forth, back and forth, until finally reaching an enormous black gate. To Cori's surprise, Burke swung it open. "Where are we?" She asked.

Burke whispered two words, explaining everything. "Welcome home."

The land was more beautiful than anything Cori had ever seen in her life. The grass was bright green and hundreds of flowers decorated the enormous yard. A colossal mansion sat on a hill, past the brightly colored flowers and green grass. It was a beautiful home, covered in rock. She had never seen anything like the house before. Out of the beautiful townhouses she saw on the way, this home was larger than most of them put together. In the distance Cori could hear waves crashing, and quickly realized how close it sat to the water.

Going downhill from the front, where Cori and Burke stood in at the gate was the arrangement of colorful flora but going downhill to the back was nothing but large beautiful rocks descending steeply and ending on the beach. The ocean waves crashed behind the home, close enough to hear, smell, and nearly taste. "Oh, Burke." Cori whispered, unable to voice her opinion.

"I told you that you would like my home," he chuckled.

"It's amazing. How do you afford this? You must be one heck of a pirate," she babbled.

Burke threw his head back in a loud laugh, "I shall explain later. Let's go in." He fumbled with the lock on the elegant, mahogany door until it slid open. "Usually," he clarified, "I have a large staff of servants living here who take care of the manner. However, since I didn't know how long we would be gone, I dismissed them all. I have a few who come a couple times a week and keep it clean but the rest will return now that I'm home."

Although it was late, Burke gave Cori a tour of his elegant house. He led her to the library, showing her more books than she had ever seen in her life. The dining room, study, and the bedroom chambers impressed her just as much. Finally, Burke showed her the Master Chambers, his own personal bedroom. "You shall sleep here," he said, giving her the best room in the home. "I want you to enjoy it and decide to stay here permanently. I plan to stay awake tonight anyway, getting things ready for my short trip to Versailles. Rest well, Mademoiselle."

Burke's giant, four post bed was enormous. The canopy top was elegant and for the first time in Cori's life, she felt like a princess. She giggled to herself and thought *I really am a Pirate Princess now.* Minutes later, she was curled comfortably in the soft bed. She was still in such a state of shock that her thoughts flew around her as she tried to fall asleep. Falco's terrifying threat, Burke's gorgeous home, Marin's easy escape, Odelia's cruel warning, and her own future entangled her mind. *Something does not add up,* Cori worried as she finally fell asleep.

When she awoke in the morning a brilliant ray of sunlight flooded through the room. She noticed that there were two large windows on either side of the bed. Walking to one window and peering out Cori saw the side of the bright green lawn and yellow, orange, red and pink flowers. Moving to the other window, she looked out at the coast and the warm ocean water splashing onto it. Dressing quickly she rushed downstairs to find Burke. "Burke?" She called with a smile. "Are you still here?"

"You didn't think I would leave without telling you goodbye, did you?" Burke chuckled, meeting her at the bottom of a massive mahogany staircase.

"No," she blushed. "Your home is amazing. It's even lovelier than *The Heart of Calais*."

Burke laughed, "I'm glad you think so because I designed them both."

Cori marveled at the man she loved. The home was wonderful but it didn't make Cori love him any differently. She wanted to be by his side either way. "Burke, I need to talk to you about something important," she whispered excitedly.

"Come then, let's set out on the front porch." He suggested, wondering what she wanted to say.

When they walked through the front door and sat in the big, wicker chairs aligning the porch, Cori began. "Do you remember when I told you that I never want anything else to do with pirates?"

"Yes, of course." Burke replied in anguish.

"Well, I have made up my mind. And I want you to know it has nothing to do with your home, or anything else.

I'm amazed by *you*, Burke. I could never live without you, nor do I want to. I don't care what your job is. I don't care if we sail the seas or stay here on land. Wherever you go, I will follow. If you truly want to be with me, then I am yours," she consented. "As long as you get out of marrying Odelia."

Burke bounded out of his chair and lifted Cori out of hers. He swung her around in circles with his heart racing in his chest as he held her tightly in his arms. Not able to wait any longer, Burke looked into Cori's deep brown eyes and kissed her lips for the first time since she kissed him almost two months before on *The Beloved Loss*, coaxing him away from the fight with Falco. Cori kissed him back, also remembering their first kiss and how much more at ease and enjoyable the second one was. Both hearts raced and there was nothing that could tear them apart. He was hers, and she was his.

He lowered himself to the ground, holding Cori on his lap. They smiled at each other in complete bliss, and Burke opened his mouth to speak. Shushing him, Cori put one of her fingers over his lips. Moving her hand, she softly rubbed the handsome little scar on his cheek. "I have one more thing to say," she whispered in his ear. "I love you, Burke Landis Belcourt."

Burke felt that nothing in the world could ever have been more amazing than that minute in time. "I love you too, Corisanda Aleene St. Aubin."

A loud rattling noise interrupted the beautiful moment as a carriage flew down the twisting lane. Angry that the moment was ending, Burke rose to his feet, holding Cori's hand in his own. "Who's coming?" She asked.

"I'm not sure," he grumbled. "I must meet Acel and Karoly in Versailles. They should be there by now. Quain should not be back from Le Havre yet, unless he raced through the night! I don't know who else it might be..."

He had to wonder no longer, a carriage came into sight. Despite the odds, it was Quain. He raced toward the house, jumped off the carriage and ran to Burke's side. "Burke," he began, out of breath.

"What's going on, Quain? You shouldn't be back until this evening? Where's Odelia? Did you not take her home?" He asked.

"Yes, I did. That's why I am here. I was there long enough for her father to see her. I don't know what you did or why you did it, but Odelia told her father that the marriage had to happen immediately. Because, because..." he stuttered.

"Because why?" Burke demanded.

"She says you made her pregnant, Burke."

Cori's knees buckled and Burke's own weak legs barely held her up. He eased her to the ground and stiffened his under him. "I DID NO SUCH THING!" He yelled when he finally found his voice.

Cori's world was crashing around her, "Why would she say that then?" Burke had no answer and they both looked toward Quain.

"I'm not sure, but she swore to her father that you made her pregnant. I told her that it was impossible; you stayed on *The Beloved Loss* most of the way home. She said that the night you spent on *The Heart of Calais* when Karoly fixed a problem in the steering, right after we left Argentina, that you came into her room that night," Quain explained.

"I did not! She came into mine, but…" Burke began.

Cori dropped her head to her hands before he could finish. That was enough of a confession for her. She ran into Burke's home alone and locked herself into Burke's grand bedchambers upstairs. A few minutes later, Burke knocked deliberately on the door. "Please let me explain," he begged.

Cori just cried in silence. Burke finally gave up, "I'm leaving, Cori. I have to get to Versailles and put an end to this rumor. I have to tell the King that it's not true. She cannot be pregnant, Cori. I never touched her. I shall be back in a couple days, just wait for me. I love you."

Burke left immediately, as he said he would, to set the story straight between him and Odelia Vadeboncour, "Quain, I love Cori. I shall marry her and only her, one way or another. I never touched Odelia. You know I'm a man of my word and I'm honorable. If I got Odelia with child I would do the right thing by her and the baby, but I didn't. She cannot truly be pregnant. She's lying, Quain."

"I believe you, Burke." Quain paused for a moment, not wanting to continue but knowing he should warn his friend, "Odelia is playing her story up and you shall have a hard time convincing Lord Orson, because he's not happy about this at all."

They reached Versailles by early evening, meeting Acel and Karoly there. The two men were waiting expectantly on Burke's arrival and rushed to him the moment the carriage arrived. "Odelia is already here," Acel informed.

"UGH!" Burke grunted. The world just seemed to be against him. "I never touched her," he sighed to Acel.

"We know, Burke. We know. And we will all testify for you, you know that!" Karoly consoled.

"Let's just get this over with," Burke replied in confusion. "Did you have any trouble with the prisoners?"

"No, thankfully. At least they all cooperated. Falco and Sharlene were suspiciously easy to deal with," Acel answered in relief.

Burke only nodded his approval and the four crewmen of *The Heart of Calais* entered King Louis XIV's enormous Versailles Palace. Ten minutes later they were ushered to the King's side in a large dining room. Odelia sat a few chairs down from the King, beside her father. Burke strolled passed them, purposely darting his eyes away. "Burke!" King Louis greeted with a smile on his face. "Thank goodness you've returned! You did an amazing job! I knew I could count on you when I wanted a job done right."

"Thank you. Louis, I want no payment. I forfeit the reward for bringing in the criminals; I forfeit the money you would have paid me for the job. All I want is my freedom. And what I mean by that is freedom from Odelia.

I never touched the girl, you know I wouldn't have done that," Burke began.

King Louis took a deep breath, feeling his friend's pain. He knew that Burke hated Odelia and that he was not the one who took the girl's innocence from her. "I must tell you the same way I told Odelia and Lord Orson earlier today. You deserve your freedom and there is absolutely no proof that you defiled Lady Odelia's virtue. I planned on releasing you from the union when you returned from this trip. However, if Lady Odelia truly is pregnant then someone must marry her! She's a Lady, Burke. That shame would haunt her and her family for centuries! Can you imagine her trying to raise a fatherless child? It would ruin her."

"I understand that and I agree. However, you should find the child's real father, if she truly is pregnant. I'm not it!" Burke continued.

Lord Orson rose from a chair, stuttering in anger "Now, wait just a minute boy! My daughter is a saint! She's a good girl! She has never known any man besides you and you obviously thrust yourself upon her. You *raped* her! And you made her pregnant the second time around! Take responsibility!"

"Lord Orson, with all due respect, if I got any woman with child or took a Lady's innocence I would take care of her. Sir, I have never touched your daughter," Burke tried.

Orson shook his head, "We had a doctor inspect her when she first claimed that you stripped her of her virtue, and he agreed that she was no longer an innocent child!"

Burke rolled his eyes, "That may very well be true! Odelia has slept with half of the country, to be sure. But I am not one of them!"

"How dare you?" Odelia cried overdramatically as she threw her head into her hands, feigning outrage.

"Furthermore, I hated the idea of you going on this trip. That was a scandalous notion in itself but you demanded. I never touched you then either, and I don't know if you're pregnant or not but it's certainly not my child if so!" Burke persisted.

Lord Orson hugged his daughter believingly, "Fine then. Let's solve this problem and get a doctor to examine her. She is pregnant, alright. I have seen her sick all morning!"

King Louis nodded his head and motioned for a guard to escort Odelia to another room to meet the King's personal physician. Lord Orson huffed indignantly and threw himself back into his chair. Acel tried to speak up in Burke's defense, "King Louis, I don't know if you shall believe us or not, but I can assure you that Burke was never near Odelia."

"Of course I believe you, Ace." King Louis replied, "It's just out of my hands…"

"It cannot be out of your hands, you're the King!" Acel demanded abruptly.

Burke calmed his cousin down, begging pardon from King Louis. "I understand," the King forgave. "As soon as this is over and done with then we will sentence your prisoners."

"Alright," Burke mumbled.

"No fear, Burke." King Louis reassured, "You know how Odelia lies! She's probably not pregnant after all, and when we have proof of that then you shall be as free as a bird."

Burke just nodded in hope. All he could think about was Cori in Calais, and if she was alright. *I love Cori with all of my heart. I do not want to lose her now after working so hard to gain her.*

FIFTEEN

Cori cried for over an hour, sobbing in Burke's floor as if her heart had been ripped away and taken from her. *Why did he do this to me? Why did he lead me to believe he loved me? He loves Odelia, after all! He wanted to marry her. He wanted a family with her. He used me to occupy his time on the journey! I was just a game to keep him from boredom before he was married.*

She wiped her eyes. *Aunt Novia was right; men lie and play games to get what they want! What will I do now? I should have stayed in Cuba with my family, the people who actually love me! What shall I do in France without Burke or anyone I know? How can I get back to Cuba without Burke's help?*

Cori was not sure what to do but after running herself a bath, fixing her hair, and changing into a clean set of clothes, she felt ready to resolve the issue. *I do not know what I shall do, but I know I cannot stay here. Burke will probably be back tomorrow or the next day, I need to be as far away as possible by then. Hopefully I can be on my way to Cuba!*

Cori packed her few belongings and left Burke's enormous home. As she walked through the beautiful yard she wondered what it would be like to call a home like that her own. The house was a dream to Cori. It was the perfect blend of sea and land, flowers and sand. She took a deep breath and made herself continue through the big black gate protecting the home from intruders. She walked down the winding road, thinking about Burke and wondering where he was or what he was doing. *He should be in Versailles right now, judging my father's crew and marrying Odelia!*

When she reached the busy streets of Calais she decided to go on a small adventure. Since the night before was chaotic and she didn't have time to look at all of the beautiful shops and homes, this seemed like a grand time to do it. It occurred to Cori that she was stalling, hoping that Burke would rush into town and prove himself a good man after all. She shook her head, silently dismissing that idea.

After walking through the town most of the evening, she sat down on a park bench staring at a small pond with ducks sitting on it. *Time to think,* Cori decided. *I cannot let myself see Burke again. It would be humiliating to face his new wife. I must let them keep The Beloved Loss! He can sell it to someone else. As for me, I could stay in France alone, knowing no one, and with no money. Or, I could go to the dock and board a boat that can take me to Cuba.*

She took a deep breath, wondering which option would keep her furthest from Burke. Cori knew that Burke would now make ventures to each location, living in France and trading with Cuba. The question was which place would be the easiest to avoid him. A tear fell from her eye as she thought about never seeing Burke again. She loved him enough to do anything in the world to be with him, even if it meant being a despicable pirate for the rest of her life. Her heart belonged to him and she knew there would never be a way to get it back. *This is how my father must have felt when he realized that he would never see my mother again.*

Cori decided that the best place for her would be Cuba where at least she would have family. She left the park and walked to the dock where *The Heart of Calais* and *The Beloved Loss* still sat. Minor repairs had been made to both, and her father's ship had a FOR SALE BY BURKE BELCOURT sign on it. She felt her heart beat faster just by reading Burke's name. Cooling her emotions and trying to hold her head high, she walked passed both boats to the next one in line. "Can I help you, Mademoiselle?" A man asked.

"I hope so. Does this ship ever sail to Cuba?" She asked.

"No, certainly not. There are too many pirates down there!" He stated.

"I see. Do you know of any that do?" Cori questioned.

"I'm not sure, some of these boats might if you ask. The best person to talk to is Captain Belcourt, he owns a large shipping company and I believe he goes everywhere. He's in charge around here," the man replied.

Cori was not sure what to say, so she just smiled and said, "Thank you."

She walked further, passing boat after boat until she finally found another with a man standing in front of it. "Sir," Cori called. "Do you take trips to Cuba?"

"No way! I don't want to be attacked by all of those buccaneers and pirates! That place is just a death trap!" He answered.

"Oh, alright. Do you know anyone who might?" Cori continued, fearing his answer.

The man nodded his head, "I would ask Captain Belcourt. He owns a bunch of ships and trades everywhere. You shall be safe with him. He's rarely attacked and never beaten!"

Cori sighed, "Okay, thanks."

At the end of the dock she met a red haired man standing in front of a shabby little vessel. "I suppose you don't go to Cuba either," she suggested.

"Actually, I do! I just returned from Cuba this morning. My home is in Ireland, but I met a man in Cuba wanting to travel to France so I came here first. Can I help you with something?" He cheerily questioned.

"Yes! I have family in Cuba. That's where I'm from. Is there any way you could take me there?" She asked.

The man shrugged, "Well, I shall be leaving for Jamaica in a couple days and could swing by Cuba to drop you off. Can you wait that long?"

"I suppose, but I have nowhere to stay until then. Does your ship have any extra space?" Cori politely begged.

"I don't have much. My vessel is a small one, as you can see. However, since my most recent passenger has already left the ship and is staying at an Inn, my spare room is now empty. It would not hurt for you to get settled into your quarters. Come aboard and I will show you around.

My name is Captain Douglass," The man replied with a wave of his arm.

Cori climbed aboard and walked around the small ship. It was an old vessel, even older than *The Beloved Loss* with very little extravagance. However, Cori knew it would get the job done and take her to Cuba for a speedy escape. She sat in her new quarters below the deck. It was cramped and tight, holding nothing but a small bed, and a bowl for sponge baths. *Well, this certainly is not like Burke's ship, but I guess it shall work.*

The room was silent. Burke paced from side to side, Lord Orson glared at everyone, Acel, Karoly and Quain sat in awkward anguish, and King Louis whispered silently to his guards. "Captain Belcourt," he called.

Burke walked to the King's throne. "Yes, Lou?"

"The doctor is taking a lot of time and I have many things to do today. I ordered my guards to retrieve the prisoners so they can await their sentence and we can get started as soon as this matter with Odelia is resolved," he explained.

"That sounds fine. I'm anxious to get home as well. If we can get all of this over with tonight I can be home by tomorrow." Burke agreed.

"If Odelia is pregnant, Lord Orson has asked for an immediate wedding. He says that you have put this off long enough and no one needs to know about Odelia's pregnancy until she is securely married. She'll be going home with you when you leave here," the King said with pity.

"That would be understandable, if she is pregnant. Trust me, she is not. I haven't touched her," Burke confidently answered.

A few minutes later the door swung open. Guards walked in holding Falco, Sharlene, Zeeman, and Klaas. They were all placed next to each other on the far side of the room. Falco and Sharlene glared at Burke with the same strange look of deception on their faces that they had worn for days. Silence returned to the room and Burke took a deep breath, ready to go home to Cori.

Finally the door opened again and the King's personal physician entered the room and sat down, followed by Odelia. "WELL?" Burke, Acel, Quain, Karoly, Lord Orson, and King Louis prompted in unison.

"Well, what?" The elderly physician asked.

"IS SHE PREGNANT?" The group questioned again.

"Oh, yes! She is certainly pregnant. About a month along, maybe two, I would say. Not far, but far enough to tell." The doctor answered.

Burke dropped to his knees, feeling weak. "I never touched you, Odelia! You know I never touched you. Why are you doing this to me? How did you convince the man you're pregnant when you cannot be?" He demanded.

"Of course you touched me, Burke! I'm a lady, I don't lie! And I am pregnant! Now marry me," she insisted.

Burke sat with his head buried in his hands, wondering what to do. Acel, Quain and Karoly surrounded him trying to give him their comfort. "I don't know what to do," Burke whispered to them.

"You have to marry her," Acel said.

King Louis spoke loudly for the room to hear, "We shall follow this evening with a wedding between Burke and Odelia. For now, let's sentence Burke's prisoners."

"Wait!" Odelia screamed, "We *must* marry now. Then you can judge the prisoners."

The King rolled his eyes and Lord Orson pulled Odelia back into her seat. Burke knew what he had to do, so he spoke up. "King Louis, I won't marry Odelia today. I shall not marry her ever. I'm in love with a beautiful woman named Cori, and I plan to spend my life with her. Strip me of my title as Count, give me prison time or whatever must be done. But I will not marry Odelia."

The King was in shock and didn't know what to say, Acel on the other hand did. "No, Burke! You cannot do that! Don't give up your title or your reputation."

"You don't understand," Burke explained solemnly for the court to hear. "I love Cori with all my heart. She's my world now, and nothing is worth losing her. I will give up everything. My home, title, wealth and shipping company mean a lot to me but she's worth giving it all up! I shall do it gladly and I know I didn't get Odelia with child."

"Burke," the King answered. "You must marry Odelia since you made her pregnant. We will discuss all of this after we judge your prisoners."

Burke shook his head at the King, "Your highness, we may certainly discuss it after the sentencing and I agree that we need to handle the prisoners first. However, you might as well sentence me at the same time you sentence them, because I can assure you that I shall not marry Odelia."

King Louis took a deep breath, sad for his friend. He motioned for the prisoners to rise. "Being caught in the act of pirating is a five year prison sentence. Zeeman and Klaas, after reading Burke's report, that will be your fate." the King ordered.

Burke wondered why Sharlene and Falco looked so happy. "Do they not know they're going to prison?" Burke asked.

"I don't know. It doesn't make sense," Quain replied in a whisper.

"Sharlene St. Aubin, you are wanted in France for thievery. You were also caught in the act of pirating. Burke says he returned a ship load of children to Argentina that you kidnapped. Falco de Vries, according to Burke's report you are wanted for pirating, kidnapping, and murder of many you attacked while working as the Quartermaster of *The Beloved Loss*. Do either of you deny these charge?"

"No." Falco said, "It doesn't matter though, we shall be released."

King Louis chuckled, "No, you won't! I'm sentencing both of you to life in prison."

"NO!" Sharlene screamed. "Odelia said that we will both be freed. You must let us go."

"Odelia?" The King asked. "Did you tell them that?"

Odelia piped up, "No, I have never spoken to them in my life."

"Odelia!" Falco screeched. "You cannot do this! Tell them your plan. Tell them that I shall be free!"

"I don't know what you're talking about," Odelia shooed, growing panicked.

Falco looked wild, as if he was losing his mind. "MAMA! She is getting out of this, do something!"

"*Mama?*" Burke, Acel, and Quain asked in unison.

Sharlene yelled, "Shut up! You're ruining everything. For the last twenty eight years of my life you have destroyed my sanity! I was a poor but happy French woman until your good-for-nothing Dutch father came along! Unlike Odelia, I didn't *try* to get pregnant!

Unfortunately, you came into my life anyway! I stole, faught, and starved just to feed and clothe you! When I finally escaped to *The Beloved Loss*, I felt like I had a life again. That couldn't have worked though, could it? You found me there too! I knew better than to believe you could get us out of this."

"I'm sorry, Mama. I just wanted to be with you," Falco growled.

"Forget it! You cannot do anything right. Let me handle this!" She barked, turning back to the Vadeboncours. "Odelia, just tell the King that we should be freed. You planned all of this and said that my son and I would both be turned loose!"

The whole room was in shock and confusion. Odelia kept insisting that she did not know what anyone was talking about, and demanding that Burke marry her immediately.

"Okay, okay! Order in the court," the King finally screeched. "I don't know what's going on around here. I didn't know that Falco was Sharlene's son, and I don't know why Odelia would tell the two of you something like that. However, we need to get this wedding underway so everyone can get accustomed to the idea. I also know that the two of you pirates are sentenced to life in prison no matter who told you anything!"

Falco wailed, "I'm telling them the plan, Odelia! I'm telling the plan."

"No! No, wait! Stop! There is no plan! Shut up, Falco!" Odelia screamed, beginning to shake.

"You cannot arrest my son or me!" Sharlene growled, "He is the father of Odelia's child!"

"WHAT?" Orson yelled uproariously.

"*Ja*! That's right!" Falco agreed. "Odelia came into the storage room where we were being held prisoner. She said that if I got her with child and everyone thought it was Burke's that the King would make him marry her. Then, she said that she had pull with the King and would get me and my mother released! I would go find Corisanda, *The Beloved Loss* would belong to me and I could leave."

Falco raised his eyebrows and continued, "So I did what she wanted. I moved behind a stack of rugs and Odelia came to visit me a few times each week. She stole Burke's key so she could get in and out. Odelia unlocked the gun trunk on the ship right before we docked, so I could steal a gun, grab Cori and leave in my ship. I was afraid I would be outnumbered and that would not work, but Odelia assured me that if I did my part of the plan and got her pregnant that she would persuade King Louis to release me. I did my part, she's pregnant, now free my mother and me!"

"NO!" Odelia bawled.

"Odelia, tell me that's not true!" Orson begged.

"It's not! This baby is Burke's! It is Burke's!" She cried.

Burke took a deep breath, "Odelia, I have never touched you. Tell the truth."

"NO! This is not what was supposed to happen. You should've married me months and months ago when I spent the night at your house! No one would have ever found out that it was not you that took my innocense. No one would have known that this was Falco's baby. You should've just married me then like you were supposed to!" She wailed, giving herself away.

Burke's mouth dropped open as Acel jumped for joy. King Louis spoke quickly before anything else could be said, "Odelia! You have gotten yourself into a mess.

Now you're pregnant with an incarcerated man's child. I'm ordering a banishment from France! Falco de Vries and Odelia Vadeboncour, I now pronounce you husband and wife! Return to The Netherlands with your bride, Falco. If you're ever caught in France you will *both* be executed."

Sharlene wailed, "Let me go!"

"No, because of this strange circumstance I shall drop your life sentence. However, you're still going to serve your term of three years for thievery in France fourteen years ago! Then you will be banished from this country as well. At that time you shall be escorted to The Netherlands to be with your son, daughter-in-law, and grandchild," The King ordered.

Then turning to Burke, he said, "You're dismissed from any responsibility of Odelia. Leave before someone changes their mind!"

Burke took the King's advice and left Versailles, rushing as quickly as he could to Calais. Acel, Quain, and Karoly followed at a distance, not able to keep up with the love-struck swain. He raced through the night and entered the big black gate surrounding his home by noon. "Cori! Cori! My love!" He called as he burst through the front door.

Burke searched through the house but found no trace of Cori. She was gone. *Where is she? Where did she go?* He wondered frantically. He left the home and ran around the house, hoping to see her. Finally facing the fact that she was gone, he rushed into town. He ran through the park, entered every shop, stared into townhouse yards and looked for her on every street. She was nowhere to be found. *Where could she have gone?* He wondered. *The only place she could feel at home is my house, The Beloved Loss or The Heart of Calais! She must have gone back to the ships!*

He raced to the dock and onto his ship. Karoly, Acel, and Quain were just arriving as well. "Have you seen Cori?" He asked.

"No! Is she not at your house?" Acel asked.

"No, Ace. She's gone!" He yelled over his shoulder as he searched the quarters. "She's not here either. I'm going to *The Beloved Loss* to look for her."

He raced onto Marin St. Aubin's ship, searching everywhere he could. She wasn't there. "Hello, Captain Belcourt!" A red headed man greeted.

"Captain Douglass, I cannot talk right now. I'm looking for someone," Burke dismissed impatiently.

"I wanted to talk to you about your new ship, the one that's for sale. I know a man who is interested in it! I brought the man a very long distance because he was insistent on buying a French ship. He wants to buy *The Beloved Loss*," Captain Douglass said.

"Can you not come back later?" Burke snapped.

"The man is in a hurry to leave. He's staying at the Inn. I told him there were other ships for sale but he has settled on *The Beloved Loss*. He gave me all of this cash, see?" The red-haired man said as he pulled out a large wad of bills from his pocket. "Will this be enough for the boat?"

"Sure, just take it and let me be!" Burke ordered, taking the money.

"Well, are you not going to count the money first and see that it's enough?" Captain Douglass asked in confusion.

"No! It doesn't matter. It's not my ship, it belongs to someone else and if I can find the true owner then money shall never be an object to her again. Just get out of my way!" Burke barked as he raced off of the ship.

Burke didn't know where to go or which way to turn. He thought about going back to his home to see if she had returned, but he knew in his heart that she hadn't. For over an hour he spoke to every passerby he could find, asking if any had met the lovely woman he was searching for. Giving up, he walked to the edge of the dock and swung his feet over the side. It was hard for him to believe that only a few months before he was sitting in the very same place while *The Heart of Calais* was getting ready to leave in search of *The Beloved Loss*.

Cori is too strong, independent, and prideful to stay after what happened yesterday morning. She's gone. She could be anywhere by now! I will probably never see her again, he sighed as he dropped his head into his hands.

Suddenly, Burke remembered what Captain Douglass had said. Someone wanted to buy *The Beloved Loss*. It was someone who knew that other ships were for sale but only wanted that vessel! *It must be Cori!* Burke thought in elation. *She wants to buy her father's ship and travel back to Cuba. That's why Captain Douglass came to buy it instead of Cori, so I wouldn't see her.*

Burke raced onto the shabby little boat that Captain Douglass traveled in. "Captain Douglass! Captain Douglass! I need to speak to you," he screamed.

"Yes, Captain Belcourt?" He answered, rushing from the helm, hoping that Burke had not changed his mind about selling his friend *The Beloved Loss*.

"Who did you buy *The Beloved Loss* for? Was it a woman?" Burke demanded.

Captain Douglass shook his head in confusion, "No. It was for a man. Why?"

464

"Are you sure?" Burke questioned.

"I'm positive, he's definitely a man. I know a woman when I see one!" Captain Douglass answered.

"What is all the fuss about?" A woman's voice called from an under deck cabin, "Captain Douglass, is everything alright out there?"

"It's just fine, Mademoiselle. I'm speaking to a friend. He's selling a boat to one of my acquaintances," Captain Douglass explained loudly as the woman emerged onto the deck.

"CORI!" Burke shouted.

"Burke?" Cori gasped.

"What are you doing here?" He demanded.

Cori shook her head, "I'm going back to Cuba, Burke. I want you to leave me alone."

Acel heard the commotion from *The Heart of Calais* so he curiously rushed to meet them. "Cori, I can never leave you alone. Let me explain," Burke begged.

"No!" Cori said as tears poured down her face. "I can handle no more of your games and lies, Burke. You're married to Odelia now, I'm quite sure. She's already carrying your child. Please just leave me alone."

With that, Cori turned on her heels and ran back to her new home on the shabby ship Captain Douglass owned. Burke dropped his shoulders in exasperation, feeling like giving up. He felt he had lost everything. Without Cori, his life was meaningless. Acel took matters into his own hands and marched to Cori's room. "Mademoiselle Corisanda, it's Acel. Let me in."

"No!"

"Yes!"

"Are you alone?"

"Yes. Just let me in, Mademoiselle."

Cori cracked the door open, peering out. Acel entered and closed the door behind him. "Cori, you don't understand what has happened," he began.

"Yes, I do. Burke toyed with my mind through the whole trip. He made me believe he loved me and I fell head-over-heels for him. He made Odelia pregnant and married her. What else do I need to know?" She cried.

"He didn't do any of that. He's crazy about you, Cori. Falco made Odelia pregnant, not Burke! Burke has searched everywhere for you, you are his world now. Can you not see that?" He explained.

"Falco? How could that be? Stop lying to me!" Cori begged, "Just leave me alone. Odelia has a baby in her stomach to prove Burke's love. What do I have?"

467

Acel could stand no more and even though Burke made him promise not to tell, he could not stop himself. "You have a free father, that's what you have! That should prove his love for you."

"My father escaped in Cuba," Cori dismissed in confusion.

"How could Marin have escaped? If he could have, what would have stopped Falco, Sharlene, or the others?" He posed.

"Well, I don't know but…" Cori tried with a stutter.

"Burke released him. He knew you were upset about him being sent to prison so he gave him his freedom. Burke turned your father loose in Cuba for *you*," Acel stated calmly.

Cori was in shock, "That cannot be true! This is all just a game."

"It's no game. Not only that, but Burke offered to give up everything for you!" He said as Burke entered the room behind him. Burke stood in the doorway, staring at Cori as Acel finished speaking. She realized how hurt Burke looked. He was exhausted, worried, and miserable. Acel took a ragged breath, finishing his explanation, "Burke offered to give up his home, *The Heart of Calais*, his money, and even his title to be with you."

"What title?" Cori asked in confusion.

Acel nodded his head at Burke and left the room, allowing Burke to fight his own battle, "Cori, I'm not a pirate, a buccaneer or anything related to it. I own a shipping company. I trade by the sea for a living as pirates do but it's completely legal. I don't attack other ships, or steal anything. My career is a very *honorable* one. Besides that, I'm a titled noble in France. Cori, I'm a Count, and I love you with all of my heart."

Cori did not know what to do or say. She sat in shock, trying to dry her eyes. "Odelia is gone?"

"Yes, she's married to Falco de Vries and they are permanently banished from France. It is a long story, but I can explain later if you will allow it." He answered, still awaiting her judgment of him.

"I promised that you could court me if she was gone," Cori whispered as a smile appeared on her face.

Burke swooped her into his arms, hugging her tightly. "Will you really?" he asked.

"It depends," Cori said as she pulled slightly away from Burke. He looked at her nervously again, wondering what she would say. "You said that courting led to marriage if it went well. What happens if it doesn't?"

"Then we would separate from each other forever," Burke solemnly replied. The thought of losing Cori broke his heart all over again.

"You cannot court me then," Cori denied, stomping her right foot.

"Why? Cori, please!" Burke begged.

"No, I want to do something that ties us together forever. I don't want to take a chance on losing you again," Cori began, trying not to smile.

Burke grinned, hoping she was not just toying with him. "Really?" He asked.

Cori nodded, "Do you want to be with me forever, Burke?"

"I would do anything to be with you forever, Cori." He answered as his heart raced in his chest.

"Then ask me to marry you," she whispered.

Burke felt that he could not breathe, as he stooped down to one knee and looked into Cori's eyes. "Will you please, please, please marry me?"

"Can we do it now?" She asked.

"Yes," Burke whispered.

"Then *yes*," Cori squealed as Burke took her into his arms again. They kissed for a long moment, knowing nothing in the world could ever pull them apart again.

An hour later they were standing at the helm of *The Heart of Calais*, overlooking the beautiful ocean as a chaplain stood in front of them. The crew of *The Heart of Calais* watched the pair with misty eyes from the deck. After agreeing to wed soon, Karoly held Leala in his arms as their daughter smiled in glee. Quain, Garner, and Davet watched the couple happily. Acel pictured himself marrying Cori's lovely cousin, Rosa. He truly hoped they took another trip to Cuba soon.

The ceremony only took a few minutes and they were pronounced the Count and Countess of Calais. Burke held Cori in his arms as he spoke to her. "Corisanda Aleene Belcourt, you told me long ago the meaning of your name. You said that Corisanda means *flower of the heart*. Well, you are definitely the flower of *my* heart. You are also the Flower of *The Heart of Calais*. Your middle name means *alone*, and I assure you that you shall never be alone again. You're my world, Cori. You're my pirate princess," he chuckled.

Cori didn't have time to reply as they were surrounded by the crew in congratulations. The men hugged her and patted Burke on the back. "When will you start a family?" Karoly asked, as he hugged Leala in his arms.

"Immediately!" Burke chuckled as Cori's face turned red.

"Will you sail with us on our trips?" Quain asked.

"Yes, you will never leave me behind!" Cori answered in excitement.

"Where are you going on your honeymoon?" Acel questioned.

They heard his inquiry but neither answered. A boat was passing that took their attention completely. No one met the new owner of *The Beloved Loss*, so when it sailed by, Burke and Cori could not help but stare. A familiar looking man stood at the helm, waving his arms at the newly married couple. Loud laughter was heard from the man as he opened the sails and sped into the ocean toward Cuba. The new owner of *The Beloved Loss*, the passenger that Captain Douglass had picked up on his journey, was a man already *extremely* acquainted with the old ship. Marin

St. Aubin sped *The Beloved Loss* away as quickly as it could take him, waving for *The Heart of Calais* to follow suit.

Everyone on the ship realized the same thing at once. Quain and Karoly rushed to set sail as Burke grabbed the powerful wheel, preparing for an exciting game of chase. Cori and Burke replied to Acel's question about the honeymoon in unison, "Cuba!"

THE END

SPECIAL THANKS

-Jagger and Jett: Thanks for letting Mommy work… some.

-Conlee: You're the best husband on Earth. XO.

-My family, "in-law" family and friends: You're all wonderful. Thanks for all your support. Love always.

-Berto Designs: The cover is beautiful! You're the best.

-Lairson Photography: Thanks for the lovely photos!

-My beta readers: Thank you so much for the amazing feedback. Your help was crucial to the success of this book.

-K.A. Robinson: I don't know how to tell you how amazing you are. Thanks for encouraging me and always being there with advice. **If anyone is reading this and you haven't read the Torn Series or Shattered Ties by Author K.A. Robinson yet, you should totally go check them out.**

-Tyeesha (Momma's Secret Book Obsession): You're a lifesaver. Thank you for the countless hours of hard work!

-Authors and Bloggers who have helped me achieve my goals: You are the most wonderful resources on the planet. Thanks for existing.

ABOUT THE AUTHOR

Brittany Jo James was born and raised in the small town of Idabel, Oklahoma. She is happily married to her high school sweetheart, Conlee, who is now a soldier in the United States Air Force. They share two rowdy sons, Jagger and Jett. Her life revolves around living for God, caring for her family and writing, writing, writing. The James family is currently residing near Anchorage, Alaska until the USAF decides otherwise.

OTHER BOOKS

BY BRITTANY JO JAMES

My Knightly Dreams:

http://www.amazon.com/My-Knightly-Dreams-Brittany-James-ebook/dp/B00EFFFVVE/ref=sr_1_1?ie=UTF8&qid=1387240717&sr=8-1&keywords=brittany+jo+james

At Least I'm Pretty:

http://www.amazon.com/At-Least-Pretty-Brittany-James-ebook/dp/B00E1WMXWG/ref=sr_1_2?ie=UTF8&qid=1387240748&sr=8-2&keywords=brittany+jo+james

CONTACT THE AUTHOR

www.facebook.com/brittanyjojamesauthor

www.twitter.com/brittanyjojames

www.brittanyjojames.blogspot.com

www.goodreads.com/brittanyjojames

To all my readers: I would be honored if you would "like" my page on Facebook, follow me on Twitter, keep up with my blog or add my books to your to-be-read list on Goodreads. Thank you for your support. I have a lot of people to be thankful for, but my readers single handedly created my career. I couldn't be an author if I didn't have readers. Thanks for everything. Don't forget to rate/review A Pirate Princess! Also, I love to interact with my readers so feel free to leave me a message on FB and I'll try to get back to you as soon as I can! Thanks again.